D. '

The Applications of Geology to the Arts and Manufactures

SALZWASSER VERLAG

D. T. Ansted

The Applications of Geology to the Arts and Manufactures

Reprint of the original, first published in 1865.

1st Edition 2022 | ISBN: 978-3-75259-064-7

Verlag (Publisher): Salzwasser Verlag GmbH, Zeilweg 44, 60439 Frankfurt, Deutschland
Vertretungsberechtigt (Authorized to represent): E. Roepke, Zeilweg 44, 60439 Frankfurt, Deutschland
Druck (Print): Books on Demand GmbH, In de Tarpen 42, 22848 Norderstedt, Deutschland

THE

APPLICATIONS OF GEOLOGY

TO THE

ARTS AND MANUFACTURES.

BEING SIX LECTURES ON PRACTICAL GEOLOGY, DELIVERED BEFORE THE SOCIETY OF ARTS, AS A PART OF THE 'CANTOR' SERIES OF LECTURES FOR 1865.

BY

PROFESSOR D. T. ANSTED, M.A., F.R.S.

LONDON

1865.

INTRODUCTORY NOTICE.

THE late Dr. Cantor, of the East-Indian Medical Service, who died in 1860, bequeathed one-half of his residuary estate to the Society of Arts, to be applied as should be deemed best for promoting the objects of the Society.

In exercising the trust thus imposed, the Council of the Society decided on employing the proceeds in establishing Courses of Lectures, open to members of the Society, illustrating and explaining the various applications of Science to the Arts.

The Lectures on Practical Geology now published in a somewhat expanded form, were delivered as one of the "Cantor" courses of the Session 1864-5.

The Author has not attempted, either in the Lectures or in this book, to do more than offer a sketch in broad outline. If entered upon in detail, the subject matter of each Lecture would demand a separate course of Lectures, and one or more volumes to itself. In the absence of these the present work may be useful, and the large and steady attendance at the Lectures seemed to show that a popular sketch of this kind was needed.

D. T. ANSTED.

ATHENÆUM CLUB,
London, 14th March, 1865.

CONTENTS.

LIST OF TABLES.

LIST OF DIAGRAMS.

LECTURES ON PRACTICAL GEOLOGY.

Lecture the First.

AGRICULTURAL GEOLOGY.

I PROPOSE, in a short course of Lectures, to introduce the subject of the various practical applications of Geology. In undertaking this task, I am not without a sense of the difficulties that lie in my way; for, on the one hand, the facts are so numerous that if I were merely to enumerate and tabulate them, I could not hope merely to place them all before you in the time at my disposal; and, on the other hand, if I were to generalize without facts and statistics, I could not expect that you should appreciate the great importance of my conclusions. But an account, in any sense popular, of the working out of the great theorems of geology, and their bearing upon agriculture, architecture, engineering of all kinds, and mining of all kinds,—their influence on the progress of the various arts of construction, and on the discovery of the materials of which things are constructed, can hardly want interest, and need not be useless because it is brief.

In treating of the applications of geology, it is convenient to take advantage of those natural divisions which the subject offers. The earth is both the place itself on or within which everything is done, and it yields all the material by which everything is done. We have to employ the earth as it is presented to us by nature, and to do so we have to discover and remove from the earth the means of using this same earth to advantage. With the aid of stone, stone implements were first made. With these, and with fuel grown on the soil, the soil itself was prepared for better crops. Copper. and iron were thus obtained, and by their aid, again, other and better implements were constructed. By slow degrees, but still at a very early period in the history of civilization, men were enabled to cultivate, to construct, to engineer, and to work metals, and in all these matters they were learning and applying geology. By practising a mechanical art they gradually learnt the principles of a science.

As it has been in other sciences, so was it in geology. I have said that practice anticipates science, and in geology the science and the principles were once thought lightly of, because the practice had advanced far without their help.

Of the applications of geology, that which has reference to agriculture is the one which I propose to consider this evening. It is one of no slight importance, and involves many details and many principles. I must presuppose, on the part of those who enter on the subject, a certain knowledge of geology; for I cannot now instruct you on the elementary truths of that science. I think, however, that it will be well to lay down, in a few words, in mere outline, a statement of those facts of geology that are chiefly concerned in its reduction to the uses of common life.

The actual surface of the earth, as exposed to ordinary view in the cultivated parts of a country, consists of vegetable soil. In parts where the soil is barren, this very soil may be almost entirely sand or stones, but it conceals the rock. In a fertile district only a very small proportion of the whole surface exposes the substratum of rock.

If we take the case of England, we shall find that almost everywhere on the east side of the country there is soil of some kind; while, on the western extremity, there are large tracts of barren rock. Every country has its own *facies* in this respect. Even where there is soil, its thickness and general character are very variable. In some districts, for instance, the vegetable earth is apparently many yards thick, and passes down so gradually into similar material that is not adapted to vegetation, as to render it very difficult to decide what is soil and what is rock. Elsewhere there is only the thinnest film of soil supporting a small growth of grass, immediately beneath which we come to a limestone, sandstone, or other rock. Whatever the thickness may be, however, there is always a termination to the soil, and below it is a subsoil partaking of a mixed character between soil and rock, while below the subsoil is the rock. This rock is exposed in quarries and railway cuttings, and may be found and examined in the fragments brought up when water is sought for, either by wells or borings. Even the channel cut through by a stream, however small, will often be found to give a useful geological section.

Rocks are of various kinds, but the varieties may be included within certain general and familiar terms. Such are limestone, sandstone, clay, granite, basalt, slate, &c. Mixed fragments of these form gravel when loose, and conglomerates or pudding-stones when cemented together. More minute fragments ground to powder are sand. Of these, some are arranged in layers, or, in geological language, are *stratified*; others present no mark of such layers or strata, and these are said to be *unstratified*. So, again, certain of them have evidently been formed with water and by water, and are therefore called *aqueous rocks*. Others appear to have been once in a state of fusion by intense heat. These are called *igneous*. Others—and these are very numerous—may or must have been formed with water, but are now so far changed as to have lost their aqueous character. These are *metamorphic*. Limestone is an aqueous rock, and stratified. Basalt, or ancient lava, is an igneous rock, and may or may not be in strata. Large masses of it appear unstratified, and may be so regarded. Slate is an aqueous rock, but metamorphic, often stratified, but not always exhibiting its stratification. Granite is metamorphic, and generally, not always, unstratified.

Stratified rocks are generally tilted. Originally deposited in nearly horizontal planes, they are often now inclined at an angle to the horizon, which may vary from only a few degrees to perfect verticality. It is even possible that beds once horizontal may be actually inverted, and made to dip the wrong way. Strata lifted up are sometimes broken.

Rocks occur in series. Often a multitude of stratified rocks are found in the same district, some of them being much more tilted than others. The older rocks may have been turned on edge, and the newer may have been deposited horizontally on the upturned edges, and then the whole may have been once more tilted. There are no limits to the contortions and disturbance of strata in mountain districts; but where there are no mountains at hand, strata are generally much more nearly horizontal and regular. This general rule is not without marked exceptions.

Stratified rocks are often interpenetrated by those that are metamorphic or igneous, but sometimes the metamorphic and igneous alternate with the aqueous. There are instances of very large tracts of such rock as granite neither in or near mountains, nor connected with disturbances; but more usually granite or similar rocks accompany upturned and metamorphosed strata.

Such are some of the simplest and most significant facts of geology, ascertainable by any one with little trouble in almost every country, and bearing on those practical questions we shall have to consider in these lectures. Rocks are the mineral constituents of the earth beneath any vegetable soil that may have accumulated upon them. They have, in some cases, been formed as deposits from water; in some cases they have been left undisturbed and unaltered, in others they have been greatly changed. They are even sometimes converted into substances so different in appearance from the original deposits as to seem to have no relation with them. But they retain enough of their original or altered nature to enable us to judge of the processes they have passed through, and very often to determine the order and extent of the changes that have taken place in them. They yield to the chemist a ready account of their composition, and to the student, who investigates them for that purpose, a clear outline of the mechanical changes they have undergone; while they are often sufficient to enable the geologist to determine a tolerably complete outline of events, and a history of changes and operations that have taken a long time to complete.

Owing also to the mixed origin of rocks,—to their having been deposited from suspension or solution in water and being afterwards changed by the operation of heat or by chemical action, and removed from their original position at the bottom of the sea or in the interior of the earth to become parts of the land above the sea-level—it has happened that most rocks are broken and fractured, the cracks being filled up more or less completely with minerals, sometimes derived from, sometimes foreign to, the enclosing rocks, but generally crystalline.

You will now be able to understand the connection that exists between geology as a descriptive or physical science and the practical applications we have to consider. Soils are derived from rocks, and many of the important properties of soils are due to the rocks beneath them. The condition of a soil in respect to water-supply and drainage is determined by the mechanical nature of the rocks beneath. Mineral manures are to be obtained from rocks in certain geological positions. So also in other departments: all that is most important in reference to building-material—whether clay, stone, lime, or cement; whether for the construction of houses or palaces, of harbours or bridges, of statues or porcelain; and whether to be dug or quarried—must be obtained from rocks, and will be best obtained by those who are familiar with geological science. In all matters concerning the distribution and discovery of water in the search for mineral fuel, and for every kind of metalliferous or earthy mineral of value, geology is needed; for the work of discovery and removal lies in and among those rocks whose history and placement geology studies.

Every kind of vegetable soil was once rock, which, by the unintermitting action of heat and cold, air and water, has been broken down by degrees into smaller and smaller fragments, until at last it is reduced to a kind of powder, dust, or mud. The part of this process performed by the atmosphere is called *weathering.* It goes on constantly—day and night, winter and summer, in a wet or dry, in a calm or stormy atmosphere. It breaks down the hardest rocks on the lofty mountain-top as well as removes the soft mud on the plain. It eats away the bottom of the deep sheltered valley, and pares away the surface of the barren exposed moor. It affects the toughest granite and the softest clay or loosest sand.

Wherever rock is exposed to the air, it becomes weathered; and weathering means ultimately a reduction to fine powder.

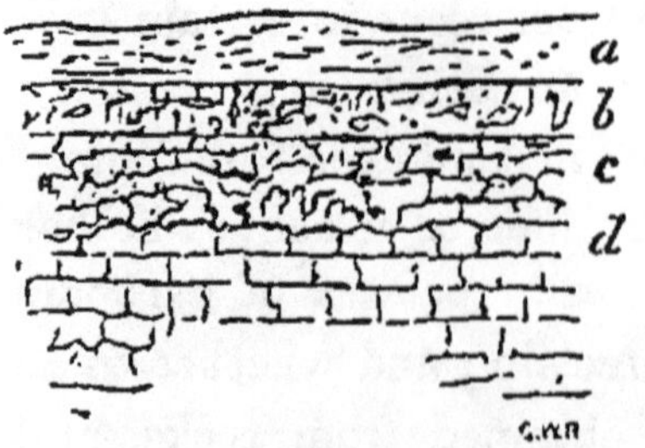

Fig. 1.

Diagram No. 1 illustrates this condition so far as regards the change that is observed in passing down from vegetable soil to the rock from which it is derived.

On the granite or quartz rock exposed on the cliff, or in the quarry, a group of small lichens is seen to grow. These only seem to ask from the rock a solid foundation; but they are insidious enemies, as, although they derive their nourishment chiefly from the atmosphere, and might be thought even to protect the exposed naked surface from the weather, they really pave the way for destruction. That which they separate from the air and employ in the construction of their leathery bodies, becomes after their death a brown pulverulent mass, or *humus*, which affords nourishment to larger individuals of the same tribe. At length there is sufficient of this humus or vegetable soil to support a higher class of vegetation. Various mosses succeed the lichens. These take root; and small crevices, such as are formed by exposure on the surface of all rocks, receive their roots. Once inserted, these roots expand and exercise an irresistible force, splitting asunder the rock and breaking up the surface. Other roots are thus enabled to penetrate yet further; and after a time the first mosses are succeeded by more vigorous branching kinds, and these again, according as the climate is dry or moist, are followed up by heather, ferns, grasses, or small shrubs; until at length each generation of plants working its way deeper into the rock and increasing the quantity of soil, there is attained a thickness of sufficiently deep earth to enable forest trees to grow, thrusting down their rootlets to a great depth in the crevices and making room for the admission of rain. In due time frost comes, rending asunder the rock and producing, in hilly countries or near cliffs, frequent slips and slides, falling into the valleys below, but soon spread over the surface and lost sight of, being washed away by the rain.

No one can have examined old walls and houses in a damp country without seeing abundant proof of the enormous power of vegetation. Even in the driest lands the same effect is recognizable. I have seen in the Greek islands the roots of olive-trees lifting out of their places huge stones weighing many tons, that once formed part of cyclopean walls. I have noticed, at the Giant's Causeway, the matted roots of grasses and other plants nine or ten feet below the apparently unchanged surface of basalt. Stones loosened and ultimately overthrown by these means may be found wherever such rocks or limestones or sandstones are laid bare. No kind of rock escapes; and the work is not only actively carried on by vegetation in a direct manner, but also indirectly and through the help of the atmosphere and rain. Rain contains materials which act on certain rocks. By degrees depressions, that ultimately become large holes, are eaten out of limestones in this manner. I have seen (also in Greece) squared blocks of limestone many cubic yards in content, bored through by holes large enough to admit of a man's leg. In this case the work must have commenced since the stones were thrown down and the wall became a ruin. Elsewhere, as in the Channel Islands (Guernsey, Jersey, Alderney, and Sark, which consist almost entirely of granite), some of the hardest and most compact kinds of rock known, or at any rate granite in contact with these hard varieties, are reduced at the surface to small detached fragments capable of being carted away as gravel, and this to a depth of twenty or thirty feet. All this is weathering, and it illustrates the mode of formation of soils in cases where such a method might seem most difficult. In softer stones similar effects are produced with extreme rapidity; but here the rain washes away the fragments into the nearest stream, whence they are conveyed to the plains below. After being thus moved about in running water, no trace is left of the events that have taken place. Thus the softest rocks show the least signs of change.

In certain soils we may expect to find the underlying rock *in situ,* in fragments, it is true, but in angular fragments and recognizable; while elsewhere the fragments are rounded and water-worn, and belong not to the rock below, but to some distant mountain or hill. This transported material is, on the whole, much more common and abundant than the other; for water has everywhere been at work, and every shower moves onwards, if only for a few yards, the material broken away by weathering from exposed surfaces. Thus *alluvial soils* are formed; and this not only at the mouths of rivers, but at all elevations above the sea. Over a great part of Northern Europe, at all heights up to a thousand feet or more above the sea, are these alluvial formations, these transported soils, and they are often of great thickness.

The solvent power of water is a very important agent in weathering. I have already alluded to its effect on limestone, and this effect is universal, differing somewhat in its mode of operation. On detached fragments water and vegetation together act as a drill. On a great mass of limestone rock, cracked at the surface and having cavities within, the water entering tends to enlarge the fissures, increase the dimensions of some of the cavities, and choke up others. Of many sandstones it dissolves the calcareous cement, and thus loosens the cohesion; of others it dissolves the silica itself. Thus in a basalt containing silica, alumina, peroxide of iron, lime, magnesia, soda, and potash, the following differences of composition were observed between an unweathered and a weathered specimen:—

	Fresh Basalt.	Weathered Basalt.	Loss by Weathering.	
				Per cent.
Silica	477	384	93	or 19·5
Alumina . . .	168	168	0	0
Peroxide of Iron .	135	131·6	3·4	,, 2·5
Lime	106	72·3	33·7	,, 31·8
Magnesia . . .	65	48·3	16·7	,, 25·7
Soda	37	12·6	24·4	,, 66·0
Potash	12	4·3	7·7	,, 64·1
	1000	821·1	178·9	

From this it appears that 65 per cent. of the soluble alkalies have been removed, 28 per cent. of the alkaline earths, nearly 20 per cent. of the silica, only 2½ per cent. of the iron oxide, and no appreciable quantity of the alumina. A somewhat similar result would be found in the case of other rocks.

All productive soils are composed partly of mineral substances and partly of certain products of the decomposition of organic bodies. This latter portion is not very definite, but is recognized under the name of *humus* or *humic acid.* It is thought that humic acid assists water in dissolving certain minerals. It consists largely of carbon, and carbonic acid is mixed freely with the water that passes through fertile soil. Humus is not generally present in soils in large proportion, but it is very abundant in peat and moor soils, having then been obtained from dead water-plants or marsh plants.

The mineral constituents of a soil are of two kinds: the one kind we may call *earth,* as being a disintegrated and often decomposed mineral substance; the other consists of those fragments that still remain of the rock from which the earth is derived or of some transported rock. The latter we may conveniently call *stones.* The former render the ground arable; the latter increase the bulk of the soil, facilitate the action of rain and frost, and in some cases change the physical character of the soil; but they contribute little to the nutrition of the plant, however well adapted their mineral constituents may be for such purpose. It is not difficult to separate the earth from the stones by stirring up a soil into mud with water. The finer particles remain longer in suspension, and may be poured off until nothing but the stones are left at the bottom.

As a general fact, the productiveness of cultivable soils is in direct proportion to the quantity of earth they contain; and the following result of a careful examination of various soils may be useful as showing their relative value in this sense. Pure sand is not regarded as an earth.

Nature of Soil.	Proportion of Earth.
	Per Cent.
Loamy soil (clay)	97
Alluvial soil (from clay-slate) . . .	92
" (from mica-slate) . . .	84
Granular marly and alluvial soil from gneiss	80 to 70
Weathered mica-slate and soils from hard schistose rock	70 " 60
Alluvial clay-slate and weathered gneiss soil	60 " 50
Red sandstone soil	50 " 40
Granite soil	40 " 30
Heath sand soil	30 " 20

Clay, lime, and sand form the staple of all rocks, and as a general rule it may be said that these are really the ingredients of chief importance in every cultivable soil, and the preponderance of either determines the nature of the soil. Clay is a silicate of alumina, insoluble, but capable of retaining mechanically and almost indefinitely a large quantity of water, forming with it a tenacious, compact, sticky paste, which is almost impermeable to water. Hence soil containing much clay is heavy and difficult to work, remains long wet when once soaked, and after rain cakes at the surface, allowing the water to descend very imperfectly. Cold and wet places are thus formed underground when clay exists below a good vegetable soil, and the roots of trees and plants reaching this water are poisoned. If the soil is dammed up so that this wet remains constantly, a swamp is produced.

Wet clay contracts considerably on drying, long and wide cracks forming in it after drought. All the changes that are needed to prepare a soil for sowing are checked in such material, and are only enabled to come about slowly. Frost breaks up the clods very effectually when sufficiently severe, and sand improves the quality ; but a deep clay soil is very difficult to improve effectually and on a large scale. Mechanical admixtures with ashes and soot, as well as with sand, are suitable to such soils.

But clays conta much potash, some phosphoric acid, and lime : these are useful properties. They also absorb ammonia and aqueous vapour from the atmosphere, and fix the ammonia very effectually. For this reason, in spite of their troublesome nature with regard to water, clay soils are regarded by the agriculturist as powerful and rich. When slightly burnt they become mellow, looser, and less apt to cake ; while some of their constituents, as the potash, pass from an insoluble to a soluble state.

In England clay lands have been effectually improved by these and analogous methods, and have become in many cases extremely valuable and fertile, especially for wheat crops, and occasionally for meadow. Drainage, by removing the superfluous water, opens the way for the permanent improvement of clay soils.

Clays are largely derived from felspars, and felspar itself has perhaps been originally derived from still older clays. Granite, gneiss, basalt, clay-slate, and some other metamorphic and igneous rocks yield clay soils on decomposition. This is owing to the facility with which the sand and other minerals mixed with the clay are carried away on disintegration, leaving the clay behind.

Loam is clay mechanically mixed with sand. It is thereby much improved in some cases. Where the mixture includes any large proportion of peroxide of iron the result is seen both in the colour of the rock and in its greater permeability to water. Most kinds of brick clay are of this nature, and so also are other plastic clays. The quantity of the silica that may exist in a soil without removing from it the usual characteristics of clay is enormously large; but when the sand is in excess, and the soil becomes actually sandy, its behaviour is altogether different.

Sand, of all substances that form soils, is that which is the least changed by weathering. Sandstones are changed by the destruction of the cement that holds them together, and this may be either calcareous or ferruginous; but the actual particles change only by mechanical abrasion, by which they become reduced from large to small.

Sand is an accumulation of granules of quartz and

quartzite, not adhering together, but lying unattached, loose, and unconnected, beside and upon one another, leaving abundant interstices admitting the free passage of water. Water is only retained in small quantities in sands near the surface, the great proportion of all that falls on such soil filtering through rapidly, as through a sieve. When exposed to the air evaporation also takes place freely through it. When wet, sand appears to adhere, but this is only temporary. The coarser the particles the more do the characteristics of sand become recognizable, and the more readily does the material act on other soils. Light soils, containing much sand, are said to have a hot, dry nature, giving up all their moisture rapidly during warm dry weather, and becoming heated and even scorched by a summer sun. So again, for the same reason, these soils are active in all their effects, but soon exhausted. Ordinary dressing and animal manures soon show a result, but are of no continued benefit, for the nutrient constituents are not retained. When, however, sand is present in an exceedingly fine mealy state, it approaches clay in its properties, forming a dense compact mass, and holding water. This transition of sand into clay is a very curious fact, and one often insufficiently regarded. Two soils having similar constituent earths, and differing nothing so far as analysis shows, may be entirely different in their value to the agriculturist. Sands of this very fine kind are often the result of great accumulations of infusorial animalcules, such as exist near the mouths of certain rivers, and are killed at the place of contact of the salt water of the ocean with the fresh water coming over lands.

Limestone exists in nature in various ways. Common limestone is a carbonate of lime, more or less pure. It is exceedingly soft, and readily acted on in the state of chalk. It is harder and more stony in the oolites and other building stones common in England and elsewhere. It is exceedingly hard, and often barren in the carboniferous or mountain limestone, and in numerous varieties of marble. All pure limestones work up into soils having peculiar properties; they are often red in colour, from the oxidation of the iron commonly present in the crevices; they are almost always cracked and broken by weathering near the surface; and often, in hilly or mountain districts, the soil and rock to a great depth consists of fragments of stone, not water-worn, but quite angular, and confusedly heaped together, obtained by the breaking up of the surface-beds of hard stone by the action of rain and weather. Such accumulations are not of necessity unfertile. The vine and fig-tree, and some other trees whose cultivation is very important, find abundant nourishment in soils of this kind. In the island of Cephalonia, where the currant-vine is cultivated to perfection on the flat lands and valleys, the best soils are entirely composed of limestone fragments, the interstices between large stones being more or less filled up by the finer and smaller fragments of the same material. Not far off, on the hill sides and in the flanks of the mountains, the grape-vine bears admirable fruit when planted on heaps of stones, with no perceptible soil of any kind, the stones lying at the natural angle they assume when thrown together. So, in the south of Italy, the vine and fig-tree are grown on lava, with scarcely any intervention of soil. In the south of Spain, and in the north of Africa, stony soils are by no means unfertile for certain crops, even when the stone is a nearly pure limestone.

Besides common limestone, magnesian limestone, or dolomite, is sometimes the prevailing rock. It consists of a mixed carbonate of lime and carbonate of magnesia, the proportions being variable, but the carbonate of lime in excess. It is generally less capable of supporting abundant vegetation than common limestone, and the soils upon it are not remarkable for fertility. It is more cellular and spongy in texture than common limestone, and therefore more absorbent, but is less acted on by water on a large scale, though occasionally cavernous.

All limestones, however, as rocks, are permeable to water, and contain a considerable per-centage of water. Many common building-stones will absorb a gallon and a half of water per cubic foot, and some magnesian limestones as much as two gallons. Chalk is especially absorbent, and acts precisely as a sponge. It will absorb one-sixth part of its own weight, and thus a cubic foot will contain nearly four gallons of water when saturated. A large part of this is rapidly given off by evaporation from the surface during hot weather.

A calcareous or lime soil, in the state of a finely-divided earth, is either a white or light-coloured, or a deep red earth, according to the absence or presence of iron. It is soft to the touch, standing in this respect midway between clay and sand. It absorbs and retains much water, but does not become sodden, always allowing more water to be added without forming pools. Its tenacity is greater than sand, but less than clay. It also shrinks much less than clay, and does not crack. It diminishes the tenacity and humidity of clay soils, rendering them more porous, more accessible to air, and warmer. Where, however, lime greatly preponderates, the soil is regarded practically as both poor and hot; but these characters are so readily altered by the admixture of clay and humus, generally at hand, that ground of a very useful nature is hence derived.

We have already seen that every soil is capable of bearing some kind of vegetable growth, and that, even on bare rock, certain lichens and mosses will attach themselves and flourish. All soils are thus more or less productive; and, while some are best adapted for one kind of valuable crop, and some for another, there are some that seem only to produce in abundance weeds and rubbish plants. Much of this difference depends on the mechanical condition of the soil, and much, of course, on the chemical composition. I have already reminded you, that both these are due to the underlying rock. Let us see what combinations are necessary to produce a productive soil.

In the first place, however, let us speak of the conditions that must be avoided. These are three:—*first*, too great cohesion. A soil may be unproductive because it is too stiff and tenacious. Dense clay, such as potter's clay, is totally unfit for cultivation, because it holds water too long, does not allow air to penetrate, and is too slowly and too little warmed. So, again, a soil otherwise productive, may be rendered unproductive if washed by rain into hollow bottoms, where it cakes into a solid, impenetrable mass. Earths of either kind, if forming a subsoil covered with a light but otherwise good soil, may cause barrenness to such soil by producing swamps, and what is technically called sourness.

But, *secondly*, a soil may also be unproductive for want of cohesion. It may be too coarse, too loose, and too open. Thus, pure gravel or sand is quite unfit for cultivation, and, for certain crops, limestone fragments are perfectly barren. Such materials hold no water except in the substance of the stone. When rain has fallen on them it sinks between the fragments of stone to a great depth, and when the sun shines, the aqueous vapour rises through them. When evaporation takes place from the surface, limestones are rapidly dried, the water rising by capillary action, and distributing itself through the mass.

Thirdly, a soil may be unproductive because it contains poisonous ingredients. It is true that this cause is rare, but it exists. The salts of lead and copper are absolutely poisonous in all proportions. Sulphate of iron is also poisonous, and alum may be regarded in the same light. Such substances occur in volcanic districts, and there we sometimes see extensive tracts without vegetation.

Lastly, soils may be unproductive from the excess of

certain ingredients which, in a different and smaller proportion, are nutritious. Thus, common salt is sometimes used with great advantage as a mineral manure, but salt water entirely destroys vegetation of most kinds, and hardly anything will grow in a soil saturated with salt. Mineral acids, again, though very useful diluted, would certainly interfere with growth, and will even destroy vegetable life, if in too large proportion.

We may now inquire what mineral and geological conditions must combine to make a soil productive, being assisted in making out the matter by the negative considerations just offered. In the first place, the soil should possess a crumbling soft consistence, which must be capable of remaining unchanged by the operations of tillage. This is a mechanical necessity, and as it can only exist under certain mineral conditions, it is very important to know how it can be produced in a soil that has it not. There are rich soils, indeed, that improve more and more in this respect as cultivation advances, but there are others that require constant care and treatment not to fall into a bad state. It is to produce such soils that a mixture merely mechanical, and one that has no effect whatever on nutritious elements, may make all the difference between a fertile and barren soil—between success and failure. It is in such circumstances that some knowledge of science, and especially of geological science, becomes not only useful, but essential, if we would avoid serious loss.

In the next place, the soil must furnish the plant with a certain kind of food essential to its existence or well-being. This food must be presented, too, in a digestible form. It is not enough to offer the roots of a plant that requires phosphorus or sulphur, the elementary substance, nor would it be of use to bury in the ground near them pure crystalline apatite or iron pyrites. The plant would starve in the midst of plenty. The food must be adapted to the plant, and if it does not exist already in the soil in that state, it must be added. The whole question of mineral manure is concerned in this, and here more, perhaps, than in any other department, geology comes in aid.

Among the mineral constituents of a soil serving as food, the following are the most important :—phosphoric acid, potash, lime, and magnesia. The quantity of these contained in the soil is extremely variable, but the following statement of the limits will be useful as a guide. It is given on the authority of Dr. Stöckhardt, a Saxon chemist.

An Acre of Land, six inches deep, would contain about—	Maximum.	Minimum.	Mean of predominating Rich Soils.
	Pounds.	Pounds.	Pounds.
Phosphoric acid .	12,000	150	2,500
Potash (total quantity)	53,000	1,500	22,000
Soluble potash .	15,000	750	3,500
Lime and magnesia	145,000	900	30,000

Although, perhaps, this estimate may not be minutely accurate, even as a proportional, and therefore still less as a quantitative statement, it shows fairly enough the relative importance of these substances. The most important is the first (phosphoric acid), for without it nourishing food cannot be grown and ripened. There is rarely an absence of the rest, though they are sometimes insufficient in quantity. Of other substances, sulphuric acid must be present to render useful most of those named in the list, and of it there is generally no want. Silica also is essential and is almost always present. To learn the proportion needed by particular plants or crops, we must refer to the constituents of their ashes. An analysis of these shows that such trees as the coniferæ contain in the ashes of one thousand pounds of dried plants only two pounds of lime and magnesia, half a pound of potash, and only a quarter of a pound of silica. Of meadow grass, however, the ashes contain a large quantity of phosphoric acid, thirty-four times as much potash, four times as much lime and magnesia, and eighty times as much silica, as in the case of coniferæ; while wheat contains the same proportion of silica as grass, but much less phosphoric acid, potash, lime, and magnesia. I give (p. 26) in a tabular form the quantities of these substances.

A glance at this table will show that various crops require very different quantities and proportions of mineral nutriment. Generally we may say, that tobacco, potatoes, clover, and peas, are greedy of such food; while the cereals generally are moderate, and forest trees eminently moderate. It must be remembered, however, that at different stages of their growth, plants require different food; that while phosphoric acid is chiefly needed for the seed, lime predominates in the leaves and stems, and potash in succulent roots; and that the time when the phosphoric acid is most needed is when the seed is approaching ripeness.

Plant.	Composition of Ashes of 1000 pounds of Dried Plants.				
	Phosphoric Acid.	Potash.	Lime and Magnesia.	Silica.	Total.
	Pounds.	Pounds.	Pounds.	Pounds.	Pounds.
Pine forest 80 years old . .	¼	½	2	¼	3
Meadow grass .	16	17	8	20	61
Ripe wheat (grain and straw) . .	4½	5½	3½	20	33½
Ripe peas . .	5½	11	16	2	34½
Potatoes (tubers and haulm) .	6½	22	11	3	42½
Beet (root and foliage) . .	4	21	7	2	34
Clover in flower	5½	20	20	2	47½
Tobacco, green (leaves & stalk)	5¼	24	40–60	8	77¼–97¼

You will now perceive how it is that particular soils are naturally very favourable for certain crops; why forest land that has been so from time immemorial, and is put under another cultivation, seems at first so rich; why certain soils, very unfavourable now for particular crops, may once have been the contrary; and also in what way a certain amount of scientific knowledge may be eminently useful to the agriculturist. A rule discovered by experience to be admirably adapted to the sands and light soils of Norfolk, may be very ill adapted to the fens of Cambridgeshire and Lincolnshire; and the farmer knowing thoroughly the treatment that will best succeed with the oolitic soils of Northamptonshire, will require to learn his lesson from the beginning if he attempt to cultivate the fertile loams of Cumberland. Not only are all the details different, but the very principles of cropping and farming can hardly be compared.

To come back to the qualifications for a productive soil, I may say that it should be composed of nearly equal parts of the three earths—sand, clay, and lime; that it should contain a certain quantity of decomposing vegetable and animal matter; that it should imbibe moisture and give it back to the air without much difficulty; that it should have depth sufficient to permit the roots of plants to sink and extend without coming to rock, to water, or to some injurious earth; that the subsoil should be moderately porous, but not too much so; and that in case of need the subsoil should be able to improve the soil by mixture with it. The proper proportion of the various earths may vary from 50 to 70 per cent. of silicious matter, 20 to 40 per cent. of clay, and 10 to 20 per cent. of calcareous matter. According as the climate is wet or dry, the soil should be friable and porous, or adhesive and retentive, and the best soil is that which, in long droughts, is never very dry, and in the wettest seasons does not become choked with water.

No doubt, any soil might be made to bear a constant succession of crops of the same kind, if the mineral ingredients removed by one crop were supplied in the same state from year to year. But this can only be done as the result of a nice calculation, and by careful and systematic farming. It requires that the farmer should thoroughly understand the nature of soils, and the habits and needs of plants, in order that he may avoid, on the one hand, a wasteful expenditure on excess of nourishment, and, on the other hand, take care that all the conditions required by the crop are fulfilled.

As a remarkable instance of the successful use of mineral manures in rendering an ordinary soil capable of bearing, for many successive years, a full crop of wheat, I may here refer with advantage to the experiments carried on at Rothamsted by Mr. Lawes and Dr. Gilbert, reported in the twenty-fifth volume of the *Journal of the Royal Agricultural Society*, published in 1864.

In this case a field of fourteen acres was selected and manured during twelve successive years with different combinations on various plots, some plots being left unmanured and others manured with ordinary farmyard manure, for purposes of comparison. The land selected had first been exhausted by previous crops of all the usual kinds, and had then been subjected to experiments of similar nature for nine years, to the year 1851. During the season 1851–2 the winter was mild, the spring cold and wet, and the summer wet and cold till September, and on the whole decidedly unfavourable for wheat crops. The results were a produce of 13¾ bushels, of 56½ lbs. per bushel on the unmanured plots, the crop yielding 860lbs. corn and 1,597lbs. straw and chaff. With farmyard manure (14 tons to the acre) the crop was 27½ bushels, of 58.2 lbs., to the acre, and yielded 1,716 lbs. corn and 3,457 lbs. straw, &c. With mixed mineral manure alone the crop was 16¾ bushels, of 55.9 lbs., to the acre, and the yield 1,320 lbs. corn, 2,787 lbs. straw, &c.; and with 800 lbs. ammonia salts and mixed mineral manure, 28½ bushels, of 54.7 lbs., to the acre, yielding 1,747 lbs. corn and 4,646 lbs. straw, &c.

The following was the result on the different plots on an average of twelve years of cropping from 1852–1863 inclusive:—

(1.) Unmanured plots: 15.2 bushels, of 56.5lbs. to the bushel, the crop yielding 964 lbs. corn and 1,662 lbs. straw and chaff per acre.

(2.) Plots manured with 14 tons farmyard manure yearly: 35½ bushels, of 59.3 lbs. to the bushel, yielding 2,232 lbs. corn and 3,869 lbs. straw and chaff per acre.

(3.) Plots manured with mixed mineral manures alone every year: 18½ bushels, of 57.9 lbs. to the bushel, yielding 1,157 lbs. corn and 1,898 lbs. straw, &c., per acre.

(4.) Plots manured with ammonia salts and mixed mineral manure every year: 36½ bushels, of 58.4 lbs. to the bushel, yielding 2,275 lbs. corn and 4,212 lbs. straw, &c., per acre.

Thus the crop which was obtained by supplying the ingredients removed in the direct form of mineral manure, was about two and a half times the quantity of corn and straw that was obtained from the unmanured land, and decidedly larger than that got from a free supply of farmyard manure every year.

"The general result," says Mr. Lawes, "is that the average annual yield was, without manure, much the same over the whole period (of twenty years); that, notwithstanding the exhausting effects of applying ammonia salts every year, the annual diminution of produce under their influence was proportionally less during the latter half of the last twelve than of the whole nineteen years of their use; that where ammonia salts and all mineral constituents, except silica, were liberally supplied every year, the produce of corn increased and that of straw somewhat diminished; lastly, that where an excess of every constituent required by the crop was annually supplied, as in the farmyard manure, the rate of increase from year to year was not so great during the later as during some of the earlier years."

The following is a list of the mineral manures supplied:—

Potash.—As pearl-ash, sulphate of potash, or silicate of potash.

Soda.—As soda-ash, or sulphate of soda.

Lime.—As sulphate, phosphate, and superphosphate.

Magnesia.—As magnesian limestone, or sulphate of magnesia.

Phosphoric acid.—As bone-ash; generally acted on by sulphuric acid in quantity sufficient to convert a considerable part of the insoluble earthy phosphate of lime into sulphate and soluble super-phosphate of lime.

Sulphuric acid.—As sulphate of potash, soda, or magnesia, in the phosphatic mixture last-mentioned, &c.

Chlorine.—As hydrochloric acid (with bone-ash), or as chloride of sodium (common salt).

Silica.—As artificial silicate of potash, formed by fusing together equal parts of sand and pearl-ash.

I have not yet alluded to the nitrogen, which forms an essential and most important part of all productive soils, nor have I spoken of the results of manuring in the ordinary sense of the word. Both belong rather to organic chemistry, as applied to agriculture, than to the geology of agriculture. From 3 to 10 per cent. of organic matter is needed to make a soil, otherwise good, available for valuable crops. It is true that some plants can live in a barren soil, while others flourish even without any attachment to the earth, but these are exceptional cases. Plants generally must have suitable soils, and a good soil must contain the remains of former vegetation. Decaying animal tissue and old bones are thus of the greatest value in assisting and forcing the growth of many plants. It will be well, then, to consider the exact nature of various productive soils before we advance another step. I select a few that are exceedingly remarkable among the known soils of the earth. The first is the Nile mud, celebrated for more than four thousand years as one of the most fertile of all soils. The second is the *Tchornozem*, a very celebrated black earth of the Aralo-Caspian plains, which appears to yield repeated crops of wheat without exhaustion. It occupies a hundred millions of acres, and feeds more than twenty millions of people. The third, the *Regur*, or cotton soil of India, is also a remarkably fertile earth, covering one-third part of Southern India, and extending far to the North. The fourth is the rich and valuable soil derived from the new red sandstone, yielding large crops of excellent grass, in Devonshire and Cheshire.

Composition of Rich Soils.

	(1) Nile mud.	(2) Tchornozem.	(3) Regur.	(4) Red marl.
Silica . . .	42·50	75·00	48·20	70·20
Alumina . .	24·25	9·09	20·30	19·20
Carb. lime . .	3·85	*	16·00	0·40
Carb. magnesia .	1·20	?	10·20	..
Magnesia . .	1·05	..	..	..
Iron oxide . .	13·65	5·56	1·00	6·00
Chloride of sodium	..	..	..	0·10
Organic matter and water .	13·50	6·95	4·30	4·10
	100·00	96·60	100·00	100·00

* Quantity small, but not specified.

These analyses are very suggestive. The Tchornozem and Regur are of considerable, but variable, thickness, amounting in some places to 20 feet, and nowhere less than 3 feet. The former bears successive crops of corn, without manure, for five years, and is then left fallow for some years. During the first years of fallow the ground becomes covered with gigantic thistles, and, after they have ceased, abundant pasturage is afforded. The rotation is about six years of each crop, and no other treatment is found necessary. Of the special matter which it contains, derived from organic bodies, a large part is nitrogen gas. The Regur also is cultivated very easily with a succession of crops, and is very rarely left fallow. It yields cotton, and two kinds of corn. The Nile mud is yearly replaced, and therefore it cannot be expected to require a cessation from cropping. Hence its great value, and the uniformity of its yield.

But it is not all soils that contain within them such great natural resources. Many that are very valuable under careful management and continued culture, would be almost valueless if left to themselves. The treatment that best succeeds in improving a soil must depend on the subsoil, the climate, and the facilities that exist for obtaining at a reasonable cost the required mineral manures.

Thus, we may take the case of the fen-lands of England, which yield, as is well known, very valuable corn crops. With many admirable properties, these lands are at first so spongy and saturated with water, that till the water is removed from them they are uncultivable. This, then, is the first process.

But, even when drained, black, peaty soil is neither fit for sheep-feeding, nor for rearing or breeding cows and oxen. The land must be *clayed*, or mixed well with stiff clay, and this is present in most parts of the fen country, underlying the peat. The clay has to be lifted and put on the surface, and this requires to be done once in five or six years. A succession of crops, consisting of turnips, oats, wheat, and clover, succeeded by fallow and again claying, is found to succeed admirably on such lands. The clay in this case acts as a mineral manure.

Among mineral manures, we may reckon as the most important those which supply phosphorus and nitrogen to the growing plant or ripening seed. These are especially necessary for food plants. In an advanced state of agriculture, in a country already well peopled, where land is valuable, any resources that will enable the farmer to avoid leaving his land waste or fallow must be regarded as valuable, and worthy of very careful investigation. Among the most important of these resources are the employment of the manure of the animals or men fed from the ground; but I must not here speak of the uses of common manure and town sewage, for they belong to agricultural chemistry, and not to geology. Nature, however, has sometimes retained for our use stores of ancient animal remains corresponding to our vast stores of coal, and these evidently and properly belong to our subject.

The want of nitrogen in soils that have become exhausted by heavy corn crops, is usually supplied by animal manure; but this is costly, and not always obtainable at the right time in proper quantity, and in the best state. Nitrate of potash, or saltpetre, is known to be a highly efficacious substitute. But saltpetre is far too costly a material to justify its use as a mineral manure under ordinary circumstances. There is, however, a kind of saltpetre called *cubic nitre*—a nitrate of soda, instead of nitrate of potash, of which very large quantities are readily and cheaply obtainable from a group of dried salt lakes in Peru and Bolivia. Owing to the position of the land in that part of South America, where there is a narrow strip only of low land between the lofty Andes and the Pacific, and where the winds blow steadily from the east, these winds become deprived of all moisture before passing the crest of the mountains, and thus no rain ever falls between them and the sea. Abounding with volcanoes, and exceedingly subject to earthquake influences, the whole coast appears to have undergone elevation within a recent geological period; and to this, perhaps, and to an occasional eruption of nitrous vapours, combined with the formation and rapid drying up of a series of salt lagoons, is due the existence of these deposits. At any rate, it is certain that in the district I have alluded to there is a tract of country measuring some 80 to 100 miles from north to south, and of considerable width, over which cubic nitre, mixed with common salt, is found at intervals in beds several feet thick, and filling up hollows. The district is 3,300 feet above the Pacific, and is about ten to fifteen miles from the coast. It is a barren desert—a striking illustration of the classical story of Midas, that the power of transforming everything into gold is consistent with the most utter poverty and starvation to the person or land thus endowed.

The value of this material, if it can be imported on favourable terms in a rough state, must be very great. It appears to be the best and readiest means of communicating nitrogen to growing plants, and might, perhaps, be one of the most valuable of the mineral manures brought to market.*

Phosphate of lime, whether used simply in the state of bone or brought into the form of superphosphate, and thus more directly efficacious, is a manure of great value, and, being obtained frequently from the mineral kingdom, is a fit subject of geological inquiry.

It is now twenty years since the attention of agriculturists was directed to the possibility of obtaining mineral phosphates of lime in a crystalline state from a known locality in Estremadura, in Spain; and Dr. Daubeney, accompanied by Captain Widdrington (who was familiar with the country by previous residence in the Peninsula), undertook to decide whether it could be economically worked and conveyed to England. They found, indeed, a bed of phosphorite interstratified with clay slate, and its thickness, where observed, was about 16 feet. It descends into the earth at a considerable

* Nitrate of potash (saltpetre) consists when pure of 13·81 per cent. nitrogen, 39·51 oxygen, 46·68 potash. Nitrate of soda (cubic nitre), of 16·41 nitrogen, 46·89 oxygen, 36·70 soda. Guano contains 14·34 per cent. nitrogen.

angle, and is not far from granite. This bed consists of several zones or bands, some of tolerably pure phosphorite, mixed with 14 per cent. of fluoride of calcium, and others of more impure and earthy mineral. The thickness of the purer part is about 3 feet, and it was traced on its line of outcrop for about two miles.

Being perfectly crystalline, it presents no direct relation to any fossiliferous deposit, but may represent all that remains of organic beings once distributed through the mud of which the slate was formed.

The distance of this deposit from any place at which it could be shipped for exportation, and the cost of transport in a country where so little progress is made in providing means of internal traffic, renders its existence useless for practical purposes of agriculture in this country. Similar bands of phosphorite, in more accessible districts, have not been described.

Some years ago, a mineral deposit was discovered in the West Indies, not less rich in phosphorus than the crystalline phosphorite of Estremadura; and, although the advantage of this discovery was more immediately felt in America, and the supply was limited, there probably remain other sources equally valuable on islands belonging to the British crown.

It was on a rock, not far from St. Thomas's, well known to West Indian travellers, and called the "Sombrero," from its resemblance to a hat,* that this discovery was made. Barren itself, like the desert of

* Sombrero is the Spanish name for a low-crowned hat.

Peru, this hummock contained enormous wealth for the agriculturist. Upwards of 30,000 tons of valuable minerals were removed and sold from it during the first year after the discovery. The more solid portions contained 80 per cent. of phosphate of lime, and the porous parts upwards of 70 per cent.

Some of the rocks and islands a little to the south of the Sombrero being examined, were found to yield upwards of 50 per cent. of phosphate of lime, but other specimens showed a mere trace.

Many years ago a discovery of phosphate of lime was made in the so-called crag beds of Suffolk, and afterwards in the greensands of many parts of the south-east of England. The former contain beds consisting of nodules of exceedingly hard material, which, when ground, are soluble in sulphuric acid, and then form a most valuable manure. The proportion of phosphate of lime in these nodules varies from 50 to 60 per cent. The crag nodules are found in the newer tertiary gravels, but the nodules themselves are believed to have been washed out of older rocks, also, however, of tertiary age. The supply seems very large, and was at one time thought inexhaustible, but it has already begun to fail, and at present not more than from two to three thousand tons are raised annually. Until prepared by crushing and solution, the nodules are not available for agricultural purposes.

The existence of a phosphatic band was discovered soon after at Farnham. It varied in thickness from a few inches to four or five feet, occasionally swelling to ten or fifteen feet, and the valuable parts were shapeless lumps of various kinds, very soft when first dug, and gradually hardening till they had the consistence of soft white chalk. They contained upwards of 50 per cent. of phosphate of lime, and were mixed with small dark brown lumps, varying in size from mere grains of sand up to a weight of three or four pounds. These are apparently of concretionary origin. They contain numerous fossilized remains of animals, and consist of nearly 60 per cent. of phosphate of lime. Many millions of tons of these nodules must exist in the beds at the foot of the chalk. They are found not only near Farnham, where they were first observed, but all along the outcrop of the same upper greensand beds at the foot of the north and south downs in the Isle of Wight, and on the south coast of England. More recently the same bed has been found and worked to an enormous extent in the neighbourhood of Cambridge, and it has been recognized near the town of Havre, in France. Marl beds have also been found in France, very valuable for manure.

The phosphatic beds of Cambridge have yielded employment to a vast number of persons, and have acquired extreme importance. Where the deposit is thick, and the quality good, the land containing the bed has, in some cases, been let for as much as £400 per acre, the lessee making good the surface after the phosphatic nodules are removed.

They are dug for commercial purposes, not only in the neighbourhood of Cambridge, but all along the line of railway between Cambridge and Hitchin, and for some miles on the other side of Hitchin, both on the Great Northern and Midland lines. They are also raised in the neighbourhood of Potton, in Bedfordshire, though apparently from a different bed. They are dug to the depth of fourteen and fifteen feet. The yield of washed stones is as high as 350 tons per acre in some of the best lands near Cambridge, but is not more than from 200 to 250 tons per acre a few miles away. The deposit is very uncertain, and there is no appearance at the surface to guide those who seek for the stones. It is therefore necessary to bore whole districts of country; and sometimes a field of ten or fifteen acres will contain a continuous deposit, while at other places there will be only small patches. There is reason to suppose that the nodules may be found in the upper greensand, far beyond the known localities, and at considerable depth. The deposit is from nine to twelve inches thick, and consists of about one part stone to three, four, or five parts clay. When dug, the stones are removed to washing mills, and the clay is carried away by water. The composition of the coprolites is as follows:—

Phosphate of lime, 55 to 58 per cent.
Carbonate of lime, 15 to 20 „
Water, sand, iron, oxide, &c.

When not covered by too much overlying deposit of chalk or gravel, the removal of the coprolites is effected after the head of earth and other material has been pared off, and generally by pits of no great depth. Although the beds are not exhausted, there is less demand at present for the nodules. The annual produce for 1864 is estimated by Mr. Lawes at from 30,000 to 40,000 tons.

It is still usual to call these nodules *coprolites*, or dung-stones, a name given originally by Dr. Buckland to the *exuviæ* of reptiles found in the lias, and also phosphatic. They are not, however, coprolitic in any proper sense. It would seem that very large organic accumulations have been made at the time of the deposit of the upper greensand, and that the animals were chiefly of high organization—either reptilian, or possibly of mammalia and birds. Mixed up with sand and foreign substances, the less destructible parts of these animals have become converted into earthy phosphate of lime, and this has separated itself in the bands that now exist where the upper greensand intervenes between the chalk and the gault.

Coprolites are obtained from the greensand to some extent in France, in the following departments, viz., Ardennes, Meuse, Haute-Marne, and Aube. The largest deposits are in the northern part of the outcropping line of the formation, where nodules are constantly turned up on the land. They are worked at a depth of from twenty to twenty-five feet below the surface near Vouziers, but the quality is inferior, not averaging more than 20 to 25 per cent. Rich specimens are found, but too few to be of much importance. The nodules are sometimes very large.

The upper greensand is by no means the only deposit in which phosphatic nodules and concretions appear. There are many such accumulations in various beds, especially in the lias, where, as I have said, Dr.

Buckland long ago observed whole beds of the excrement of fishes and reptiles. Fish-beds and other deposits where animal remains abound, and organic matter predominates, have been found in beds even of Silurian age; and there can be no doubt that stores of such material are laid up in many places where they have been accumulating for ages, and changing but little after their first deposit. Those that can now be brought once again into use, providing mineral food for plants, and enabling them to serve as vegetable food for animals, are well worthy the careful investigation of practical men.

Limestone and gypsum are both occasionally used as mineral manures, and in certain cases they may be valuable. It is not, indeed, very often that limestone can be obtained at a reasonable price, and yet be absent altogether from a soil capable of improvement by it; but the mere mechanical admixture of the salts of lime is occasionally useful. Much more usually, marling, manuring with mud, and warping or bringing upon land muddy water, and leaving it there to deposit a slime, are resorted to. These materials absolutely enrich a poor soil, besides improving its mechanical condition.

It has been well said, "Too light a soil is a spendthrift, too heavy a soil a miser." The first makes away with more than its means allow, and consumes its capital; the second retains in a useless state that which ought to be made widely useful. By the alterations just suggested, even when the mineral manure contains in itself no material that is absolutely needed, a wise frugality, a happy medium between these two extremes, is ensured. Burnt lime is extensively and successfully used as a manure. Its value is greatly affected by the amount and nature of the impurities contained in it.

There is another very important department of practical agriculture that requires a knowledge of geology to be properly carried out: it is drainage—a mechanical means of carrying off water that exists on the surface, or within the soil, in excess. Water is absolutely necessary to plants; it affords them direct food; it assists in preparing food for them, and rendering it digestible; it conveys to them other food; it renders the soil suitable for them; and it helps to regulate the conditions of temperature. In all these respects it is impossible to exaggerate its importance; but it is possible to have this valuable material at wrong times, and in wrong places; and as water, like fire, is a good servant, but a bad master, it becomes desirable to regulate its application, and remove it when in excess. Drainage performs this by preventing stagnating pools from interfering with nourishment, and carrying the water down to a convenient distance below the surface, whence it is either allowed to run off by natural channels, if there be a fall, or is lifted by machinery into such channels.

Ploughing, and especially deep ploughing, disturbs the ground and exposes it to the air; but it is not till drain-pipes are laid, and carry off water wherever its accumulation would be injurious, that the soil can be said to be permanently and properly available for high cultivation. It will be evident that this operation belongs rather to engineering than to any other department of applied science. No one who has not watched the process can at all understand the extent and efficacy of a good well-contrived and systematic drainage—of the rapidity with which the work is done, and the almost immediate improvement that ensues. Not only is the soil thus rendered drier, more crumbling, and warmer, but it also becomes more active and healthy: more active, because air is able to enter, instead of water, within the interstices, thus producing a quicker weathering of the inorganic, and decay of the organic contents; and healthier, because the access of air prevents the generation of acids, which are disadvantageous to land plants. At the same time undue tenacity of the soil is prevented, thus enabling roots to penetrate. It was at one time supposed that by deep draining the rain-water would carry down and remove manure out of the soil, but this has not proved to be the case. Drainage is chiefly important in heavy clay lands.

I need hardly point out to you in this place the extreme value of good geological maps in enabling the agriculturist to judge of the prospect of improvement, not only by drainage, but by mixing soils, and by the discovery of mineral manures. By means of such maps on a fit scale,—and they are now obtainable for a great part of England at an extremely small cost,—all that is most important in the relation of geology to agriculture may be seen at a glance. By their help the nature of the subsoil and the rock below becomes known. By them questions of drainage and water supply may be determined, and improvements of many kinds suggested. Without this knowledge of the underlying rock, on the other hand, the agriculturist works in the dark, must grope about at great cost and uncertainty for what may be immediately beneath his feet, and he may send to a distance for material in his own fields.

Although none can doubt the great value of such geological maps as we already possess, and may shortly expect to see completed, for most parts of England, it must be admited that the neglect of information concerning the superficial stratum of gravel is much to be regretted. For the agriculturist a second series of maps, having the subsoil everywhere marked, is exceedingly desirable, and we may hope it will some day be obtained.

But if geological maps are useful generally, they are especially so in draining operations; for much of the work of this kind must be carried on out of sight, and must be dependent on the state of the rock below. Where this is open, porous, or fissured, water passes away readily and air is supplied freely. Where it is close and impermeable, drain-pipes must be used, and must be arranged so as to take advantage of the run of the beds and the outcropping of any different stratum of rock.

The passage of water through those rocks that we generally regard as impermeable is so slow as to be practically unrecognizable. Through permeable rocks it is not rapid, except where there are open cracks and fissures. But all rocks so far admit the passage of water that after long drought they become dry to considerable depths, and after long rain the water passes down to some distance. This is due to capillary action, and is subject to the laws that govern the passage of fluids in capillary tubes.

The agriculturist, in endeavouring to estimate the effect of draining operations, must carefully bear this in mind.

There is one important point in regard to drainage that is too little recognised by agriculturists, and that is purely geological. It is in reference to the depth at which water naturally stands in rock, and the influence of this on drains that descend below an impermeable, or nearly impermeable, subsoil, such as in most cases is the cause of swampy and undrained soils. There is in every rock, but especially in porous rocks, such as sandstones and limestones, a surface below which the rock contains water to saturation, and above which it is comparatively dry. This surface is constantly changing its level, though by no means immediately affected by the season. When, then, in undrained land, the rock is reached above the surface of permanent saturation, there may often exist means of drainage to some outfall at no great distance by taking advantage of the comparatively dry state of the rock. The surface of permanent saturation will be in a general sense parallel to the surface of the land, and it is but little affected by the waters of any stream running on the surface, which are almost always confined to their own beds.

An ingenious practical method of drainage, suggested some years ago by Mr. Dumolo, seems to me to depend on this principle. It consists in putting main drains, at a depth below that at which water naturally stands, during dry weather, in a pit dug into the rock. It is found practically that such a drain will receive and carry away water from a swamp, and discharge it into a stream or at a natural outfall, if found within a convenient distance at the same level.

The drainage of fens and meres is an operation that may involve the lifting of large quantities of water, but in other respects differs nothing in principle from ordinary draining. In all cases the ultimate result of draining must be a lowering of the soil,* and thus there is a tendency to repeat the former condition, and render drainage more necessary than ever. But the tendency of most agricultural work is to raise soil by a constant addition of new matter in excess of the amount removed by the crops. In some cases also it has been found possible to adopt the process of warping, or introducing muddy water, and removing the water when cleared of its mud by being left stagnant. When this can be done the ground is raised, and may even be placed out of danger from subsequent flooding.

* In the recent draining of Whittlesea Mere, in Cambridgeshire, the subsidence amounted to 3 feet 6 inches.

Lecture the Second.

SPRINGS AND WATER SUPPLY.

To obtain a sufficient and permanent supply of good fresh water, either for agricultural purposes or for the use of men living in towns and cities, is a matter of such extreme importance that every inquiry connected with it is well worthy of attention. It is in a very direct manner connected with geology: for all the conditions under which water exists in the earth depend on the arrangement of rocks and the facilities for circulation among and between them. I hope to point out to you in the present lecture the facts on which water-circulation and water-supply depend, and thus enable you to understand and appreciate the efforts that have been made in our own country or elsewhere to obtain supplies by artificial means when and to the extent they are required.

The one great source of water is the ocean; the one great means by which it is transferred from the ocean to the land is the atmosphere; and the constant circulation of water not only through the atmosphere in the state of aqueous vapour, but through the earth in its liquid state, is the great fact to be borne in mind by the practical geologist in his investigations concerning the sources of water, and by the engineer, who has to consider in what way any required quantity may be best obtained and conveyed. I shall therefore occupy no time in preliminary description or discussion, but proceed at once to point out to you the nature of this circulation, the behaviour of different rocks when subject to the presence of water under more or less pressure, and the result of the alternation of permeable and impermeable rocks, continuous and broken strata, and other structural phenomena on the progress of water through the earth.

Over the vast area, consisting of nearly three-fourths of the whole surface of the earth, now covered by the ocean,—an area of 145,000,000 of square miles,—there is ever present an atmosphere of aqueous vapour, which, with the other air, is constantly being carried along by the winds, and at length reaches land. In passing over the land, the air becomes changed in temperature and in its electrical state, and ceases to retain the aqueous vapour mixed with it. From vapour the water passes into cloud, and from cloud to rain. Water or rain falls on the fifty millions of square miles of land, this water having previously been sucked up from thrice that area of sea; and the rain that falls in the course of a single year on the land would, if accumulated, cover its whole surface to a depth of nearly three feet.

Such, in a few words, is the circulation of water through the air. It is incessant, and the annual average is constant; but the quantity of cloud and rain vary extremely in different places and at different seasons; for while some spots receive so much water that they might be submerged by it to a depth of many yards in a year, others are perfectly dry, and know neither cloud nor rain from one year's end to another.

If we trace the history of the rain that falls, we shall find first that a large proportion is attracted to the summits and flanks of mountain-chains, to upland valleys and lofty plains; secondly, that the selected spots for the chief rain-fall have the sea at no great distance, and are subject to winds blowing more freely and frequently from the sea than from extensive tracts of dry land in the interior of the country. As the temperature of the air is known to become lower as we ascend to the upper strata, and as cool air cannot retain so much aqueous vapour as warm air, the air is deprived of its moisture, and rain falls whenever moist air rises towards and passes over a mountain-chain. Much of the rain reaches the earth on slopes looking towards the sea, and down these slopes it must pass to reach the sea again. A large quantity of water is thus conducted by various natural channels to rivers, and these cross the low lands and enter the ocean. But it will be evident that out of the whole of a large district only a small proportion consists of river-courses, even if the channels of the smallest rivulets are all included, whilst the rain falls alike on the whole surface. The soil becomes wet, and, according to its nature, either retains the moisture in pools or allows it to pass down. The subsoil behaves in like manner; and much moisture from very heavy and continued rain cannot fail to reach the underlying rock.

Evaporation removes a great deal; but there must always be an important residuum, and of this we must give account.

Of the rocks which water thus reaches, some are sands and open sandstones or broken limestones, and others disintegrated and fragmentary rocks. These allow water to enter them easily and rapidly, and almost as easily they give back the water at need. Others are very differently constituted: some consist of porous strata, between or amongst which are beds shutting off entirely the passage of water. Many of the natural clays are of this nature; and water passes between such clays as through a pipe, and is almost prevented from rising. So again, many rocks are broken and disturbed by faults, or by anticlinal and synclinal axes, while veins often replace the crevices and are filled with crystalline mineral. The nature of rocks then, the mode in which they are arranged, and the mechanical conditions under which they are presented to the action of water,—these are the points that govern the course of that part of the rain-fall of a district that is absorbed into the soil before running into rivulets or other streams, and that escapes from re-evaporation into the air and from immediate use by plants or animals.

Rocks, as I have pointed out in the last lecture, are either limestones, sandstones, clays, slates, or granites. The use of these expressions in a wide sense will, at any rate, suffice for the purpose I have now in view. Of such rocks the first two are permeable, or allow water to pass more or less freely among and between their particles when in the solid state; the latter three are not in this sense permeable. Assuming, then, an alternation of these materials in any order,—it matters not what,—there will be an alternation, or a series of alternations, of permeable or impermeable beds. Water reaching a permeable bed will certainly enter and be absorbed in the substance of the bed, besides traversing all open passages, whether minute or on a large scale. Water reaching the impermeable beds will remain on the surface, or will run down into cracks and fissures in the substance of the rock.

All rocks contain water. Even the driest and most compact marbles in their driest state hold from ·4 to 4 per cent. by weight in their composition. Granites contain water: some even in the ordinary dry state contain one pint and a half of water in every cubic foot, and are capable of absorbing half a pint more. This is independent of the water of consolidation. In every case, under the least favourable conditions, we may assert that none of the rocks commonly met with near the earth's surface, and regarded as non-absorbent or impermeable, contain less than two pints of water in every cubic yard. In other words, as a cubic yard of ordinary stone weighs nearly two tons, we may say that each ton even of the least absorbent rock will contain a pint of water.

But there is a wide difference between the water that rocks cannot be freed from and the water they allow to pass freely through their interstices. Let us consider the different varieties of rock each by itself. Almost all were originally deposited with and from water in the sea, a river, or a lake. Many have since undergone great change by exposure to heat, pressure, and chemical action. Almost all have become much altered, and often could not be recognized if compared with the original mud of which they were formed. All have been dried, and have since been subjected to the action of rain-water passing through the earth. The water passes between and among the particles, partly by pressure and partly by capillary action, and often it has contained acids assisting it to make its way.

The quantity of water capable of being held by common loose sea-sand amounts to at least two gallons in a cubic foot. In ordinary sandstones nearly half that quantity would be contained; and in the best building-stones belonging to the sandstone group, from four to five pints of water are contained in each cubic foot of the stone in its ordinary state. It will give a better idea of this quantity to say that, in an area of such sandstone in its ordinary state, occupying ten square miles, and ten yards in thickness, the quantity of water contained is from four to five hundred millions of gallons. This would fill a reservoir of a hundred acres to the depth of ten feet. If, then, there be beneath the surface, at any depth, and between impermeable beds, a space ten miles square of sandstone, ten yards thick, this sandstone would be capable of containing between forty and fifty thousand millions of gallons of water; and if these sands were fed from above by the rain-fall of a district of one hundred square miles, on which the rain-fall was twenty-six inches per annum, of which one-third part entered the earth, it would need three years to accumulate the quantity named. It is evident, then, that the underground store of water must generally be greatly in excess of the mean annual supply. It will be important to remember this in estimating the value of an underground source of springs fed by a drainage area of measurable extent. The underground store, though really dependant on the rainfall ultimately, is rather dependant on the average than on any particular season.

But sandstones are rarely without bands of clayey matter, separating their water contents into sheets of moderate thickness, and owing to faults and hitches, and occasionally to vertical bands of compact and often crystalline mineral, an underground sandstone district is generally broken up into boxes of various dimensions, each one of which is independent to some extent of the rest. Like all other stratified rocks, sandstones have been subject to great tilting of the strata. They thus sometimes stand at a considerable pitch, which is tolerably uniform over great distances. Sometimes the dip is very moderate, and occasionally there is even a reverse dip. We shall see hereafter how important are all these conditions to the available water contents of a sandstone district, and how entirely the quantity of water procurable at a given point depends on these unseen, but often known and recognizable, geological phenomena.

Although sandstones and sands are pre-eminently

water-bearing beds, there are some varieties passing into pudding-stone on the one hand and quartzite on the other, that contain no available water whatever in their mass. The water they hold is water of consolidation, and is not given off under any conditions short of the destruction of the stone by calcining. Of this water the practical geologist takes no account. It is an indication of the origin of the rock, but is not otherwise to be regarded. Even in such rocks, however, it rarely happens that there are not systematic fissures and innumerable small cracks, wherever there is an exposed surface. Into these water cannot fail to penetrate, and the supply from them is sometimes large. The weathering of the rock often commences in this way, for though water occasionally dissolves silica, this produces little chemical effect on a large scale. It is almost entirely from natural joints produced by contraction or fissures, during elevation, that the supply, if any, is obtained.

Limestones differ from sandstones in many ways independently of their composition; and their water capacity as well as their behaviour as water-bearing rocks are among these points of difference. Thus, the least absorbent of the common limestones of England holds as much water in its ordinary state as a good compact variety of sandstone fit for building purposes, namely, from four to five pints in the cubic foot; while a cubic foot of Bath stone will absorb double that quantity, and some varieties of magnesian limestone nearly three times as much.* A bed of such stone in the earth, ten yards thick, would contain in an area of ten miles square as much water as would fill a reservoir of three hundred and fifty acres to a depth of ten feet.

Chalk is still more absorbent than the building limestones, for a cubic foot of soft chalk will hold as much as two gallons of water, or as much as loose sand. Such chalk will take up half its own bulk of water, and yet hardly appear wet. By exhaustive pumping, however, a large quantity of water may be obtained from chalk; for the rock seems to act as a sponge, the water tending to sink to the bottom. In most solid limestones the water contained in the solid mass does not readily come away by pumping, being kept up by friction as well as by capillary attraction. Friction seems to act more effectually on limestones than on sandstones, as water passes from one part to another of the wet rock much more readily in the latter than in the former. Thus the quantity of water that can be drawn out of ordinary unfissured limestone when fully saturated is very small, while the quantity from soft sandstone is very large.

But if limestone is inferior in some respects to sandstone as an absorbent, it is, on the other hand, more available as a water-bearing rock, as being far more cracked and fissured, both on a large and small scale, both at and near the surface, and at all depths. It differs also in being sensibly acted on by water, both mechanically by abrasion and wear, and chemically by becoming dissolved and carried away to be re-deposited elsewhere. The cavernous nature of limestone is one of its most remarkable features, and it is difficult for anyone not familiar with the rock to judge of the extent to which this is traceable in its mass. But limestone is also almost always stratified, and at the intervals of strata there are either open spaces allowing a free passage to water, or bands of clay and other material preventing the passage of water. Limestone also, like sandstone, is often faulted, vertical fissures, either open or filled with clay, dividing any large area into a multitude of smaller areas, each one of which has its own water system, though all communicate with more or less freedom. The cracked state of limestone at the surface, and wherever weather can act upon it, tends also constantly to increase, and causes still more water to enter the mass; for water as it falls from the clouds, and after passing through vegetable soil, is always sufficiently charged with carbonic acid to render it a ready solvent of carbonate of lime in all forms.

Clays, though practically impermeable, often contain as much as ten per cent. of water (by weight). When dry and least absorbent, and when hardened into shale or slate, this rock still contains six or eight per cent. of water; and other clay rocks, such as the varieties of schist, which are extremely numerous, are similarly constituted.

Water is therefore present in great abundance in the rocks that are near the surface of the earth. It is present in the substance of all, and in the interstices of the particles of which they are made up. In some rocks, as in sands and loose sandstones, the water would readily run out and fill any cavity, if such existed naturally or were produced artificially. In others the rocks may be wet, but do not yield their water readily into such cavities. In others, again, there are natural cavities, very numerous and often very large, and always more or less filled with water, under ordinary conditions. So much water is thus held in rocks beneath the earth's surface that under the surface in all those parts where rain is frequent we may consider that, within a depth of 1,000 feet, there is water, which, if collected, would be a sheet of the same area, never less than six inches deep, and in some rocks as much as 200 or 300 feet. In certain parts of the soft chalk it is even possible that the sheet of water might be half the depth of the rock; for I have myself proved by experiment that some chalk is capable of absorbing more than half its own bulk before it is fully saturated.

Of the rain that falls upon the earth at any place during a given period, it is calculated that not more than one-third runs off the surface and enters the sea by rivers. This calculation cannot in the nature of things be very exact, and must vary greatly at different seasons and in different climates, but it may be taken as the best known approximation. What, it may be asked, becomes of the rest? Part of it, we know, is evaporated; part of it feeds animal and vegetable life; but there remains an ample supply to enter the earth. Most soils absorb water, and allow it to sink down to the subsoil. Beneath the subsoil is the rock; into this the water penetrates, either by absorption, the rock acting like a sponge, or by the innumerable crevices and larger fissures that break it up into convenient fragments. Down all such natural channels the water passes. Occasionally it meets with a permeable rock, and through this it runs—now through a large mass, slowly, and with much friction and interference, and now into open cavities, or through channels that serve as conduit pipes, and convey it horizontally, or even bring it up again under the influence of the pressure of a column whose height has reference to the level of the spot at which it first entered as rain.

This steady and perpetual circulation through the interior of the earth is due in a large measure to the natural inequalities of the surface of the land. With lofty mountains traversing the larger and even many of the smaller tracts of land—with many parallel and transverse systems of lower mountains—with extensive areas of lofty table-land—and with wide and numerous plains and innumerable valleys, there is a complete framework adapted to assist in this great work of conveying water not only over but through the earth. As most part of the rain falls on the mountains and high ground, and the rocks are usually tilted towards the plains from those parts of the land which form axes of elevation, the tendency of water to run down a slope which is not less marked in the interior of the earth than on its surface, ensures the conveyance of ample supplies. In many cases these must exist under pressure, arising from the fact that the channels formed between two impermeable rocks are of the nature of closed pipes. But inasmuch as the dip or inclination of the strata is not always or even generally the same as the natural slope of the surface, and that the faults remove rocks frequently to a considerable distance vertically, it will happen that the water entering the strata above will sometimes find an issue at some lower level at a considerable distance, where it will well up at a fault, or at some artificial cutting, or in some other way will reach the surface again, though always at a lower level than that at which it entered. When water issues naturally at the surface by any of these means, it is called a spring. It may be a spring of the ordinary kind, when there are no marked mineral contents in the water; or a mineral spring, when foreign ingredients are present in large proportion, and are adapted, it may be, for some medical purpose; or it may be a thermal spring, whose temperature is above the mean annual temperature of the place of observation. Each case is interesting and economically important. Besides these springs welling forth at the surface, there are many others only reached artificially, and not rising to the surface at all.

Natural springs occur in surface rocks, such as sand or gravel, when these rest on impermeable strata, and receive a larger quantity of rain on their surface than is carried off by evaporation or streams. The water accumulates as an underground pond or lake (Fig. 2, *a*) below, instead of upon the surface. It will not rise above the ground, nor will it generally approach the ground; but its depth is rarely very great, and it is reached by wells (p). The quantity of the supply must vary with the rain-fall of the season, and in dry seasons these springs generally fail, or at any

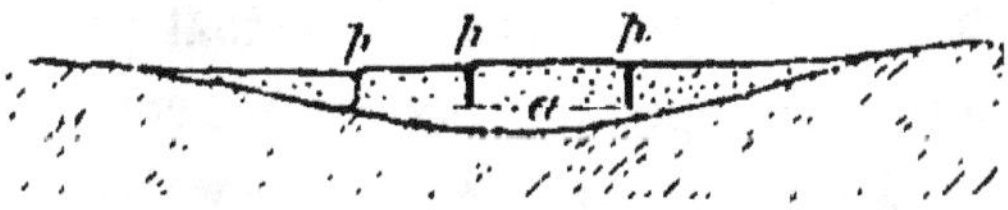

Fig. 2.

rate get much lower than usual. The quality of the water may appear good, but is liable to injury from any cause that affects the surface, and thus in large cities such sources of supply are unsafe, owing to the filtration into them of organic matter from sewage and graveyards. Wells in such localities sometimes yield upwards of a hundred grains of solid matter to the gallon.

Springs of this class are called land springs. They are common wherever there is gravel, or where surface deposits overlie impermeable rocks. For agricultural purposes they are valuable, but they are not fitted to supply large towns.

A second class of natural springs includes those which issue on hill sides in valleys, or on plains surrounded or fringed by higher land, either hills or mountains, and which depend on the outcrop of certain strata which contain and carry water, but rest on other strata or other rocks that are impermeable. This condition is illustrated in the diagram, Fig. 3, where at the points c, a'', such beds are represented as intersected by the line of the surface: in one place, on a hill-side; in the other, in a valley. It will readily be seen, that the issuing of springs under these circumstances is a very simple and easily-understood matter; and they are often the means adopted by nature to remove the excess of water over very extensive districts. Though simple enough in principle, the actual phenomena in reference to these springs may become complicated and obscure. In the first place, the water may come through a certain bed (*a*), and this may be either

Fig. 3.

covered by, or cover, impermeable beds. In this event, the actual source of the supply may be distant, and much above the level of the point of emergence. A considerable tract may entirely or partially drain into a single channel, and this may run a long way without any opportunity of escape being offered. When it issues, it may therefore be already a considerable stream. But this also may either issue at once as a large body of water, or may drain out in a multitude of springs from a number of points on a continuous line of outcrop. In the latter case, each individual spring may be small, though their combined value is large. Groups of springs of this kind are often very important. They are so long on their way through the earth, as to divide the irregularities of season over a considerable time, and thus become independent of season. The water having filtered through the earth for a long distance, is fresh and wholesome. It may, indeed, be too much loaded with solid contents to be available for culinary and household purposes, but it may be extremely soft and pure. It is unimportant, in calculating the value of such sources, whether they come out on a hill-side or a valley-bottom; and by artificial means it is often possible to connect the water of several springs into one, and, by removing accumulations of rubbish which choke the outlet, increase considerably the total amount of flow. Springs of this kind may also be tapped on their way to the natural outlet, which will thus be rendered much smaller than before. At any rate, the supply brought is strictly limited, and therefore what is taken at any one place is taken from the general stock.

It may be, however, that the whole of the upper rock is porous and rests on an underlying, impermeable stratum. The supply is then much more abundant at certain seasons, but far less regular, so that little more dependence can be placed on springs breaking out under these circumstances than on land-springs. Good examples of such springs exist in the Cotswolds, where, all along the contact of the oolites with the lias, groups of springs are known to issue. A few days after rain most of these springs become swollen, and run very freely. When a few weeks' dry summer weather occurs, the supply of water falls off very greatly, and many of the springs altogether. In this case, it is true that the dip of the beds, though towards the escarpment for a short distance, soon changes, and bends towards the east; but the main cause of the irregularity of the springs must be sought for in the fact that, though crop-springs in one sense, they are land-springs in the nature of their supply. The diagram, Fig. 4, will illustrate this condition. The

West.

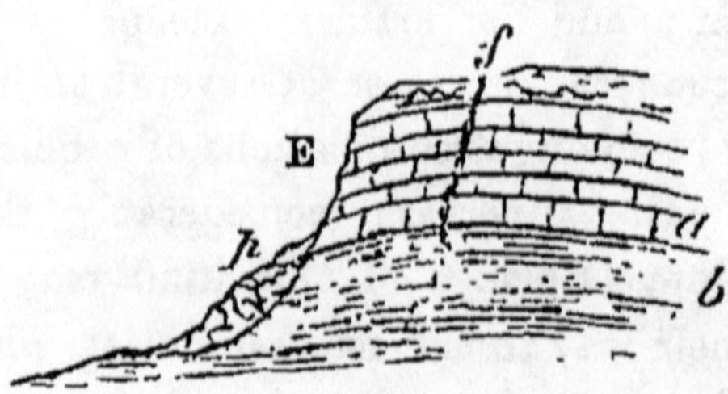

East.

Fig. 4.

inclination of the beds of lias (*b*) is towards the east, but close to the escarpment (E) the beds at the base of the lower oolite appear to dip towards the west. At *p*, at the contact of the lias and lower oolite, the springs issue, but they drain off little more water than that falling on the rock west of *f*. The supply is thus inconsiderable, and, as all the beds to the surface are porous, it is also irregular, and rapidly affected by rain-fall or drought.

In the districts whose structure is indicated in the diagram, Fig. 3, it is not difficult to obtain water by boring, or sinking a well to the water-bearing bed (*a*). The wells marked *p* will yield water, which may rise in the well to some height, if the source of supply of the water is above the level of the ground where the well is sunk. Such wells will partake of the nature of the springs issuing at *c*, and will, of course, take off water that would otherwise have reached those springs.

A third class of natural springs is illustrated in the diagram, Fig. 5, which represent beds, *a*, *a′* (bearing water), interrupted and broken by a fault, *f f′*. The beds are supposed to rest on impermeable strata, and

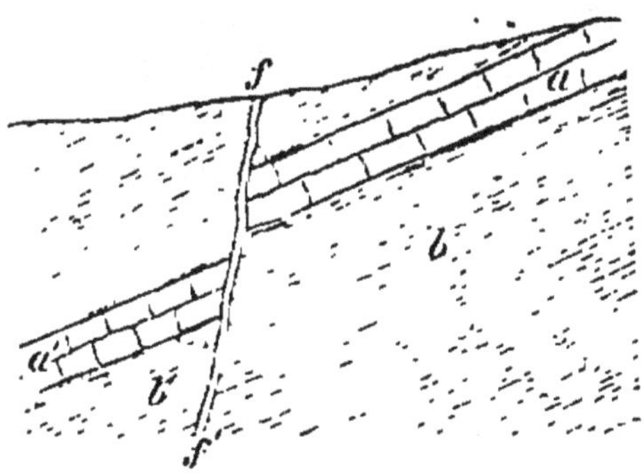

Fig. 5.

to receive water either from the outcropping porous beds, or from the surface, generally by crevices and weathered rocks. Impermeable beds are supposed also to overlie the porous beds. In this case, however, there are several possibilities. If the fault is open, the water passing down *a*, on the slope of the bed, may pass below the point where *a* recurs on the other side of the fault, and leave *a′* entirely dry. Referring to the diagram, Fig. 3, it is evident that the water in *a* may thus sink to another porous bed, *b*, and this may come to an open fault, *f f′*, where it rises again and supplies *a''*, in this way producing complication. But if the face of the fault towards *a* in Fig. 5 is open, and the face towards *a'* closed, the water may rise at *f* in a strong natural spring, unless it runs away downwards to some other more convenient outlet. If, again, the fault is open, but only so far as the connecting of *a* and *a'* are concerned, it will have no effect whatever in producing a spring. Whilst, then, wherever there is a fault in certain districts, there is almost always a spring, it is not more difficult to understand the reason of the exceptions to this general rule, than the explanation of the phenomenon itself. A fault acting as a wall, because it is filled with clay, will in most cases be accompanied by a spring, though not always at the exact spot where we might be inclined to look for it.

Another class of springs is the *Artesian spring*, so called because of some old sinkings successful in obtaining water at several places in the county of Artois (now the department of the Pas de Calais), in France. Springs of this kind occur naturally in many

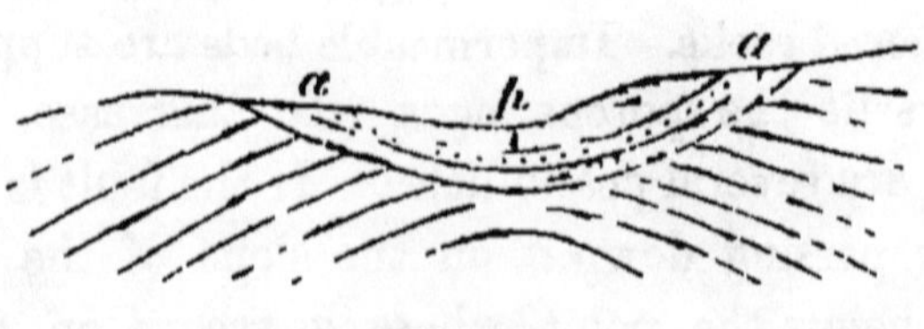

Fig. 6.

places, and have been obtained artificially from the earliest times. An idea of their nature may be obtained by a glance at the diagram, Fig. 6. A permeable bed, *a*, between two impermeable beds, crops out at the surface, and there receives the rain-fall and surface-water. The level of this outcrop is higher than that of a part of the surrounding country beneath which the strata pass, owing to their dip. The permeable bed thus represents a bent tube, and may be kept full of water under a pressure corresponding to the height at which the porous bed crops out. If, then, a well is sunk or a hole bored, as at *p*, the water will rise in it, not only towards, but even in some cases far above, the surface, in a jet. The history of these wells, which, from the principle they involve and the extent to which they may profitably be applied, are extremely important, is sufficiently interesting to justify a few words of allusion.

The most ancient of such wells that are known are to be found in the oases of the deserts in the north-eastern part of Africa. In the oasis of Thebes they are very numerous. They appear to have been sunk through about 80 feet of clay and marl by a shaft of 6 feet to 10 feet square, and then bored through 300 feet of limestone, beginning with a six or eight inch bore. At the bottom of this limestone water-bearing sands were met, and the water seems to have run over the top of the well. In the Lybian desert some such wells have been cleared out in modern times, and successfully restored to use. These wells are not less than 4,000 years old. Others, of very ancient but unknown date, were sunk by the Chinese, who have long known and used the method with success. The Chinese method of boring has of late years been introduced into Europe.

But the chief Artesian wells, and the oldest in Europe, are those in the north of France, and they seem to have spread thence through the other countries of Europe. They are sunk through the lower tertiary strata to the chalk, from whose upper beds the water is generally derived. The chalk extends in France from the Belgian frontier, in the north, to Poictiers, in the south; and from Troyes, in the east, to Le Mans, in the west. The central portion is covered with tertiary strata, which are not very thick, and of which the upper members are for the most part impervious, and the lower permeable. Thus, the construction of this class of wells is easy and inexpensive.

So simple is the operation of boring in this district, that an Artesian well was on one occasion commenced at Fontes (Pas de Calais), in these tertiary strata, at 6 *a.m.*, and finished at 3 *p.m.* the same day. The depth bored was 20 mètres (65½ feet), and a jet of water rose two feet above the surface, supplying nearly a hundred gallons per minute. The expense is not stated, but it must have been extremely small. In England, in soft strata, 60 feet can be bored for about five pounds sterling.

The Artesian wells of Artois date back certainly to the twelfth century, and there is one at Lillers, said to have been sunk in 1126, and to have yielded always, so far as is known, the same quantity of water. In Italy, at Modena and Bologna, and in Germany, at Vienna and elsewhere, ancient and successful wells of this kind exist; but it is only since the commencement of the present century that they have become general in Europe. In and around Paris there were already, in 1845, not less than eighty deep Artesian wells through the tertiary strata into the chalk. All of these were successful; many of them yielded a very large supply of water, and their cost was not excessive. The supply varies very much from different wells within the same district and in different districts, but is tolerably constant in the same well. One very remarkable well, sunk at Brou, on the Marne, in 1845, to a depth of 75 mètres, supplied nearly 800,000 gallons per day, the original cost being only £200. This is an extreme case; but a supply of from 30,000 to 150,000 gallons per day is a common yield, and the expense of sinking is extremely moderate. The yield, though in other respects constant, is not unfrequently interfered with by the choking of the passage, either from sand forced up from the bottom, or from the falling in of the sides.

As a specimen of the larger operations in Artesian wells, I may refer you to the sinkings for the supply of the city of Paris, commenced in 1833, at Grenelle, and continued, at intervals, till 1841, when water-bearing strata below the chalk were reached at 1,800 feet, at a total cost of nearly £15,000. The first rush of water was at the rate of nearly a million of gallons per day, rising 120 feet above the surface. This continued for some time, and may be regarded as permanent, so far as the water supply is concerned. Nothing but a thorough confidence in the geological conclusions as to the stratification of the district, could have secured a successful issue to this undertaking. It was hoped that water would be obtained at about 1,300 feet, at a cost of about £4,000.

Artesian wells are common also in England, not only in and around London, where the geological conditions closely resemble those of Paris, but at Cambridge, through the gault, at Liverpool through the new red sandstone, and elsewhere. London and Paris are both built in valleys, on tertiary strata, covering basin-shaped depressions in the chalk to a considerable but variable depth, and in both localities the bottom beds of the tertiary series consist of open water-bearing sands, covered with impermeable plastic clay.

In both, therefore, the method of Artesian borings is applicable, first to the chalk itself at a moderate and known depth, and afterwards through the chalk to the sands below it at an unknown depth. The Artesian wells of London are, however, confined to borings through the tertiaries into the chalk, and do not include any sinkings to the greensand. No doubt, the existence of well-marked sands between the lower chalk and the gault in England, and the thinness of the sands and irregularity of the gault in France, render the chances of sinking better with us than on the other side of the Channel; but, on the other hand, the thickness of the chalk itself seems to be generally much greater.

The depth of most of the Artesian wells of London is less than 400 feet, and none of them are much above 500 feet. Some enter the chalk to a depth of 200 feet, or more, and, therefore, obtain their water to some extent from that formation; while others only reach the chalk, and obtain water from the sands. The tertiary strata pierced are rarely more than 250 feet in thickness. The water, when reached, seldom rises higher than from 40 feet to 60 feet below the level of the Thames high-water mark, and thus considerable expenses are incurred in lifting it. It still remains a question how far deep sinkings and borings through the chalk to the greensand would yield a supply sufficient in quantity to justify the increased cost of boring, and whether in such springs the water would rise sufficiently high to do away with the necessity of pumping.

The wells at Cambridge are very numerous, and penetrate the gault to the lower greensand at a depth of from 100 feet to 150 feet. The cost is very small, and the supply at first rose to or above the surface. It is now 10 feet or 12 feet below. The supply is large and steady, and the number of wells within a few square miles amounts to several hundred.

The wells in the new red sandstone at Liverpool and elsewhere are also very numerous, but nowhere very deep. The cost is not very great, and the supply of water is generally large. The town of Wolverhampton is supplied in this manner, and many places in the midland counties depend on this rock for their water.

The quality of the water obtained from Artesian wells is a matter of some importance. It might have been expected that water passing through so long a course of strata would absorb mineral matter, and become very impure, but such is not necessarily the case. Clay is capable either of removing mineral salts from water when they are already present, or yielding various salts if the water be pure; and thus waters passing through a great thickness of clay may be either remarkably pure, or very hard. It would be easy to quote examples of both these conditions. The waters of deep wells in London contrast very unfavourably in this respect with those of Paris, as will be evident on reference to the table in the next page.

The qualities of water for practical use in cities and houses may be estimated in many ways:—first, for drinking; secondly, for cleansing; thirdly, for manufacturing purposes, as dyeing and paper-making; and, lastly, for general sanitary purposes. A water that is excellent for drinking purposes may be totally unfit for washing or dyeing, and a water quite fit for cleansing may be a very flat and indifferent, and even an unwholesome, drinking water. Anything but salt water is sufficient for watering roads and flushing sewers. Waters from shallow wells are apt to be loaded with the impurities of surface rocks, such as carbonates or sulphates of lime, and various salts of magnesia, iron, and alumina. Generally the water from deep wells is both wholesome and fit for washing and brewing; and even if this is not the case when the spring is first tapped, the quality often improves with time.

The following tabular account of the analysis of the water of a few wells from known localities, and a few springs, will be useful.

NUMBER of GRAINS of SOLID MATTER per Imperial GALLON contained in the WATER of certain SPRINGS.

	Trafalgar Sq. Wells, Lond. terminating in chalk 252ft. below surface	Hampstead W. W. Co.'s Well, on top of Chalk.	The Mint, 202ft. below surface of Chalk.	Grenelle, Paris, below Chalk.	Surface Spring at crop of Chalk, Bushey Meads, Watford.	Gorbals Water at Glasgow.	Streams at Rivington (Liverpool).	Critchmere Springs, near Farnham.
Carb. lime	3·26	0·30	3·50	4·76	17·00	3·61	1·08	..
,, magnesia	2·25	..	1·50	0·99	0·43	..	0·54	trace
,, soda	18·05	16·32	8·63	..	..	..	..	..
,, iron	..	..	..	..	..	0·07	0·07	..
Bicarb. potash	..	..	..	2·07	..	..	..	..
Sulph. lime	..	..	..	..	1·20	0·87	..	1·07
,, potash	13·67	..	..	0·86	..	0·30	..	0·03
,, soda	8·75	15·50	13·14	..	—		..	..
,, magn.	..	..	..	..	—	0·12	..	..
Chlor. potass.	..	..	..	0·76	traces	..	2·37	0·26
,, sodium	20·06	11·50	10·53	..	1·82	0·88		0·88
Phosph. lime	0·03	..	..	..	traces	..	..	..
,, soda	0·29	..	..	..	..	..	..	..
,, iron	..	..	trace	..	..	..	..	1·00
Silica	0·97	1·50	0·50	0·40	1·14	0·15	0·52	..
Apocrenic acid	0·10	..	..	..	..	..	..	..
Crenic acid	0·14	..	..	..	..	..	..	..
Extractive matter	0·67	..	..	..	..	..	..	..
Organic matter.	..	1·08	trace	0·20	..	1·15	0·72	0·90
	68·24	46·20	37·80	9·86	21·59	7·15	5·30	4·14

Of the different minerals there are some that produce the condition called hardness, and interfere much with the use of the water for detergent purposes, though they are not otherwise injurious. The alkaline salts, however, render water soft, and thus the large quantity of salts of soda and potash in some of the waters from deep wells does not interfere with their value for household purposes. Carbonate of lime and magnesia, on the other hand, and the salts of iron, though they render water hard, leave it well fitted for drinking purposes.

Besides the cases to which I have chiefly alluded in this account of Artesian springs, there are others that belong to the same class, though the conditions appear slightly different. These are illustrated in the new red sandstone, where such a section as that represented in the diagram, Fig. 7, is not uncommon. In this

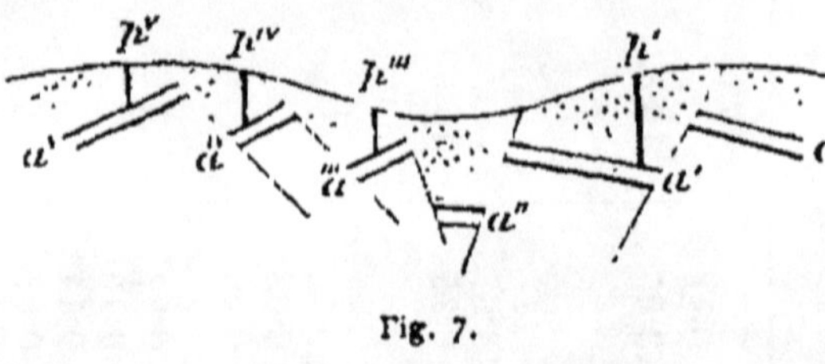

Fig. 7.

case, by a succession of faults partially and imperfectly permeable, the rock is broken up into a series of boxes, not without communication, but separated by material through which water passes very slowly. Borings sunk to a particular water-bearing bed, *a a'*, &c., will have very different depths, and yield very different quantities of water, rising to very different heights above a fixed level. The quantity of water obtainable from wells, under such circumstances, is limited. It is dependent on the annual rain-fall of the district, but within certain limits is capable of increase, the channels of communication becoming enlarged and opened with the exhaustion of the supply from a particular bed.

I pass on now to a fifth class of springs—a class somewhat exceptional, and generally occurring in connection with disturbances of strata, or the presence of metamorphic rock. The springs of this class are almost always highly charged with mineral matter and gases, including free carbonic acid gas, nitrogen, hydrogen, oxygen, and sulphuretted hydrogen gas, with a long series of salts of most of the metals. So large is the quantity of matter brought by these springs to the earth's surface from the interior, that, according to a calculation by M. Lecoq, who has recently published an elaborate work on the subject, certain known mineral springs of the central plateau of France, whose waters have been carefully examined,

Fig. 8.

bring to the surface upwards of 16,000 tons weight per annum of various salts. The diagram, Fig. 8, illustrates one of the modes in which these waters rise through broken strata, at an anticlinal axis ; and Fig. 9. shows the manner in which they sometimes

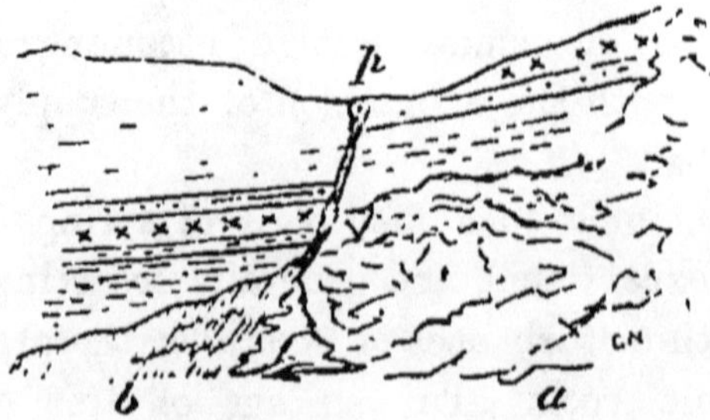

Fig. 9.

proceed from among metamorphic rocks, often in connection with faults. These springs are generally thermal, or possess a temperature independent of the surface, and higher than the mean annual temperature of the place at which they emerge. This temperature varies, sometimes reaching the boiling point of water. The water rises from great but unknown depths, often under extreme pressure. It often issues in large quantities, rising above the surface in a jet. Occasionally used for medicinal purposes, and the heat being sometimes available economically, these springs are generally well known in the districts in which they occur.. They are found in all parts of the world, and at all levels above the sea, but they are usually most abundant in mountainous regions, or near volcanoes.

The flow of springs is not always uniform, and this is the case with all kinds of springs and in all countries; but, with a few remarkable exceptions, deep springs are much more uniform in all respects than those which come from near the surface. For the cause of small and irregular variations we must probably look to the effect of the seasons, but these may not produce a visible result till long after the cause of change has ceased to act at the surface. There are, however, certain marked periodical variations of supply in particular cases, that require a more definite explanation. These are known as *intermittent springs*, and are almost confined to limestone districts. The river Mole, in Surrey, issuing from the chalk, is an example of this kind of spring. It appears abruptly at intervals, which are nearly regular; then runs strongly for a certain period, and as suddenly stops. A reference to the diagram, Fig. 10, will explain

Fig. 10.

the mystery. There exists, no doubt, in the chalk hills adjacent, a reservoir (*a*) filled gradually by percolation from the rock above, or by numerous small channels, but with only one outlet, which by some accident of the stratification, curves upwards a few yards before turning down again, and following the strata to emerge at *p*. So long as the water in *a* is not higher than the top of the curved part of the water-way no water can run out, but as soon as this happens, the bent tube acts as a siphon, and when it once begins, continues to carry out the water till it has emptied the reservoir. It will be evident that the limits of height of the curved pipe that apply to the siphon must apply also here, and therefore that the accident of such an exit for the water is likely to be very rare. It is not necessary to allude to modifications of this construction equally possible, and some of them known to happen. All these cause irregularities in the delivery of the water by its natural channels, and some of them appear very singular and exceptional.

Such are the phenomena of springs, natural and artificial, and such the methods adopted by nature and imitated by man to bring the water from the interior of the earth once more to the surface. It cannot be necessary that I should show you how essentially connected is this subject with geology, nor how completely a selection of the right locality for sinking in search of water must depend on a knowledge of rocks, of their superposition, and of the disturbances, upheavals, and disruptions they have undergone. It is more important that I should proceed at once to point out the application of this great subject to the supply of towns.

It is impossible to bring together a large assemblage of human beings within a confined area without some arrangement that shall secure a permanent supply of so essential an article as water. For this purpose most large towns are situated on, or very near, running streams, thus ensuring, at least, a certain quantity of this element, whatever the quality may be. But as the town increases, the waters of the stream do not alter, or rather they become reduced in quantity by the large use made of them along their course, near an important city; and they are also deteriorated in quality by the cultivation of the neighbouring lands, the accumulation of an excess of animal life on such lands, and the drainage both from the field and the farmyard into the river. Wherever also there is a large population—at least, in the western world—the sewage is greatly in excess of the demand of the agriculturist, and, becoming a nuisance, is conducted with other nuisances into the river as the great highway for all matters that can thus be got rid of. Thus the waters of the river as it passes the town become both smaller and more impure as the need of water becomes greater. Springs are then resorted to for potable water, and the river-water is only used for washing and cleaning of various kinds. The rain-water also is collected and stored for these purposes, for which it is well adapted when pure. But rain-water within a town is rendered foul by the admixture of smoke and vapours of various kinds arising from living beings and manufactories; and thus this supply, even if otherwise important, is of little value.

All available means have been resorted to from time immemorial to obtain and conduct water from natural sources of supply to large cities, where it is so much needed. The Romans conveyed water in this way from distant places in the mountains, where the supply was constant; and when at a convenient level they conveyed it by magnificent aqueducts to the spot where it was needed. Long before the Romans constructed these extravagant but noble works, the Greeks and their predecessors had conveyed water over the surface in closed pipes, taking advantage of the known principle, that water will always stand at the same level if there is free communication, no matter how irregular the form and dimensions of the channel. These same methods are resorted to at the present day, and with similar success. Where water can be obtained readily and in large quantities from springs, these are employed, and from them, no doubt, very constant supplies may sometimes be obtained by means of exhaustive pumping. In this way Paris has been enabled for a long time to struggle against the need for a more perfect system. In this way large quantities of water were formerly, and, indeed, are still, lifted to the surface in London and its neighbourhood. Most of the principal towns in England have, at one time or other, depended on this source of supply. We must, then, regard springs as a most valuable means of obtaining water for the use of large populations.

But springs often fail after a time. The constantly increasing demand of a growing population for manufacturing as well as domestic purposes becomes felt, and the new wells sunk are both more costly and less productive than those originally provided. And not only so, a very serious and important deterioration takes place in the quality of the water. Owing to the quantity of organic matter in a decaying state present at and near the surface, especially near sewers and gas-pipes that leak, and graveyards that are already crowded, the pure water below becomes affected by material which filters through from the surface into it, and the yield of the wells becomes so affected that it is not only disagreeable, but poisonous. In early times most of the cities of Europe, before they had attained their present dimensions, were decimated at certain intervals by some fearful pestilence, arising from the want of water and the accumulated filth at the surface. Now, we no longer have periodical visits of the plague; but year after year, as surely as summer arrives, insidious fevers and other diseases carry off their thousands, and of these victims a large proportion are poisoned by malaria arising from the bad condition and insufficient quantity of the water. This is not the case only in London, Paris, Vienna, and other great capitals, but in our large provincial towns, and even sometimes in those towns to which people resort for health and amusement.

A supply of water, however, is not a thing that can always be secured easily and without cost. It is an engineering operation for which the aid of the practical geologist must be sought. Most engineers of the present day are so well aware of this as to combine geology with their other attainments. To obtain an ample supply of pure water for a town, resort must be had to contrivances suggested by, or adapted to, tho physical condition of the country surrounding the town, and thus local as well as general knowledge becomes necessary.

Thus, while in some cases springs may be resorted to with advantage, in others rivers or canals may be used; in others, streams may be intercepted at or near their source; in others, again, mountain-lakes or tarns may be rendered available; and occasionally the rainfall of a limited district may be collected and stored in reservoirs or artificial lakes, whence the water, conveyed in closed pipes, is carried along underground or on the surface to a reservoir in the immediate vicinity of the place where the supply is needed. Examples of all these methods, more or less successfully carried out, may be found in the various towns of England. It is for the intelligent engineer, knowing the structure of the country, the prevalent rocks and their condition, and the various local requirements, to decide in any case which particular method shall be adopted. But his calculations must have reference to more than the mere surface-conditions, or the springs may fail when most needed, the canal may leak or become poisoned, the rainfall of the district may be insufficient or imperfectly collected, or the reservoir may fail at the hour of greatest need.

I have explained to you the conditions of the interior of the earth under which springs rise naturally or may be obtained artificially; but there are certain practical limits to the supply of water from springs even the most favourably circumstanced, which now require consideration. Chalk, loose sand, and some sandstones, will certainly yield to pumping a large quantity of water, and this will be replaced from time to time by rain, while the quantity of water contained in a given area of such rock, saturated to a certain depth, may very greatly exceed the quantity required for the town or city built on the surface. But it by no means follows that the water is obtainable by wells and borings because it is present in the rock. The loosest varieties of rock are sufficiently close in texture to offer great difficulties to the free passage of water; and even from wells of exhaustion the quantity of water removed in a given time is not only incapable of being increased, whatever the extent of wetness, but the rock is only drained of water within the content of a cone whose base is at the surface and whose apex is the bottom of the well, and the area of whose base is rarely more than half a mile in radius. The two rocks that yield the largest quantity of water are chalk and soft sandstone; and concerning both these experiment has shown that as such rocks commonly exist, and without large open fissures and natural reservoirs, little more than a million gallons per day can be expected from a single well. To yield this maximum, also, such wells must be at least a mile asunder. But even these are the indications of possible results, and could not be calculated upon. It is only in the event of reaching a natural reservoir of large size, existing under pressure in the interior of some limestone rock, that a large permanent supply could be obtained; and such reservoir would in time be exhausted if the removal of the water were in excess of the supply from the surrounding rocks. In the case of deep Artesian springs, where the supply comes from a distance and represents the rainfall on a large area of outcropping beds, the case is different in some measure; but even then it has always been found that there is a practical limit to the quantity obtainable, and that one well interferes with another if the distance between them is very small. This is the case even when the drainage area is certainly large enough to supply many times over the whole quantity removed.

The expense of Artesian borings, though varying much according to the particular circumstances of each case, is rarely very great. Except the great sinking and boring at Grenelle, near Paris, already alluded to as one of the greatest works of this kind in Europe, the cost of boring has rarely much exceeded 10*s.* per foot if the depth is under 200 feet, one pound per foot if from 200 to 500 feet, two pounds a foot from 500 to 1,000 feet, and three pounds per foot from 1,000 to 2,000 feet. Including shafts to some depth, and lining the shaft with brick and the bore-hole with metal, the cost even for the deeper operations is not considerable. There are thus powerful inducements at all times to resort to this expedient. On the other hand, it must not be lost sight of that there have been some very costly instances of failure after boring to a great depth in promising strata.

When, owing to a greatly increased population, a deterioration of the quality of the water, or a diminution of the regularity of the supply, it is necessary to have recourse to some other contrivance than springs, the old Roman method of constructing an aqueduct, or a canal conveying water from some distant point, has sometimes been resorted to. The river that passes by the town, or one of its tributaries, at once suggests itself for this purpose. Thus, in the case of London, the "New River" designed by Sir Hugh Myddelton replaced the imperfect resources of the day, and was thought a great success. But as population collects round a great city, opportunities of this kind of cutting off water even at a considerable distance are gradually becoming more and more scarce, while it becomes always more difficult to keep the stream clear. Such contrivances gradually cease to be applicable, and only when the aqueduct, canal, or pipe is connected with great and permanent reservoirs can this supply be recommended. But the construction of a reservoir is a very serious matter, as is known by fatal experience in some recent instances. It is not twelve months since the bursting of a newly-constructed reservoir in the neighbourhood of Sheffield produced a serious loss of life and property. Thus it is the case that even in this mode of obtaining a supply there are important points to be considered. I may state these as, *first*, the ultimate source of the water; *secondly*, the storing it in reservoirs; and, *thirdly*, the conveying it to its destination.

Where there is a natural lake of pure water sufficiently large and well supplied to ensure a permanent supply, no better source can exist. Thus it has been proposed to convey the waters of Bala Lake, in North Wales, to supply London with water; and the idea, though it has not been carried out, was by no means so extravagant as might at first be supposed. The enormous cost of conveyance is, of course, a great barrier against the adoption of any such plan; but the possession of a vast natural reservoir, always full of the purest water, is no slight matter. But if there is no lake, the outflow of natural springs, where they first issue from the earth, if sufficiently large in quantity and good in quality, may be made use of. Such springs are generally subject to periodical variation; but if the total annual amount is sufficient, the surplus in the season of maximum flow may be stored without difficulty. Thus many of the sources of the Thames are powerful enough to be worth taking for the use of London. But to this abstraction of the water of a stream running past the metropolis there has always, and with great reason, been a strong objection. The quantity of water entering the sea at the mouth of the Thames is so little more than sufficient to ensure a permanent stream that it cannot afford to lose any tributary, however small. So it is generally in a thickly peopled country like England. There is also another objection, not geological but extremely influential, which renders these sources rarely available. Almost all the streams of England are so far peopled on the line of their course, and the waters so thoroughly utilized, either for fishing, for mills, for manufactures of various kinds, or for navigation, that the abstraction of any such quantity as is needed for the supply of a large town is very sensibly felt and very greatly objected to.

Even when springs are sufficient and available, it rarely happens that the flow is so regular throughout the year and in all seasons as to justify the careful engineer in dispensing with a reservoir. In level countries reservoirs must be almost entirely artificial but in hilly districts it is usual to take advantage of natural irregularities of the land, and select the head of a valley, where by a single embankment a convenient space can be enclosed. Such embankments are common, and when properly constructed are not dangerous; but the existence of a weak point in the stratification on one side or at the bottom of the valley may be the cause of an accident, as well as any fault in construction; and the consequences are so serious as to render a thorough geological inspection desirable before the work is commenced. It was the opinion of the engineers and practical geologists who examined into the matter after the accident, that the Sheffield reservoir was faulty in this way. A slide, or land-slip, of part of one of the walls of the reservoir may take place in consequence of the existence of a porous bed cut by the valley, but at too high a level to admit water until the reservoir is filled; or such an accident may be caused at the bottom if the base of the embankment does not pass deep enough below the surface to render any slipping impossible, regard being always had to the stratification.

Reservoirs are equally necessary, and the same caution must be used in the original selection of the site and in the mode of construction of these works, where the rainfall of a district is to be collected and transferred to a distant spot. In Lancashire and Yorkshire there are several instances of this arrangement, and for the most part they are eminently successful. The rainfall of the district, the form of the collecting-ground, the rock of which it is composed, and the dip of the rock,—these are all matters of consideration and of preliminary inquiry, and need the knowledge and experience of a geologist. An idea may be formed of the importance of this source of supply when it is known that Manchester, with a population of half a million, is supplied from the drainage of a gathering-ground of 18,000 acres, at a distance of sixteen miles from the city; Liverpool, with a population nearly as large, from an area of 10,400 acres, twenty-six miles distant; Newcastle-on-Tyne (population 120,000) from 4,000 acres, twelve miles distant; Bolton (population 60,000) from 500 acres, four miles distant.

The average annual rainfall of these parts of England greatly exceeds thirty inches,* more than one-third of which runs off in streams, and might therefore be collected in reservoirs and stored. The total water that can be collected in the year may equal, or even exceed, a supply of 30 gallons per day per acre for each inch of annual rainfall. The usual estimate of quantity required for all purposes in a large city or manufacturing town is at the rate of twenty gallons per day per head of population.

It may be useful, in conclusion, to give a general

* In the neighbourhood of Liverpool the average is nearly 60 inches.

idea of the probability of finding water in the various British rocks that are most familiar, and the circumstances under which the water exists in each case.

The upper tertiaries of England, including the gravel, rarely afford anything more than land-springs. From the boulder clay, indeed, water is obtained, though not often in large quantity. It is obtained in such cases from under the clays, and therefore, in so far, from outcropping beds below impermeable strata; but the clays are irregular, and no important supply can be expected in this way. It is not till we penetrate the lower tertiaries, and reach the permeable sands between the London clay and the underlying secondary rock, that we obtain large supplies from Artesian borings. The sands within the London clay also contain water, and some springs have been got from them. The supply from the sands below the London clay is extremely large.

Chalk is a rock containing, by absorption, an enormous quantity of water, which is distributed throughout the whole mass, though chiefly abundant in the lower part. The lines of flint favour percolation, and occasional spaces in the interior of the rock exist, and are generally full. At intervals in the chalk there must be beds that hold back water better than the rest, and thus many wells have been successfully sunk only a certain distance into the rock. Though generally permeable, chalk in many places seems to keep back water, especially in the upper part, where the interstices are, perhaps, choked by the fine particles of argillaceous mud washed into them from the London and plastic clays. Water may almost always be obtained by sinking into the chalk to a sufficient depth, though not always in large quantity or rising high.*

Wells sunk through the chalk into the upper greensand are not always more successful than those terminating in the chalk; but the gault below the upper greensand being quite impermeable, water may generally be expected on reaching this bed. In the gault there is little water; but the lower greensands below are everywhere in England extremely wet. Almost indefinite supplies might be expected therefore from sinking to this rock, but the limitations already made to the quantity obtainable from a single well, or from wells within a given distance of each other, apply here not less clearly than elsewhere. The water of the lower greensand is irony if got near the outcrop of the bed, but when filtered through other beds, especially when passing through much clay, it becomes more pure.

Little water can be got from the beds of clay at the top of the Wealden series, nor is the Hastings sand very much to be depended on. The Kimmeridge clay and the Oxford clay also are so retentive and separated by bands of permeable rock of so little importance as to have little value as water-bearing beds. It must not be supposed, indeed, that water is not to be got between or even amongst these two important bands of clay, but it depends on local conditions, and its

* I am informed that 6,000,000 gallons per day have been obtained, without exhaustive pumping, from a single well in the chalk near the mouth of the Thames.

presence cannot safely be assumed without proof. The Portland rock above the Kimmeridge clay includes overlying stones and an underlying sand, the former of which hold water chiefly in crevices, but the latter in its mass.

The lower oolites contain much water in various beds, the alternation of clays and open limestones being very frequent. In those parts of England where these rocks come to the surface, the wells are not very deep, but the supply is tolerably constant. In all cases the wells have to be sunk into the limestone to its plane of saturation, wherever that may be, or even through it to the clay, as the rock does not otherwise yield a supply.

The lias holds back water, so that at its contact with the lower oolite there is almost always a line of springs, and under favourable conditions the supply is large and constant. Wells sunk into the upper beds of the lias rarely fail in obtaining water, but the quality is not always very good.

Wells sunk through the lias where the thickness of these clays is not too great, almost invariably obtain water from the new red sandstone. Wells sunk in the new red sandstone are also almost certain of success, to some extent; but, owing to the number of close faults, the quantity cannot be depended on, and the water is apt to be salt. The new red sandstone is eminently a water-bearing bed, and the numerous alternations of marl and sand render it possible to obtain water from almost all depths. From a well sunk at Gorton, by the Manchester and Salford Waterworks Company, into the new red sandstone, as much as 2,000,000 gallons per day have been obtained by the aid of radiating galleries from the bottom of the shaft and by exhaustive pumping.

The magnesian limestone is a rock full of cavities, and very cellular. The cavities and cells are filled to a certain level, and water may, therefore, be obtained from this rock. Large quantities of water are present not only in the magnesian limestone, but in the underlying coal-measures and carboniferous limestone. In the coal-measures, at the underclay beneath each seam of coal, and in the limestone in the cavities, wherever there is an impermeable band between strata, or at faults, water is found. The faulted condition of the carboniferous and older rocks in England greatly affects the water capacity of the rock. The old red sandstone is a variable rock, sometimes containing much water in sandy beds, sometimes in cavities, and, at intervals, between the strata. There is generally a good store of water wherever this rock prevails.

In Silurian rocks there are many alternations of permeable and impermeable rocks, and water appears in the intervals. More, however, is to be got from faults and fissures, which are very numerous, than from any strata. The limestones of this period are, for the most part, argillaceous, and, therefore, hold back water; and they are less cracked and fissured than the carboniferous limestone and oolites.

Slates, schists, and all varieties of granite, hold water only in fissures; but from these it may be sought for, in some cases, systematically. Where there is a considerable rainfall, these rocks sometimes afford large supplies, and wells have been sunk into all of them with success. Little dependence can be placed on such rocks, however; for the fissures, though often systematic, and not unfrequently open, do not always communicate readily from one to another. A remarkable instance of successful sinking in granite exists in the island of Jersey. The object was to supply water to Fort Regent, built on a bold projecting mass of syenite to the south of the town of St. Helier, the summit of the hill being 170 feet above the level of high water. The rock has some appearance of stratification, with vertical joints, but there was nothing at the surface to indicate water. The sinking was commenced, in 1806, in the solid granite, and was continued to a depth of 234 feet, all compact rock. At this depth a spring was reached which rose 70 feet in the shaft, and has continued at that level. Water in small quantities was found at various points, but not enough to check the work. In this work about twelve hands were employed, and from nine to thirteen feet per month were sunk, the total expense amounting to about £2,600. More than twenty-five cwt. of gunpowder was employed in blasting operations.

Lecture the Third.

MINERALS FROM SUPERFICIAL DEPOSITS.

Sands and Stream Ores, Clays, Cements, Plasters, and Artificial Stones.

IN the previous lectures I have spoken of certain applications of geology in which I have regarded the earth as the basis of operations, or as consisting of rock masses through which water circulates. I now propose to speak to you of the various mineral substances contained in the earth, or of which it is composed, and which are used for special practical purposes. Of these there are several classes :—

(1.) Sands used in various manufactures, either as part of the manufacture, as in the case of glass, or for moulds for metal-casting.

(2.) Sands consisting partly of, or containing, valuable minerals, as gold, diamonds, tin ore, &c.

(3.) Plastic clays, or clays tenacious enough to be worked up with water into definite shapes, used either simply sun- and air-dried, or after burning.

(4.) Varieties of limestone used in construction, but not till they have been calcined.

(5.) Building stones of all kinds, only requiring to be shaped in order to be available for use.
(6.) Coal and some kinds of iron-stone and copper ore forming strata in the earth.
(7.) Ores of metals not bedded, but existing in mineral veins, or in crevices and fissures in rocks.

For the discovery and working of each of these, geological knowledge and experience are necessary.

The number of different minerals in common use for economic purposes is very large; probably much larger than is generally thought. Most of them have to be sought for when wanted, and to know where to look for them is one of the objects of practical geology. In my address this evening I desire to confine your attention to the first four classes of minerals found in the earth.

SANDS.

Silica sand is a material valuable in glass-making. It is not rare; but the samples that are free from lime, iron, alumina, and other foreign substances, are much less common than might be supposed. They are obtained from rocks of various geological age; among others, from the beds at the bottom of the tertiary series at Alum Bay, Isle of Wight, where the quality is very good, and adapted for the best flint glass. Other good kinds are got from the Hastings sands. There is a bed of such material, eight feet thick, in the lower greensand at Aylesbury; others from the sands of Reigate, and others again from the older beds in the north-west and north of England and Scotland. Although there is no geological limit for the existence of those sands, they are principally derived from sandstones that have been metamorphosed, or from quartzites. It is generally found that less pure sands alternate with those that consist almost entirely of silica.

While pure sands are needed for glass-making, certain varieties of loam and sand are preferred for casting. Some of these are grit-stones, and others are very sandy clays ; the quality needed depending on the nature and fineness of the casting and the fluidity of the iron. The sands from Mansfield are considered to be particularly favourable for casting.

Vast quantities of shelly sand are removed from the coast of Cornwall into the interior, for agricultural purposes. This operation has been going on for at least 250 years, and so important has it always been regarded, that nearly two centuries ago the cost of removal by cart was estimated at upwards of £30,000 per annum, an enormous sum to be expended at that time on agricultural improvements. Roads have been constructed expressly for this traffic, and the quantity now annually removed cannot be less than 8,000,000 cubic feet. These sands average from 60 to 65 per cent. of carbonate of lime, and they contain a certain proportion of organic matter. Their use is by no means confined to the mere mechanical division of the soil, which would be effected by the siliceous sands. They also act directly as a manure, partly by the carbonate of lime, of which they are composed, and partly by their organic contents. They are taken principally from the neighbourhood of Falmouth Harbour on the south, and between Trevose Head and the Land's End on the north coast of Cornwall.

A peculiar kind of sand is obtained from the river bed of the Parret, in Somersetshire, not far from the city of Bath, and being made up for convenience in the form of a brick, it is commonly known as *Bath brick*. It is used for polishing. It consists chiefly of the very minute cases of infusorial animalcules accumulated in beds in vast quantities, and consisting of almost pure silica in a fine state of division. *Tripoli*, or rotten-stone, is a somewhat similar, but yet finer siliceous powder, obtained from beds of limestone of the carboniferous series. These mealy substances are remarkable as being different in their properties, as economical products, from any other varieties of silica, although they do not appear to differ much in chemical composition. Tripoli is usually of a dark brown or dark grey colour, whereas Bath brick is paler and more yellow. The polishing powder of Bilin, near Berlin, is of the same nature and has the same origin as the Bath brick.

Sands and gravels are not only valuable for their silica or other earthy minerals, of which they are composed. They often contain, mixed up with these grains, fragments more or less abundant and of various sizes, consisting of such metals and minerals as are capable of being broken or ground up into minute particles, and are not very readily decomposed by weathering. A search among sands may thus result in the discovery of diamonds and other precious stones; of amber, of iron ore, of tin ore, and, above all, of gold. All these occur largely in alluvial deposits. Some are extremely rare, others more common than is generally thought. Some occupy but a very small space in the sand or gravel that contains them, but others form the principal part of such material in certain localities. It will be necessary to speak of these alluvial and diluvial deposits with reference to the minerals to be obtained from them.

Diamond washings are carried on almost exclusively in India and Brazil, although these precious stones have been found in many other places, as in Siberia, Africa, California, and Australia, and almost always where the sands also contain gold. The process of exploring is simple enough; the only implement made use of in India being a sharp pick-axe, with which men accustomed to the work dig into every promising spot. The diamond matrix is first picked out from the loose pebbles and larger pieces of gravel by the use of water—this requires a practised eye,—and the selected mass, consisting of smaller grains, is next carefully spread out on a flat surface, where it can be examined with greater care, and grain by grain. The earth most sought for is a red ochrey clay, containing a small proportion of oxide of iron; but the diamonds are also found in the loose mud. An educated eye is the chief requirement in this department of practical geology.

Alluvial ores, or ores and metals found in alluvial

deposits, may conveniently enough be included in one general description. Except gold, the oxides of tin and iron are the only metals or metalliferous minerals thus found in important quantities, and the treatment of tin ore and gold, though not very different in principle, requires separate notice. Iron ore, to exist as a valuable mineral in sand, must be so entirely preponderant that no doubt can exist as to its nature. Very large supplies of stream tin were once raised in Cornwall, and stream works are still important. The chief quantities are now found in the island of Banca, in the Eastern Archipelago, and this source of supply seems to increase rather than diminish.

The gold of commerce is chiefly obtained from sands and gravels. These are derived from the disintegration of some parent rock or vein, but they are often so entirely detached from the rock that there is no clue to its origin. Such sands are found in many of the river beds of Europe, and in gravels near the banks of such rivers. They are well known, and far richer in auriferous contents, on the plains and in the vallies of certain parts of Siberia; in many parts of Africa, especially on the west coast; in Brazil, and elsewhere in South America; in Mexico, and in California and Columbia; in the West Indian Islands; in the south-eastern part of Australia; and in New Zealand. These are but a few of the very long list of localities from which it is now known that gold may be, or has been, found in sands and gravels in paying quantities.

There are, however, two positions in which the gold is found. One is in contact with existing river beds, and the other in ancient detritus and gravel, not now affected by water. Examples of both these are found in Europe. The mud and sand banks of the Rhine and Danube, and the sands of the Tagus are all auriferous. The percentage of gold may be small and variable in certain parts of their course, but gold is to be found throughout the muds of the bed and banks of the streams. Twenty-four grains of gold dispersed through a hundred-weight of sand has been considered enough to justify working. A grain of gold is worth about twopence, and it is evident that the kind and extent of manipulation must not be very costly which can leave a profit after extracting only one ounce of gold from a whole ton weight of rubbish. But in a river bed water is always at hand, and gold is many times heavier than mud. The whole principle of alluvial washings is to take advantage of the different specific gravities of the treasure and the rubbish, and thus the work can be carried on at very small expense, and the hand labour of individuals is sufficient without other apparatus than a rude wooden pan or shovel.

The washing of gold alluvia is indeed a very simple matter. A wooden bowl held in the hand and shaken artistically in and with water separates, with singular rapidity, all the heavier from the lighter mud. The latter is floated off time after time, until at length a delicate narrow line of rich yellow colour is seen edging the last fine mud left in the bowl. A few more turns and this yellow residuum is obtained as almost pure gold, in the shape of a fine powder.

Thousands of gipsies and others earn a precarious livelihood during the summer months in the rivers whose golden sands, however glorious to the imagination, are really of very small profit to the country they traverse, or the inhabitants who work them.

There is nothing but experience to justify the geologist or the miner in forming an opinion as to the value of an auriferous stream of this kind, but each country, and even each principal river bed, has its own indications. In some, the gold is found in very minute particles of dust, or flat spangles, that can be floated by the slightest current of water. In others, the particles are more distinct grains, and therefore resist more completely the current. Sometimes, in sheltered places, heavier grains or nuggets are found with the gold. Magnetic and other iron ores, native platinum, and several very rare metals, besides gems and fragments of quartzy minerals, often occur.

No doubt these river deposits may have been brought down at once from great distances, and even from the higher mountains where the gold-bearing veins crop out; but much more usually the auriferous mud in modern rivers is but the remains of some bed of auriferous sand and gravel long since accumulated. Thus, in the river Rhine, where gold has been worked during the present century between Bâle and Mannheim, the mud is derived from some sand bank or gravel island at a distance above the place of working. It is only in the middle of the larger gravel, on the margin of the bank nearest the head of the stream, and rarely for a thickness of more than half an inch, that the gold is concentrated. In the ancient deposits of the river, forming a zone three miles in breadth, gold also occurs. In these cases the gold is found in flakes or spangles so exceedingly minute and thin that it needs from ten to fourteen hundred to weigh a single grain. A cubic yard of the mud will contain from five to forty thousand of these spangles, and you may imagine that some ingenuity is needed to separate enough particles of such dimensions to pay for the cost of the operation.

Compared with Siberia and South America, these Rhine sands are very poor, the Siberian gravels yielding five times, and those of Chili ten times as much, while of late years California, Columbia, Australia, and New Zealand have yielded supplies compared with which all those formerly known fade into insignificance. It may be well to allude to some of the varieties of auriferous gravel, and the general nature of such deposits as are most suggestive.

The Siberian gravels, worked for a long time with great success, are extremely coarse, being composed for the most part of a shingle of moderate-sized and small subangular fragments of the adjacent rock. They occur along the eastern flank of the Ural chain, both in the lateral, or north and south, valleys, and in those which run transversely, or from east to west. The former are generally the richer, and it would seem that the modern streams have but little influence on the deposits. The gold alluvia of Siberia appear to be of definite geological age, and to belong to the boulder gravels deposited by ice during the glacial period. These gravels contain the bones of large mammals that have long since departed from northern Europe and Asia.

The Brazil auriferous deposit is called locally *Cascalho.* It is either an indurated soil that can be broken up with pickaxes, and afterwards exposed to a current of water, or a loose gravelly stratum of rounded quartzose pebbles, and pounded gneiss and schist. It generally rests on granite, and is covered by earthy matter. Its thickness is very variable, and the condition of the pebbles indicates the distance of the deposit from the rocks whose disintegration it represents. In the mountains the pebbles are angular, and in the plains round.

The Californian gravels, like those of Siberia and Brazil, are alluvial, and consist of coarse and small stones, mixed with mud and fine sands. Some of these are the actual beds of the existing streams; but there, as in almost all countries, it is evident that the great deposit of such material has been already effected, and is not now in progress, at least in the places where the gold must be sought.

In Australia, the gold-bearing district is chiefly in the south-eastern part of the country, and the gravels, while of the same general character as those already described, are very much deeper, and seem to carry gold throughout. Shafts sunk through the gravels to a depth of a couple of hundred yards succeed in reaching gold gravels, and the heaviest and largest lumps of gold have often been found at the lowest depths.

The most important recent discoveries of rich gold alluvia are those of British Columbia, New Zealand, and Nova Scotia. In all these the gold has been found by the method of *prospecting*, and the first discovery may almost always be described as accidental. Rivers are found running down from mountains, such as in known gold districts contain gold veins. In these rivers, or in their smaller tributaries, or, finally, in the creeks and gullies opening out from the mountains, there are always accumulations of sand and gravel—alluvial, and often diluvial. These contain the gold—the minute specks, the visible grains, and, now and then, the great nuggets. The latter are found often enough to afford a sufficient temptation to the adventurous miner, and, at rare intervals, the excitement becomes very great when several of unusual size are found in the same locality. As a specimen of the successful explorations, I may mention an incident that occurred soon after the first discovery of gold in the gravels of British Columbia. Five partners commenced working at a place called Cariboo, during the summer months of 1861. At first their claim was not very promising, for during the first three days they obtained little or nothing. On the fourth day they raised about 4 oz. of gold. On the fifth day this increased to 10 oz., and on the sixth to 41 oz. The yield went on increasing until it reached 387 oz. in one day, and the last day's work resulted in the obtaining of 469 oz. Four labourers were employed, at eight dollars per day, in clearing away tailings. The total value of the gold raised during the two months' work of these five partners was upwards of £20,000, and the dimensions of the claim were only 80 feet by 25 feet superficial.

While the search for gold in the auriferous gravels is thus sometimes rewarded by the discovery of a locality where nuggets of moderate or large dimensions are mixed up with smaller pepites and dust of gold, there are other cases where, after long search, some one or two magnificent results have been obtained. Among the most remarkable of these was the discovery of the "Welcome" nugget, found on the 11th June, 1858, at Bakery-hill, Ballarat. It belonged to a party of twenty-four persons. It was found at a depth of 180 feet, and was a water-worn pebble, measuring twenty inches by twelve and seven. It contained nearly 10 lbs. of quartz, clay, and oxide of iron. Its original weight, when brought to England, was 2,166 oz., or 135 lbs. 6 oz., and it contained 2,019¾ oz. pure gold, the value of which was £8,376. Several nuggets, weighing from 12 to 45 oz., were found before reaching this giant.

The economical working of these auriferous deposits is a matter of extreme practical importance. The methods adopted for the ordinary deposits must be nearly the same as those in use in Cornwall for reducing tin ore. As a specimen of Cornish work, then, it is useful to know that a single engine, working at 55-horse power, has broken up for washing no less than 30,200 tons of tin stuff in a year, at an average cost of 1s. 3½d. per ton. The cost of crushing gold quartz would, no doubt, be somewhat greater than this; but it is clear that where the sands or gravels are sufficiently abundant, and the result sufficiently certain to justify a large expenditure for machinery, the operation may be profitable, even when the percentage of the precious metal is extremely small.

The gold gravels sometimes contain, besides the

metal which gives them their chief value and their name, the following crystals and native metals. All are, generally, more or less water-worn. Sapphire, topaz, spinel-ruby, zircon, tourmaline, garnets, olivine, platinum, palladium, osmium, stream tin, diamonds, and several varieties of quartz. These are independent of oxide of iron, which is almost universal.

I have now briefly pointed out the conditions and circumstances under which valuable auriferous sands and gravels are present in the earth. They seem to us to be chiefly distributed in countries where deposits belong to a comparatively recent geological period. But this is the case only because our opportunities of observation are now limited to the results of the latest denudations, and because the surface of the existing land has so recently been subject to the action of water. That much of this apparent water-action arises from weathering and the conveyance of broken stones and mud over the surface by rain, and by streams derived from rain, there is no doubt. Thus it is that the gold alluvia may be regarded as at once proving how recent are all existing lands, in a geological sense, and yet how very long a time must have been required that these lands should have been covered to a thickness, often amounting to some hundred feet, of the broken fragments of mountains, which may once have been lofty, but which are now lowered into hills.

In endeavouring to follow up this subject and point out the differences, as well as analogies, that exist between gold alluvia and deposits of stream-tin and other metalliferous ores, worked in a similar manner,

I may conveniently refer to Cornwall. At all times there have been accumulations of transported material due to fresh water, and their magnitude and extent must everywhere depend on the quantity of land exposed, on the elevation of the land above the sea, and on the position of the land in reference to the poles and the equator. In our own island these facts and their results have already been studied, and useful conclusions have been arrived at. The gold alluvia, though in some respects enormously more important than any others, in a commercial sense, are not common in most countries, and are not therefore so useful for our present purpose.

It has long since been observed that all the productive streams yielding tin ore are in the valleys on the southern side of the Cornish peninsula, although most of the richest veins of such ore are on the northern side. Most of the valleys have been explored, and those on the northern side are pretty uniformly barren. Here we have evidence of a drift from the north conveying the tin, and a similar conclusion must be drawn from the facts known concerning the principal gold drifts north of a certain line in Europe and Asia.

But you may ask how it is that such a drift, produced by a submarine current or wave flooding the land, can have resulted in the deposit of the stream ores?

This involves a further consideration of the mode in which the surface of the granite districts of Cornwall has been decomposed and disintegrated, and those who are familiar with these districts, and know the infinite multitude of small veins and branches, carrying tin ore, that traverse the easily decomposed granites of St. Austell and its neighbourhood, will not doubt that if a body of water were now to rush across that part of our island, the decomposed granite would be very readily and rapidly removed, the broken up quartzy strings containing tin would be rolled into pebbles, and the tin-bearing pebbles would be separated from the mere stony pebbles, owing to their much higher specific gravity, which is considerably more than double that of quartz, felspar, mica, or granite. Owing to their greater specific weight these pebbles would first come to rest, and if once drifted into hollows would not easily be removed. On the other hand, the lighter material would be much further transported. There would thus be a tendency to accumulate a fundamental layer of tin-stone pebbles at the bottoms of the valleys, and in sheltered spots, which would remain quiescent while the lighter stones were conveyed far away on the surface.

It is very difficult for anyone merely travelling across Cornwall to form an idea of the original extent of the accumulations of tin-stone gravels that have been the object of incessant exploration for several thousand years. Even on the highest grounds there are perpetual indications of former workings, at intervals, along the whole distance from Dartmoor to the Land's End, and in many of these the ground has certainly been turned over twice or thrice, the stones which, at one time, were neglected, having since become valuable, as the deposits have become more and more ransacked. There is, however, still left sufficient unmoved ground to illustrate the general geological facts of the deposit, especially on the lower grounds, and near the sea-level. The examination of the evidence concerning such deposits reveals some startling facts, and I will give an outline of some of these observed in 1829, which are especially interesting now, in connection with recent discoveries concerning the probable antiquity of the human race. The facts are mentioned by Sir H. de la Beche, in his admirable account of Cornwall (p. 401). The works to which it especially alludes (Happy Union Works, near Pentuan) have been long since abandoned.

Section of Stream-ore Deposits, near Pentuan.

	Thickness. FT.	IN.
1. Rough river-sand and gravel, with sea-sand mixed.—Sharpened wooden piles were discovered in this bed (their tops 24 feet from the present surface), just on a level with the present low water at spring-tides. These piles crossed the valley, and seem to have belonged to a causeway or foot-bridge ..	20	
2. Sand containing timber-trees, lying in all directions; bones of animals, including red-deer and whale, human skulls, &c... ..	20	
3. Silt or clay	2	
4. Sand with marine shells, yielding salt water.—(The water above and below is fresh) ..	0	
5. Sludge or silt with recent shells, hazelnuts, wood—apparently formed by human hands; bones and horns of deer and oxen, &c. ..	10	
6. Dark silt with decomposed vegetable matter. —*An ancient soil*	1	
7. TIN-GROUND.—Thickness, variable and depending on the inequalities of the rock below.—		

	FEET.
The tin usually at the bottom, with fragments of adjacent rocks often angular.—The tin in fragments, from size of grains of sand to ten pounds weight; and with stones of ore weighing two hundredweights or more, containing copper and iron pyrites as well as tin ore.—Roots of trees from above penetrate this gravel	3 to 10

Other stream works point to a similar history, and mark great changes in the level of the surrounding country since their deposit, as well as causes of drift which are now altogether unknown in the district. The upper limit of the tin ground in the section given above is not less than 48 feet below the level of high water at spring tides and 30 feet below the level of low water. It has certainly been covered in former times by vegetable soil, and the land at that time possessed human inhabitants.

It must be observed that in many other places in Cornwall, where on account of the extreme economic importance of the subject the gravels have been penetrated through to the underlying rock, there is unmistakable evidence of an alteration of level—a general depression of the surface—to the extent of at least fifty feet within the human period, without the smallest evidence of any great earthquake disturbance or any change in the dip of the rocks. It is also certain that the depression has been general over an extensive area, and that it has been very gradual. On the other hand, there is equally good evidence in Cornwall itself and in the adjacent county of Devon, that in many places there has been local elevation, to an extent even much greater than this depression, and also within the human period. I must not here enter on this subject beyond the mere statement of the fact; but in referring to it, I would point out the great value of accurate measurements and careful records of all facts connected with the gravels, whether they are rich in tin-stone, as in Cornwall; or whether they contain the fragments of gold that are being so eagerly sought for in Australia, New Zealand, California, Columbia, and other places; or, lastly, whether they are only remarkable as containing in one deposit bones of extinct species of quadrupeds and works of human labour.

It is not everywhere that the course of the northern drift can be traced in the northern hemisphere by means of tin-stone or gold; but the same principle of observing the relative specific gravity of deposits to determine the direction of the drift is universally applicable. And it must also be remembered that, while sometimes, as in the cases we have been considering, the valuable minerals, being heavy, are left behind and deposited at the bottom; in others, where they are lighter than other stones, they are floated onwards, and either caught up accidentally, or remain permanently at the top. This is the case with amber—the ancient resinous excretion of certain extinct pines. On the shores of the Baltic pits are occasionally sunk through loose sandy downs, to the depth of a hundred feet, with a view of reaching the fragments of this substance in the uppermost of the regular strata below the sand. Elsewhere the amber is floated or drifted to the shore during severe storms, and is then picked up before it is caught and covered up by the blown sands.

CLAYS.

I pass on now to the consideration of plastic materials. These are for the most part varieties of clay; and there are not less than four used largely in the arts, each having its own peculiar properties, and each available for some special purpose. They are known as brick clay, fire clay, pipe clay, and pottery or porcelain clay.

Brick clays are very widely spread, and few countries are without some varieties of greater or less value. In England they are common in most of the geological formations and often form very thick and extensive beds. The clays of each particular locality are almost of necessity used for brickmaking and other common purposes in the district where they occur, since clay will not readily bear the cost of conveyance. The finer kinds are in this respect different, being conveyed in a manufactured or prepared state from that part of the country where they can be best procured to all other parts with which there is communication.

Brick clays of the common kind consist of a coarse and irregular admixture of silicate of alumina—which we may regard as pure clay—with sand, lime, iron, carbon, mineral alkalis, and a host of impurities for the most part accidental. The admixture with sand is essential; and the proportion of free sand in the clay, as well as the actual composition of the clay as a silicate of alumina, admit of great variety. The clay must, indeed, be free from large stones; but the admixture of a percentage of silica-sand, which results in a combination that contains as much as 90 per cent. of silica, is not at all incompatible with the formation of an excellent brick. The mealy state of the silica, curiously illustrated in Bath brick and already described, is found to be injurious to the quality of a clay for making bricks.

The number of common or stock bricks annually manufactured and used in England must greatly exceed one thousand million; and to supply this demand, brick-pits have been opened in the neighbourhood of every town in which dressed stone is more expensive than brick. Generally, a sensible quantity of iron, lime, potash, or soda, would be an unfavourable sign in a brick clay; for too much of any of these substances would cause the brick to run into glass when left in the kiln to burn. By this burning process the clay loses some of its properties, amongst others the capacity of mixing with water, and its plasticity. It becomes permanently hard, not softening in water, though absorbing it readily. Bricks resist weathering if the brick earth be of good quality; and if iron has been originally present in the clay, it is converted into peroxide, and changes the dull brown of the clay into a bright red. To make an even and average brick, the material must be freed from small pebbles and grit as much as possible. It is also ground up with some care into a uniform mass and mixed with water, after which it is left to dry before being made up. In preparing it for use, it must be mixed with coarse sharp sand, and besides sand the ashes of coal are very useful in this stage of the manufacture. If tempered or exposed for some time to the weather, clay is always improved and makes better bricks or tiles. In a good brick clay there should not be more than 2 per cent. of lime or potash.

Fire-clay is the name given to varieties that will bear intense heat without running or melting in the kiln; and the fire-bricks made from it will also bear exposure in the interior of furnaces. This material is also used for gas and other retorts. It may be supposed, therefore, that the alkalies, alkaline earths, and other substances, such as iron-oxide, which would help to flux it, are absent. Carbon and hydro-carbons are not unfrequently present in fire-clays, and some of the most valuable are found as the floors beneath seams of coal. Many excellent clays of this kind are met with in the coal measures of England, Belgium, and France; but they are almost confined to those coal measures which belong to the carboniferous series. The best are those from Stourbridge (Worcestershire), Newcastle-on-Tyne, and the neighbourhood of Glasgow. All are greatly improved by working with water and long exposure to the air and weather, and in making the clay into brick, fragments of old fire-bricks already burnt greatly improve the composition. The following is the composition of good samples of these clays:—

ANALYSIS OF FIRE-CLAYS.

	Stourbridge.	Glasgow.	No. 3.
Silica	63·70	65·20	66·16
Alumina	22·70	33·41	22·54
Lime	?	·32	1·42
Magnesia	?	·13	trace
Iron oxide	2·00	.49	5·31
Phosphates	?	·45	..
Water and loss . .	11·60	..	4·5[illegible]
	100·00	100·00	100·00

Of these analyses the first is by Berthier and old. The lime and magnesia do not seem to have been observed. The second is more modern, and the clay has been deprived of its water before the analysis was made. The excess of alumina in the latter is very marked. No. 3 is a variety used in the potteries for making *saggers*, and also in glass-works for crucibles; it is a kind of pottery clay.

Of the finer kinds of plastic clays there are many varieties: some being well enough adapted for coarse pottery; others for finer kinds of brown and red ware; others, again, for the whitest and best kinds of common ware. There are also the pure white pipe clays and, lastly, the minerals known by the Chinese names *Ka-o-lin* and *Pe-tun-tse*, of which excellent qualities are found in Cornwall and West Devon, in Central France, and in Northern Germany. The former may belong to various deposits. The latter seem, without exception, to be due to the decomposition of the felspar in certain kinds of granite.

The following analyses of various kinds of clay used in manufacture will form a useful introduction to the remarks I shall have to offer concerning them :—

ANALYSES OF VARIOUS FINE CLAYS.

	Pottery Clays.				China Clays.		
	(1) Yellow Clay.	(2) Brown Clay.	(3) Blue Clay.	(4) Pipe Clay.	(5) Sandy Clay.	(6) Kaolin.	(7) Kaolin, average.
Silica	58·07	49·44	46·38	53·66	66·68	46·32	44·60
Alumina	27·38	34·26	38·04	32·00	26·08	39·74	44·30
Iron oxide	3·30	7·74	1·04	1·35	1·26	·27	·20
Lime	·50	1·48	1·20	·40	·84	·36 }	1·60
Magnesia	trace	1·94	trace	trace	trace	·44 }	
Water	10·30	5·14	13·57	12·08	5·14	12·67	8·74
	99·55	100·00	100·23	99·49	100·00	99·80	99·44

(1) A pottery-clay for coarse ware; burns yellow. (2) A common kind, only used for black and common red ware; will not bear exposure to great heat. (3) Best pottery clay; burning white. (4) Used for pipes, but contracts too much for pottery; burns white. (5) A coarse china clay. (6) Finest china clay. (7) Average of kaolins.

Pottery clays are found abundantly in England, in the counties of Devon and Cornwall. They are more soapy and plastic than brick clays, and require to resist heat to any extent. When pure, indeed, they are practically infusible; and unless they contain an excess of iron or alkaline earths, they resist the most intense heat of the furnace. They contract in burning, and often with much irregularity. They part with their water only under exposure to the furnace; and the iron they contain becoming converted into peroxide communicates a colour, varying in intensity with the quantity of the metal. Thus the more ferruginous clays yield the deepest red; but as the iron also acts as a flux, these are the most fusible, and require the greatest care. The grey varieties are generally the safest. The presence of a small percentage of magnesia, though in the analysis No. 2 it happens to form part of a very impure specimen of clay, is not necessarily injurious.

The uses of pottery clay are so various, involving some manufactures little superior to ordinary brick or tile, and others hardly inferior to porcelain, that no precise line can be drawn concerning them, nor does analysis strictly define their value. The raw material seems generally to be the result of a natural separation of coarse and impure parts of a common clay by the aid of water and long exposure to weather; and thus there are certain deposits of it in particular localities. In this respect pottery clay may be compared with deposits of alluvial gravel, of stream ore, and of china clay. Pipe clay is a variety containing an excess of silica and very little iron, but otherwise differing little from the best kinds of pottery clay.

China clay and china stone, as I have already remarked, are elaborately formed by a process of natural or artificial washing from the decomposed felspar of certain kinds of granite. The most valuable materials of this kind found in England are from Cornwall, and artificially prepared; and a short account of the natural deposit and the preparation will be sufficient to explain their nature.

Kaolin is of a loose earthy texture, and light, having a specific gravity varying from 2·21 to 2·26. The composition is different as obtained from different localities, the limits being very wide indeed. The average composition is given in the table, but samples sometimes contain as much as 10 or 12 per cent. of free silica, either as fine or coarse sand, mixed with the clay. Natural china clay varies much more in quality than the artificial production bearing the same name.

The preparation of kaolin for the potteries is extremely simple, and consists in washing the decomposed rock in such a manner, in a succession of tanks, that the heavier and useless particles of quartz, mica, or other minerals, may either fall from the water in which they were mechanically suspended, or be carried forwards by the velocity of the stream; while the fine particles, consisting of the remains of the decomposed felspar are allowed to settle quietly in tanks prepared for them. Afterwards, the water being removed and the sediment partly dried, the latter is conveyed to proper sheds, where the drying is completed. They are then cut into cubical masses of a certain size (nine inches to one foot per side), and the material is ready for the market.

The decomposition of the granite is such as to leave the quartz in stones, which are generally crystalline and more or less angular. These are got rid of in a first or second catch-pit, through which the whole mass is carried along by a current of water. The kind of granite that most readily decomposes is that whose felspar is of the variety called *albite*, a pearly-white variety in which soda replaces the potash of ordinary felspar. Besides these granites, many of the porphyritic rocks of Cornwall, called *elvans*, decompose readily, and yield plastic clays useful for various purposes, but not so well fitted for porcelain as the soda granites.

The operation of washing, carried on artificially for the preparation of the finest kaolins, has been performed naturally on a large scale, though not quite so thoroughly, both in Cornwall and Devonshire. In the preparation of this material the decomposed granite has been washed through an extended valley, so that while the coarse particles of quartz were left behind in the upper part of the valley, nothing but the particles of fine clay were conveyed to the lower part. These are removed, after being cut into brick-shaped pieces and partially dried. They are cut from large pits, from the top of which the local gravel has been removed. The lumps of this clay, or china stone, as it is called, are somewhat larger than the cubes of kaolin, and they are not to be depended on for purity.

The export of china clays and china stones from Cornwall and South Devon is very large, and they are used not only in the potteries, but for paper-making and calico-dressing. More than 10,000 tons of the finer and three times as much of the commoner kinds are annually made use of in the Staffordshire potteries.

CEMENTS AND PLASTERS.

Besides clays of all kinds used in their natural state, before or after burning, there is another class of substances, called cements and plasters, which I may here notice. The use of these is very ancient, as some of them were employed in the earliest architectural constructions, to fasten together the bricks or stones of which buildings were made. They are of various kinds also, and are available under very different circumstances. The most common and familiar is that called mortar. It is obtained by first calcining common limestone in a kiln, and converting it into quicklime by depriving it of its carbonic acid. After calcining, the resulting quicklime is a white or greyish, powdery and cracked substance, which, on the application of water, absorbs a certain quantity with the evolution of much heat, and falls into a fine powder. This powder, further moistened, made into a thin paste with water, and mixed with two or three times its own weight of sharp sand, is common mortar. Slacked lime, or hydrate of lime, as moistened quicklime is called, absorbs carbonic acid from the air, and in time mortar is reconverted into limestone, but the operation goes on under peculiar conditions, and the result also is peculiar; for a film of silicate of lime is formed round each grain of sand, and thus the whole mass, and the stones between which it is placed, become in time more compact than the particles of natural limestone.

As, however, there are different kinds of limestone, more or less impure, there result limes of very different qualities and properties. These require special treatment to obtain from them the best result. The purest carbonates of lime, such as marbles or chalk, make what is called a rich lime, setting firmly only in dry air, while the very impure carbonates, in which clay is largely mixed with the limestone, result in the production of hydraulic limes, which set more or less rapidly in moist air, or even under water. Some of the impure limestones are used in the manufacture of cements by the admixture of definite proportions of foreign ingredients. Sometimes, by the admixture of certain substances (as puzzuolana) with the rich limes instead of sand, hydraulic limes are produced. There are few subjects connected with the application of geology that are more important than the determination of the material that should be used, and the treatment adopted in various countries in the manufacture of cements, mortars, and stuccos.

Commencing with nearly pure carbonates of lime, it is not difficult to trace the changes that take place in their conversion into cement. I have already alluded to these and need not now repeat the statement. A layer of such mortar, not too thick, placed between bricks or stone, which are themselves absorbent, and kept in dry air, dries gradually, and holds together such substances with extraordinary tenacity. But this is a work of years, and sometimes even centuries must run out before the extreme of hardness is attained. It is not unusual to find imperfectly-hardened mortar in very old constructions. The mortar that fastened together the bricks in the old Roman walls, common in many parts of Europe, is now almost everywhere so far hardened that a fracture takes place in the brick rather than the cement. The same will perhaps be the case in time with some modern mortars, provided, indeed, the buildings whose walls they cement last so long.

Limestone is widely distributed, and almost every variety, however impure, can be burnt for lime. In the manufacture of good common mortar to set in the air, pure limestones and those of fair ordinary quality are available; but in using them attention must be given to their composition, and even texture. Thus the hardest limestones and marbles make the fattest lime, other things being the same; but each variety yields a lime of different quality—distinct in colour, in weight, in the greediness with which it absorbs water, and in its ultimate hardness.

The method of calcination also varies, but the general result is that, after burning limestone, the resulting quicklime is lighter than the original stone, and differs from it essentially. To determine the nature of lime and its peculiar properties, perfectly fresh samples should be placed in a small open basket, and immersed in pure water for five or six seconds. Removed from the water, the loose unabsorbed water must be allowed to run off, and the contents of the basket emptied into a stone or iron mortar. According to the nature of the limestone, the lime will now exhibit some one of the following phenomena :—

(1.) It will hiss, crackle, swell, give off much hot vapour, and fall into a powder instantly ;

(2.) It will remain inert for some short time, not exceeding five or six minutes, after which the results stated in (1) will be energetically declared ;

(3.) It will remain inert for more than five minutes —the time extending sometimes to a quarter of an hour. It then gives off vapour to a moderate extent, and cracks without noise and without much evolution of heat ;

(4.) The lime will crack without noise and with little steam, but not till an hour or more has elapsed ;

(5.) The lime will become scarcely warm to the touch, will not fall to powder, and will crack to a very small extent.

In each case, before the effervescence (if any takes place) has quite disappeared, the slacking should be completed by the addition of water, not thrown upon the lime, but by the side of it, and the result should be frequently stirred, more water being added, till the whole is brought to the consistence of a thick paste. When the mass has cooled, which will not take place for two or three hours, the whole should be beaten up again until a firm but tenacious paste is produced, resembling clay prepared for pottery manufacture. Vessels being then filled with this paste, as obtained from each variety of limestone, the day and hour of immersion should be marked upon them, after which they are to be left to solidify.

We thus obtain a test of the nature of the materials used, which may belong to one of five classes :—(1) rich limes, (2) poor limes, (3) moderately hydraulic limes, (4) hydraulic limes, (5) eminently hydraulic limes. The word hydraulic as applied to lime means only that it possesses the property of *setting*, or becoming solid in moist air, or under water.

Rich limes are obtained from the purest and hardest limestones. When slacked they increase to double their volume; if employed alone they remain unaltered, even for years, and they are soluble in pure water. Limestones that contain from one to six per cent. of foreign substances, such as silica, alumina, magnesia, iron, etc., yield rich limes, the purest yielding the richest.

Poor limes are obtained from limestones in which foreign substances, such as sand, carbonate of magnesia, oxides of iron, and manganese, are present to the extent of from 15 to 30 per cent. These increase in bulk but little on slacking, do not set under water, and are soluble, like the rich limes, except that they leave an earthy residuum.

Between eminently rich and eminently poor limes

there is, of course, every gradation, and matters of great practical importance are governed by the condition of the limestones used and the nature of the foreign substances present. It is considered that fossiliferous limestones make bad mortar, as the slacking is irregular. Limestones containing much silica swell in setting, and may dislocate the masonry executed with them. Where alumina is in excess the lime is apt to shrink and crack. Where carbonate of magnesia is combined with carbonate of lime, as in the magnesian limestones, the original bulk is retained. Moderately pure limestones, with a mixture of foreign substances, are well adapted for ordinary purposes.

Hydraulic limes, or cements, as they are sometimes called, are extremely interesting and of very great value in construction. They are known under various names, and are either obtained naturally from the burning of certain varieties of calcareous rock, or are manufactured artificially by mixing limestones with the requisite foreign ingredients, or by combining quicklime with foreign materials. Roman cement, Portland cement, Parker's cement, and many others, are varieties of artificial cement well known to architects and builders, but as all these are essentially the same it will not be necessary to trouble you with the details of manufacture or special properties of each.

Nodules in clays and argillaceous bands in clay deposits are the localities that yield the largest quantity and best quality of limestones for burning into hydraulic lime. In all these the limestone is argillaceous and combined with other impurities, among which iron oxide and carbon are very frequent. It is not clear that oxide of iron alone, or carbonate of magnesia alone, exercise any influence in rendering limes more hydraulic; while, on the contrary, it is certain that tolerably pure clays, combined with pure calcareous mud, make some of the best artificial cements. It is generally considered that from 15 to 25 per cent. of a limestone should consist of silicate of alumina, in order that it may burn into a good hydraulic lime. Such a limestone exists in the *septaria*, or calcareous nodules, in the London clay at Sheppey, the Kimmeridge clay at Weymouth, the Oxford clay, and many other clays. Similar material occurs in the bands at the bottom of the lias at Barrow-on-Soar, in Leicestershire, in other bands in the lias at Whitby, and elsewhere. The Barrow lime is got from eight calcareous bands, averaging not more than nine inches thick. These bands are continuous and of very uniform quality, yielding an excellent cement, and a certain amount of change, or metamorphosis, must probably have taken place before a really valuable limestone for hydraulic purposes is formed. The cement stones require to be burned carefully and ground down to a fine powder. The best cement is the lightest.

Very excellent hydraulic cement is made by the artificial admixture of the river mud of calcareous and clayey districts with chalk, in certain proportions before burning. Admixtures of burnt clay or burnt brick, as well as the natural earths called puzzuolano and trass, have also been found to render fat limes hydraulic.

The *Portland cement*, largely manufactured at the mouth of the Thames, is a mixed river mud, while *Roman cement* is more usually formed of the nodules fished up or found in the cliffs near Harwich. In making these cements the whole of the materials are carefully pounded together under water and afterwards dried and burnt. The cement is sometimes manufactured into artificial stone, and is largely used for this purpose when made up with ten or twelve times its weight of broken stones and pebbles. Portland and Roman cements make an excellent concrete, not unlike some kinds of Portland stone in colour. Stones thus artificially made will bear a strain varying from twenty to sixty pounds to the square inch. Portland is in this respect stronger than the older manufactured Roman cement, but for many purposes there is nothing to choose between them. Several varieties of these cements are made and sold.

Gypsum (sulphate of lime), very largely developed in some parts of the middle of England, and chiefly in the beds of the new red sandstone series, is sometimes collected and burnt, like common limestone, to manufacture a plaster or cement. The calcining of gypsum does not involve its decomposition, but the water of solidification being driven off by this means, there is left only a soft white powder called Plaster of Paris; when this is again united with water the water is reabsorbed and the mass becomes first plastic and then solid; but it cannot be brought back to its original condition as a crystalline, semi-crystalline, or compact mineral. When mixed with weak glue instead of water, plaster of Paris becomes converted into *stucco*, a material also very largely used.

If, instead of being used with water, plaster of Paris in fine powder is thrown into a vessel containing a saturated solution of alum, borax, or sulphate of potash, and after soaking for some time is taken and rebaked, once more powdered, and then moistened with a solution of alum, a hard plaster is obtained that takes a high polish. This plaster is called *Keene's cement* if made with alum, *Parian* with borax, and *Martin's* with pearlash.

Pozzuolano is a substance already alluded to. It is the name given to a natural volcanic earth or trass, of a reddish colour, originally found in the vicinity of Pozzuoli, not far from Naples. Similar material has since been obtained in large quantities from extinct volcanic districts, especially at Vivarais, in central France, at Brühl, near Andernach, on the Rhine, and even near Edinburgh. In the latter case it is also a volcanic material, but of very ancient date. It varies in colour but retains its mineral characteristics. The following analyses of these materials may be useful :—

	Pozzuolano.	Trass.
Silica	44·5	57·0
Alumina	15·0	12·0
Lime	8·8	2·6
Magnesia	4·7	1·0
Iron oxide	12·0	5·0
Potash	1·4	7·0
Soda	4·0	1·0
Water	9·2	9·6
	99·6	95·2

Combined with limes instead of sand, these volcanic minerals have the property of rendering even the richest limes hydraulic and fit for use for every description of works executed in the sea or in fresh water. They are thus extremely valuable, and have been used from time immemorial with great success. They may be mixed either with fat or hydraulic limes, but in the latter case the proportion must be smaller to produce the same result, and thus the determination of the quantity must be a matter of economical calculation. Coal-cinders, slags, and scoriæ, and even wood-ashes, when their soluble alkali is removed by washing, all have a considerable effect in hastening the absorption of the moisture, and facilitating the setting of the limes with which they are used. Artificial pozzuolanos are sometimes manufactured, and I have already remarked that tiles and burnt clay or brick answer the same purpose, though less perfectly.

Besides the cements, burnt clays (*terra cottas*) are frequently used as artificial stones, but, from their great and unequal contraction and the facility with which they are acted on by frost, they are rarely satisfactory. Many other ingenious methods of imitating stone have been from time to time adopted. One of the most remarkable of these was introduced some years ago by Mr. Frederic Ransome, and deserves special notice. It consisted of sand moulded with fluid silicate of soda, the neutral fluid silicate being easily and cheaply obtained by exposing flints in a steam boiler to the action of caustic alkali, at high temperature.

In his first experiments, Mr. Ransome supposed that by mixing sand and fragments of stone with the fluid silicate into a kind of paste and exposing them to the air, they would be permanently solid. But he found that stones thus made very soon became disintegrated in the moist atmosphere of England, and could never indurate. To remove this serious objection to their use he subjected them to the action of heat, in a kiln, and found that at a bright red heat the cementing material, or silicate, parted with some of its free alkali, the portion thus renewed combining with some of the sand to produce an insoluble glass, unaffected by exposure to any of the acids present in the air, and not cracking on exposure to frost when damp. This artificial stone could be made so porous as to be well adapted for filtering slabs, or it could be so far compacted by mechanical pressure before burning as to yield a material equal in appearance to Craigleith stone, and not inferior in its power to resist atmospheric action, and even absorption. Very useful rubs and whetstones were also made, and these have almost replaced natural stones. Paving slabs, garden vases, balusters, tombstones, and various architectural features often constructed of terra cotta, were produced of superior quality and greater durability. The stone thus made, however, after some exposure, was found to become unsightly, owing to an efflorescence of sulphate of soda, the result of impurities in the preparation of the material. Some modification of the treatment resulted in a marked improvement in this respect, but it is difficult to avoid disagreeable markings, which are the result of weathering, and, though they do not render the stone more destructible, they greatly diminish its beauty.

The moulding of Ransome's artificial stone was easy and perfect, and the shrinkage in the kiln extremely small. When finished, it could be cut with the chisel and worked like a freestone, if required. Its power of resistance to transverse strains was found, on experiment at Woolwich, to be greater by one-fourth than that of excellent and known sandstones used for building, three times as great as best limestones, and eight times as great as Bath and Caen stones. To crushing weights its resistance is also remarkable. A two-inch cube sustained twenty-one tons, while Darley Dale sandstone yielded at sixteen tons, and limestones at much less.

Ransome's "patent siliceous stone," as this composition was called, though made with great facility and at a very moderate cost, and though on the whole successful and advancing in public favour, was too expensive to come into general use on a very large scale; and while pursuing his investigations on the same subject and in the same direction, the ingenious inventor found that a much cheaper, more rapid, and more satisfactory result was produced by making stones and sand into a paste with the fluid silicate in the usual way, and obtaining the required form by moulding that paste, and then, instead of burning in a kiln, fixing the form instantaneously by dipping it into chloride of calcium for a very short period. A rapid double decomposition then takes place, the chlorine of the latter salt combining with the soda of the fluid silicate, and leaving the silica free to combine with the calcium, which is thus converted into silicate of lime. The chloride of sodium being very soluble is washed out, but the silicate of lime remains and cements the particles of sand, just as hydraulic cements solidify, fastening the whole firmly together and producing a completely made stone without drying or burning. This stone, called "patent concrete stone," is now largely manufactured. It is difficult to form an idea of the rapidity of the process and the perfection of the result, without seeing the manufacture.

Before concluding this account of artificial stones, I must not omit to make some mention of the varieties of concrete, and of the vast blocks of this material that are now commonly manufactured in a perfectly solid mass. These replace the accumulations of rubbish and loosely aggregated stones, once thought sufficient for filling up intervals between walls of solid masonry, especially in piers, harbours, and other important public works. The term *concrete* is generally applied to a species of rough masonry, consisting of gravel or broken stone mixed with lime, the lime being slacked upon, and in immediate contact with the gravel. Occasionally lime is used that has previously been worked into a paste, but in this case the result is more properly called by the French name *beton*. Both methods have been followed from very ancient times, certainly by the Romans, and probably earlier. The main uses of concretes are to distribute the weight of heavy constructions, and for backing coursed masonry where the walls are required to be of great thickness.

The quality of a concrete must depend on the materials made use of, and these are differently affected according to the nature of the work. Good concretes should set rapidly and completely, for to have any value the work in which this material is used must be made quickly; and therefore either hyraulic limes, or mixtures of pozzuolano or analogous substances with common limes, are necessary. The former should be used when they can be obtained, even at an increased cost, and therefore it is the more needful that the builder should be well aware of the nature of the material yielding such limes, and the probability of its existence in any given locality.

But though hydraulic lime is so desirable, the quantity used should not be in excess. Some care in selecting the rough stones, both with reference to size and shape, caution in not making the concrete till the lime is already converted into mortar, and in not throwing the mortar from a height, but wheeling it into its place and ramming it—these are all highly essential, and though not strictly belonging to the geological part of the subject, such precautions cannot be too earnestly impressed on all who have to employ hydraulic limes in this manner.

The strength and rapidity of setting of concrete may be varied by admixture of different material. The following are the proportions of materials as given by

Treussart, an authority in these matters, quoted by Mr. Burnell in his useful treatise on limes and cements. Two sets of proportions are given as fitted for different uses. The first is a very energetic concrete that should be used the instant it is made:—

30 parts very energetic hydraulic lime, measured in bulk before slacking;
30 „ trass of Andernach, burnt clay, or pounded brick;
30 „ sand;
20 „ gravel;
40 „ broken stone (hard limestone).

These proportions diminish one-fifth after manipulation. The mortar is made first, and the stones and gravel added. Broken limestone is recommended as affording the best result, but other stones might be used.

The other composition is less rapid and should be left twelve hours exposed after mixing:—

33 parts energetic hydraulic lime;
45 „ pozzuolano;
22 „ sand;
60 „ broken stone and gravel.

Artificial blocks of concrete are made in large cubes with a framework of iron to lift them into their places. They require to be constructed with great care, of the best materials, and carefully rammed. If dried too rapidly they are apt to crack, and therefore they should be arranged to consolidate slowly, and after perfect mixture of the whole in the mould. These blocks are admirable when successful, but might be very mischievous if carelessly constructed.

Bituminous cements are largely used in some countries for street pavements to replace large flags. In our own country, where we have abundant supplies of natural flagstones, they are less thought of. In France they are extensively and successfully adopted, and where carriage is expensive they might be available in the interior of England. The material used for these pavements is of two kinds, one being nearly pure, the other a natural mixture of bitumen with sand or carbonate of lime. *Asphalte* is the technical name for the bitumen commonly employed for pavements. It is found, in France, at Seyssel, in the department of L'Ain, at Gaugeac, in the department of Les Landes, at various places (Lobrann and Bekelbronn) in the department of the Bas-Rhin, and also in the Puy-de-Dôme department. Abundant supplies are found in Albania, Wallachia, on the shores of the Dead Sea, and in Trinidad, and no doubt many other places would yield this material; especially in the Northern States of America and in Canada. Mineral pitch is found in the island of Zante.

The best asphalte is black, brilliant, and hard in the air at ordinary temperatures, but it softens in the sun. To be of any value it should be absolutely free from sulphate of iron, and indeed, from sulphur in any form. When used it requires to be mixed with mineral pitch in a boiling state, and then formed into a cement in the following proportions, a little quicklime being added while the bitumen is boiling

Pure mineral pitch ...	7 pints.
Asphalte	37 lbs.
Powdered stone dust .	7 gallons.

For street paving, a bed of concrete of hydraulic lime and gravel must be prepared. The cement must be laid in slabs, evenly spread and compressed with the trowel, and well rubbed to a uniform close surface. Bituminous cements are made by mixing powdered calcareous stone in variable proportions with pitch or tar in a state of ebullition.

There are many other applications of cements and many contrivances in use in the arts, requiring some geological knowledge to apply them to the greatest advantage. I must not, however, dwell on these. It will, I think, be evident from the remarks I have offered, and the facts I have brought before you, that a vast variety of cases occur in which some acquaintance with the nature, history, and origin of rocks, and some idea of their metamorphoses and of their associations, will greatly help the practical man in obtaining and making the best use of the material he intends to employ. It may also suggest to him material that has not yet come into use.

Lecture the Fourth.

MINERALS FROM STRATIFIED DEPOSITS.

Stones used in Construction, Fuller's Earth, Salt, and Bituminous Shales.

FROM the consideration of the materials obtained from superficial accumulations, not regularly stratified, there is a natural transition to those presenting the phenomena of stratification and those apparently metamorphised or igneous, both of which are removed either by open quarrying or by subterranean operations of the nature of mining. All parts of the earth, to as great a depth as we can penetrate, yield useful minerals; but these are of very different uses, of various degrees of importance, more or less abundant, and need a great variety of contrivances to obtain them and render them available. I cannot hope, in the short time at my disposal, to point out all the materials or all the methods; but, by directing attention to the principal classes, I may clear the way and prepare for a more elaborate and personal study.

As we proceed in our course of inquiry and gradually open out fresh fields of investigation, we find the subject of applied geology present itself continually in larger proportions. Year by year also fresh applications are made, and those already familiar are brought into more general use. There are few districts where the ground beneath our feet does not even now afford recognized treasures; and these are constantly increasing in value to those who know how to use them. There are no countries where the earth does not contain, and willingly give up, these treasures, if they are sought for prudently and properly.

I propose, on this occasion, to bring under your notice the main facts that have been determined concerning stones of various kinds used for constructive purposes, whether strictly ornamental or generally useful. The number of them is very large, and I can only pretend to speak of them in groups. They are very varied in value, in appearance, in the uses that are made of them, and in the places and circumstances of their discovery. On the whole, they may be regarded as obtainable by quarrying and open works, as belonging to rock masses and strata rather than to veins, and as present on a large scale where they exist at all. In all these respects they agree with such minerals as coal and iron stone, but they differ from the ores of copper, lead, and other metals, which commonly exist in mineral veins.

So far as their uses extend, the stony minerals we have now to consider may be divided and grouped in many ways. They are required for constructive purposes on a large scale: (1) as squared or rough stones, fit for building walls, houses, churches, and palaces; (2) slabs and slates for paving and roofing purposes; (3) pitchers and kerbs for road-making; (4) blocks for the finer kinds of construction, as columns, capitals, and other ornamental work; and (5) blocks for artistic purposes, as statuary and inlaid-work. It may happen that the same kind of stone is used for two or more of these purposes, as marbles and granite, which, in countries where they abound, are used indifferently for rough walls, houses, palaces, buildings, roads, and statuary. As a rule, however, the less perfectly crystalline, softer, and rougher kinds of stone, being cheaper and more easily worked than the others, are used for commoner purposes; the more ornamental and harder kinds, capable of receiving a high polish, being reserved for the more artistic uses.

Commencing with what are commonly called building materials, we may regard them as of three classes —granites, sandstones, and limestones. Practically, there is another division of the whole number into two classes; namely, those which can only be worked by the pick or by wedges, and those which can be worked by the mallet and chisel. The latter are called *freestones*, and include marbles, all limestones, and stratified sandstones. The former include granites, quartz rocks, and indurated schists, conglomerates or pudding-stones, in which quartz predominates, and some agglomerated sandstones that cannot be fitly called pudding-stones. Of these some are rarely used on a large scale, except in the immediate vicinity of the rocks whence they are derived, and thus, practically, the number of those we have to consider is reduced within reasonable limits.

Granites (generally of a pale colour) are procured

on a large scale from Cornwall and Devonshire, where, owing to the great magnitude of the quarries, the extent of the demand and the character of the stone, they are worked with extraordinary facility and cheapness. They are obtained of better general quality and more ornamental character, and both of pink and grey colour, but at a much greater cost, from Peterhead and Aberdeen. Others, much harder than either and of a darker colour, but too tough to be available where large squared blocks are needed, are got from Guernsey and Herm, from the Malvern Hills, and from Mount Sorrel and Grooby, in Leicestershire.

Varieties of granite, on a smaller scale, fit for monumental purposes, have been obtained from Jersey. Ireland yields some useful kinds. Magnificent granite, of extreme hardness, was formerly used by the Egyptians; and granites from India and China have been long known. The Norwegian granites, and some from Sweden, are well adapted for public works, and can be obtained at a low price, of excellent quality.

Granite, generally and theoretically, consists of crystals of quartz, of felspar, and of mica embedded in crystalline quartz. Practically, all porphyritic rocks are called granites. In many of these rocks the mica is replaced by hornblende, the result being the variety called Syenite. The mica and hornblende are sometimes absent or present in very small proportions. The quartz sometimes preponderates, and is sometimes almost absent. The felspar is sometimes in distinct crystals and sometimes only crystalline The felspathic portion of the stone also is sometimes felspar proper, but occasionally *albite*, in which the alkaline element is chiefly soda instead of potash. The crystals vary in size and in the mode of their distribution, so that the granite may be coarse or fine grained. Some kinds of granite are brittle and others singularly tough; some very easily break along lines of natural fracture and are comparatively soft while yet fresh from the quarry, while other kinds resist any regular fracture and are only reduced to a desired shape with extreme difficulty, even when first obtained.

The following is regarded as the average composition of ordinary granites and the maximum and minimum of the various ingredients. It is the result of the comparison of a large number of observations.

COMPOSITION OF AVERAGE GRANITE.

	Maximum.	Minimum.	Mean.
Silica	76·98	66·0	72·8
Alumina	17·77	11·0	15·3
Potash	8·88	4·0	6·4
Soda	2·50	..	1·4
Lime	1·50	...	0·7
Magnesia	2·00	..	0·9
Iron oxide	2·50	0·5	1·7
Loss by ignition	1·50	..	0·8
			100·0

Chemically, therefore, true granite is a silicate of alumina and potash, with a little iron and lime, and with soda sometimes replacing the potash and magnesia the lime. This analysis, however, only indicates the ultimate elements, and not the mineral composition of the rock; and, to a certain extent, granites must be regarded as mixtures of crystalline minerals in various proportions. Thus it is also useful to observe that an average granite may be expected to contain from two to three-fifth parts of crystals of quartz or crystalline quartz, about the same, more or less, of felspar, also partly crystalline and chiefly in definite crystals, and the remainder (one-tenth part) of mica. But the mica may form two or three-tenths and the quartz three-fifths, or more, while the proportion of felspar, as well as the particular composition of the felspar, both vary extremely.

Good ordinary granite possesses a mean specific gravity of 2·66, so that the cubic foot weighs 166¼ lb., and the cubic yard as nearly as possible two tons. Fourteen cubic feet to the ton is the usual estimate. Its toughness or resistance to crushing weights is very great, and is believed to vary a great deal in different samples. For practical purposes it is safe to assume that fresh unweathered granite will bear any direct crushing weight to which it can be exposed.

Granite contains a certain amount of water capable of being driven off by continued exposure to a heat insufficient to produce any other change. This quantity differs much in different specimens, even of the same stone, but it may be said to be represented by the "loss" in the table of analysis. It averages, therefore, about 0·8 per cent. Taken in its ordinary state, and containing this quantity of water, it is still sometimes capable of absorbing about one-fourth more (or 0·2 per cent.), when placed in water for a few hours. This quantity is, however, rather larger than could be expected of a good sample. Expressed in another way, I may say that a cubic yard, or two tons weight of granite, contains, in its ordinary state, something more than 3½ gallons of water, and some specimens can absorb nearly a gallon more on being placed in pure water for a short period. It is important to notice this fact, as the influence of frost on a stone is in proportion to the water it takes up, and determines its durability.

To a small extent, granite is soluble in pure water. Portions of certain varieties of granite are also taken up to a considerable extent by hydro-chloric acid. The solubility of granite in pure water and hydro-chloric acid are among the tests of its value. An indifferent granite was found to lose 0·25 per cent. of its weight in the former, and 5 per cent. in the latter. This is in excess of the mean, but good observations are wanting in this inquiry.

For various public works, both ornamental and useful, granite is admirably adapted. Among these may be named bridges, harbours, piers, and quays. For certain public buildings also it is well fitted, but generally its extreme hardness and the great cost of working it into ornamental forms limit its use to works of practical utility where durability is very essential. The monumental works of Egypt are examples of the small change produced on syenite by time and exposure in a warm climate; and other public monuments constructed of this stone in Russia and

Scandinavia, in more modern times, are proofs that it will resist for many years exposure to the cold and changing temperature of an almost arctic region. But good varieties require to be selected, and some kinds of granite are not more proof against weather than the poorest limestones. Partly by the decomposition of the felspar, partly by the disintegration of the quartz, and partly, perhaps, from other causes, some granites have become so rotten by exposure as to be reduced to mere powdery gravel.

The rocks called in Cornwall *Elvans* are porphyritic or granite veins, and are much used locally. Some of them are unsafe and apt to decompose; others are regarded as durable and valuable building stones.

Basalt is a material not often used for any other constructive purpose than rough walls; but it forms an excellent road metal, and thus enters into the list of available material. The following is the composition of some volcanic rocks:—

	Basalt.		Pumice from Lipari.
	Beaulieu.	Saxony.	
Silica	59·50	44·50	70·00
Alumina	11·50	16·75	16·00
Lime	1·30	9·50	2·50
Magnesia	..	2·25	..
Potash	1·60	..	6·50
Soda	5·40	2·60	..
Iron protoxide	19·70	20·00	..
Iron peroxide	·50	..	·50
Manganese protoxide	..	0·12	..
Water	..	2·00	3·00
	99·50	97·72	98·50

It will be evident that in the ordinary basalts a very large percentage of iron is a prevailing feature, while the percentage of potash and soda is not excessive. The peculiarly tough nature of the better kinds of this rock, and the mode in which it weathers, peeling off and leaving round hard nodular lumps, separated by rotten powdery rubbish, are due partly to composition and partly to the mode of formation and cooling of the rock. The columnar form of basalt and the impossibility of obtaining large stones are due to the same causes. Greenstones are varieties of basalt, and rocks of this kind exist in many countries where at present there are no volcanic phenomena. The name *trap* is commonly given to rocks of this kind. They are useful for road metal, owing to their toughness, but are often very easily decomposed. The columnar structure of such material in some places, as in the Giant's Causeway in Ireland, the island of Staffa in Scotland, many places on the banks of the Rhine, between Cologne and Coblentz and elsewhere, renders basaltic and trappean rocks, due to ancient and extinct volcanoes, very available for various purposes. Thus they are largely used in Germany as milestones, and even replace wood as posts. Quarries of columnar basalt often present a very curious and picturesque appearance.

Diallage rock, under the name of Crousa Down Stone, has been used in, and exported from, Cornwall. It is used with advantage for ornamental work. The same may be said of Schorl rock, which is a very beautiful material.

Of the other rocks that are not freestones it is sufficient to say, that quartzite and quartz conglomerates, or puddingstones, are little fitted for structural purposes, and are generally too brittle to be very good for road metal; they are rarely used except for rough walls. Indurated schists offer the same difficulties to the tool, and present no advantages to counterbalance these defects. They are durable, but not ornamental, and very difficult to work into any convenient form.

Indurated sandstones are more valuable than trap rocks, and are occasionally employed in engineering works. Flag-stones, as their name imports, are valuable for paving, and are greatly used for this purpose, but they are not generally available for any other purpose. The Caithness flags, however, and some of those from Yorkshire, are sometimes used in forming party walls, for which they are considered well adapted. The advantages offered by the best of these materials are due to their extraordinary hardness, the density of the texture, their non-absorbent properties, and their power of resisting, not only hard wear, but all atmospheric influences. They are, however, on the other hand, very difficult to manipulate, and being composed of heterogeneous ingredients, some one of which, if it should fail, may cause the disintegration of the whole, they cannot safely be recommended except for special uses. Paving and road material must be considered among these, and the stones for such works are generally to be found in this list.

In quarrying granite one of the most important

practical questions is connected with the nature and position of the systems of joints and natural fractures that affect the rock. These vary in different localities, but they generally have reference to the geological axis of the district, and the main direction of elevation, as indicated by the dip and strike of the older rocks. It must also be remembered that in all granites it is only certain portions of the mass—certain *veins*, as they are sometimes called, or strata, as they often appear to be—that are really valuable. In some quarries these veins are of small extent compared with the whole mass of the stone, and are enclosed on either side by walls of very rotten material. Being a crystalline mass, elaborated for the most part from a vast body of miscellaneous material, granite is almost always irregular in its composition; but the larger the mass the less are the irregularities perceived, because each variety occupies a larger space absolutely, though perhaps much the same in proportion, in the larger and smaller granitic bosses. Thus, in England, the fine and durable qualities occur in more considerable veins in Cornwall and Scotland than in Guernsey or Charnwood Forest, and though all contain valuable material, the granite for extensive works, where large blocks are needed, should be sought for rather in the former than the latter localities.

We come now to the consideration of the Freestones—the stones that may be worked with mallet and chisel, and that can be sculptured without much difficulty, and at no extreme cost of labour, time, or money, into any required form. Of these some are crystalline ; but these are few in comparison, and generally expensive from their rarity. They are chiefly the varieties of marble, including statuary marble in the first place ; the coloured and black marbles, such as those found in Derbyshire and Devonshire, in the second place ; and the crystalline dolomites in the third place. They include also alabaster, malachite, spars; serpentine, and some other minerals.

Of fine marbles, of pure white colour or slightly veined, there are examples on a small scale in many countries, but it is only at present from Carrara, and formerly from Paros, that the great supplies have been obtained. The Parian marbles have not been worked for a very long period. They are more waxy in colour and texture, and somewhat harder than the Carrara, but equally beautiful, and quite as well, if not better, adapted for the finest purposes of art. The Carrara quarries, however, are the only important resources for the artist at present.

Carrara marble is obtained from a large number of quarries within four or five miles of the Mediterranean, nearly midway between Leghorn and Genoa, and close to the beautiful bay of Spezzia. There is a railway-station on the railway from Pisa to Spezzia, at Massa Carrara, close to the quarries, which are now, therefore, very accessible. The veins of marble are in the Apennines, where the mountains of that chain approach nearest the Gulf of Lyons, and they include many varieties, of which the principal are—(1) white granulated statuary marble without veins ;

(2) the same with delicate veins, available for statuary, but of somewhat inferior quality and not fetching so high a price; (3) *ravacioni*, or Sicilian marble, a variegated kind; and (4) *bardiglio*, a deep blue stone. The demand for large blocks of the finest kinds is very active, but the others are also saleable, and are readily taken for exportation to all parts of the world, but chiefly to England, France, Germany, and America. The marble is quarried by first loosening the large masses by blasting, after which wedges are applied until the blocks are thoroughly detached from the rock. The statuary marble blocks are removed in the rough, but the others are roughly shaped into oblong squares. The blocks are conveyed to the foot of the mountain, either by letting them roll down as they will, or lowering them from one terrace to another by aid of ropes. From the foot of the mountain they are conveyed on strong cars drawn by oxen, as much as ten yoke of oxen being sometimes attached to a single block. The access to the quarries is greatly impeded by the continued accumulation of rubbish. The number of quarries is enormous, the whole mountain side having been laid open from time to time. Many of those in active work do not yield statuary marble, and many more are abandoned. There are from three to four hundred abandoned quarries within a few miles. From two to three thousand men are employed constantly in the quarries now in work, which number from thirty to forty for common kinds, and ten or twelve for fine marbles.

The annual production varies, but exceeds 50,000 tons, of which but a small part is exported to England.

Marbles of inferior quality and value are found in most countries, and are quarried like limestones. The best black are rare, and the best kinds are at present found in Derbyshire, where they form part of the carboniferous series. Red are also rare and valuable when pure and of even deep tint, though both in Italy and elsewhere they exist. Yellow are chiefly found in Italy. The mixed colours are more common, and those that depend on fossils for their effect, though often very beautiful, are not very highly valued. There are numerous varieties found in England, chiefly in Derbyshire and Devonshire. Ireland, also, contains many kinds only partially worked. India is rich in marbles of almost all kinds: some certainly available for statuary work, but they are little used by European artists. Some of the Irish marbles, and some from India, closely resemble Parian marble both in colour and texture. On the continent of Europe, Belgium, France, Spain, Portugal, and many parts of Germany all yield excellent varieties of common marble, sometimes in sufficient abundance to be worked very cheaply for ordinary purposes. The fine ancient marbles—*rosso antico* (red), *giallo antico* (yellow), *verde antico* (green), and *nero antico* (black)—are hardly rivalled by the modern kinds, although the best Derbyshire and Sienna marbles are very little inferior to the ancient black and yellow kinds.

An extremely beautiful variety of marble, called

Oriental alabaster, is obtained from Egypt. It consists of a stalagmitic deposit from waters that have been loaded with carbonate of lime. It is wonderfully transparent.

SERPENTINE is used as a kind of marble. It is a silicate of magnesia, coloured very richly by metallic oxides, especially those of iron, nickel, and chrome. One kind, obtained from Cornwall, where the Lizard rock contains veins of extreme beauty, is remarkable for its brilliant red and mottled colour contrasted by veins of the purest white, and taking a very high polish. It is well adapted for small ornaments; but when used for church work, such as fonts, internal columns, &c., its appearance is injured by its numerous veins and cracks. The polish, though brilliant, does not stand exposure to weather or damp air. The Italian serpentine (*ophite*) is a different mineral, and far less brilliant, the rich red tints being absent, and the colour generally mottled dark green. It is used, however, for similar purposes, and is of nearly the same value. It is comparatively soft, and very easily worked. Irish Connemara marble is a variety of serpentine, and is a very beautiful material for columns, tables, altars, and other decorative purposes. Its colour is much paler than the Tuscan, which it otherwise resembles.

ALABASTER is widely distributed, and when of pure white or grey colour, and transparent, is a very beautiful material. It is also very easily worked, and therefore inexpensive, but it will not stand exposure to damp air, and in our climate can only be used, even for internal work, in tolerably dry localities. For external work it is quite useless, except in very dry climates. Alabaster is obtained in large quantities in England, but the finest kinds and most abundant sources of supply are in Italy and Greece.

MALACHITE, one of the ores of copper, is obtained in Siberia and Australia, in masses sufficiently large, and sufficiently resembling marble in its behaviour under the chisel and saw to be used for decorative purposes. Its delicate green colour and regular markings give it a very peculiar appearance. Its value, when manufactured into veneers, is nearly one-fourth that of the same weight of silver.

SPARS, especially fluor spar, of a rich blue or green colour, are occasionally used for inlaid work, and in this respect resemble some varieties of marble. The appearance of these stones is very beautiful, and the natural colour is sometimes modified by the action of sulphuric acid or by partial burning.

From the ornamental stones I pass on to the ordinary freestones. These are either limestones or sandstones; the former consisting of two groups—the limestones properly so called and the magnesian limestones, or dolomites. Let us first consider the case of the sandstones, which are in many cases the most durable, though the least manageable. As it would be impossible even to allude to all the varieties in common use in England only, much less in Europe or the world, I shall chiefly direct attention to those known in the London market, and a few others that possess a wide reputation.

Of all sandstones for building, the Craigleith is one of the best. It is obtained from the carboniferous rocks in the neighbourhood of Edinburgh, and in the county of Linlithgow, in Scotland. The colour is lightish grey, and the grain fine. The cement is chiefly siliceous, very slightly calcareous, and there is a little mica in the planes of bedding. It consists of 98 per cent. silica, and only about 1 per cent. of carbonate of lime; the remainder consisting of bituminous substances and mica. The beds vary in thickness, the thickest being ten feet. The number of workable beds is very large. A cubic foot of the stone weighs about 146 lb., and will absorb four pints of water. Good samples resist crushing weights to the extent of 5,800 lb. to the square inch. The stone darkens, but is otherwise very little affected by exposure to a smoky atmosphere and frost. It is, however, an expensive stone. Other coal grits are good, but they are rarely equal in colour or composition to Craigleith.

The Dundee and Arbroath stones, obtained from the old red sandstone, on the east coast of Scotland, are dark-coloured and flaky, but hard and well adapted to resist atmospheric action. The Dundee stone is often of a dark purplish brown colour, owing to the presence of much iron oxide, and the tint is too sombre to be pleasant for buildings. The Arbroath is greenish grey; not very pleasing in colour, but not objectionable. Very large blocks of uniform appearance may be obtained, and they are valuable for flag pavements.

The Yorkshire sandstones of the millstone-grit series are often very durable and afford excellent material both for building and paving purposes. The Stenton quarries, near Durham, have supplied a stone which, in the keep of Barnard Castle, has lasted for five centuries without decay, and another building (Eccleston Abbey, Yorkshire), built of a similar stone, in the thirteenth century, is in equally good condition. Very excellent material, known as the Park Springstone, is obtained from near Leeds, and others from the neighbourhood of Halifax and Huddersfield. The composition of all these may be described as fine-grained quartzose sand with some felspar cemented with argillo-siliceous cement, and having plates of mica in the planes of stratification. They are generally coloured by oxide or silicate of iron, the colour varying from bluish green to pale ferruginous brown. These stones weigh about 145 lb. to the cubic foot, and support a crushing weight about equal to that of Craigleith. But the Yorkshire flags absorb water readily and part with it freely, and thus, though as paving-stones laid horizontally they are very durable, they are apt to peel when placed in walls. They are also unsafe when in contact with damp earth, or where water has only occasional access and there is no thorough circulation of air.

Sandstones of the lower new red sandstone series of whitish or reddish-brown colour, consisting of fine siliceous grains with magneso-calcareous cement, are quarried at Mansfield, in Nottinghamshire, and come into the London market. There are two varieties:

one of a red colour, weighing about 148½ lb. to the cube foot, and the other nearly white, and somewhat heavier, weighing 149½ lb. Both are rather absorbent stones, the former especially, as it absorbs nearly 5¼ pints of water to the cubic foot, while the white variety takes up little more than 4½ pints. These stones are said to wear well, but the new red sandstones generally are not very safe for use in a moist, smoky atmosphere. At Liverpool much stone from this rock is used, and it is necessarily employed very largely in the large tracts of country where it comes to the surface and can be quarried at very low cost, but the result is not favourable. Near Stafford, and in the buildings of that town, the same material is used, but here also it is apt to decay. An excellent and rather light sandstone of the lower secondary period, better than most of the varieties from contemporaneous beds, is worked near Whitby, in Yorkshire, and largely exported.

Of other sandstones, those of the Wealden period are well known, but the materials from the neighbourhood of Tunbridge, where stones of this kind are much quarried, are too irregular in their composition and too easily acted on by weather to justify an extended use for other than local purposes. Some of the sandstones of the cretaceous series are better, though these are also absorbent and acted on by frost. The Godstone and Maidstone fire-stones and the Chilmark siliceous limestone are very valuable for certain purposes, and if kept from the damp they last an indefinite time, but the use of the two former should be confined to internal work, at least in our doubtful climate. Chilmark stone is rather a siliceous limestone than a sandstone. It is remarkably heavy, weighing 153½ lb. to the foot cube. It is also remarkably non-absorbent, taking up less than 1½ pint of water in the cubic foot.

On the whole, the sandstones, consisting for the most part of detached grains of larger or smaller size, and generally of indestructible material, cemented together by some foreign substance that has been held in water, depend very greatly on the nature of the cementing medium for their durability. Where this is calcareous or marly, or even irony, it is apt to be affected by weather, but where it is siliceous it is safe. When the sandstone is laminated and the strata are easily separated, water enters readily and ultimately produces disintegration, and thus many that are apparently strong and durable may decay very quickly. Those sandstones that contain marly bands and occasional alternations of loose sand, are usually bad for all purposes of construction. In point of colour most varieties of sandstone that are not easily decomposed, are either too pale or too decidedly brown to be agreeable, and those that have warm tints cannot be trusted. The Craigleith, which is the best, is somewhat too white to be pleasant to the eye, and it would certainly blacken if used in London.

Many sandstones, whose laminated structure prevents their being safely used in construction for external walls and facings, are extremely valuable as slabs, either for foot-paving, curbs, or other purposes, and may be used with advantage for party-walls. Such laminated grits are, however, indifferent road metal when broken up, and in this respect they are greatly inferior to granitic and basaltic rocks.

Limestones, especially in England, are more available for ordinary purposes of construction than sandstones; they are more easily worked, and therefore cheaper; they are more varied in quality and appearance; the useful kinds are more thoroughly distributed; the colour is generally more pleasing, and they are susceptible of much ornamentation. In France and in the south of Europe there are limestones far more compact than any of our oolites and of the same geological age.

Of ordinary limestones, the Portland, Bath, Ketton, Barnack, and Caen varieties are the best known and most used in London and its neighbourhood. All these are important and each requires notice as their properties are very different. A multitude of other stones are in local use, some from the carboniferous series and even silurian rocks, and others from the liassic, oolitic, and Wealden series, not included in the above list. Even the chalk is used occasionally for constructive purposes, though chiefly in the interior of buildings.

Portland stone is perhaps the best, as it is certainly the hardest, the least absorbent, the most durable, and the most resembling marble of all our English building materials. An examination of the eastern part of Greenwich Hospital is sufficient to convince any one that this kind of stone, well selected, is as good as can possibly be desired. Like all limestones, it is acted on by the atmosphere to a certain extent and in certain exposures, but on the whole it resists exposure admirably.

Chiefly developed in the island or peninsula of Portland, whence its name is derived, the upper member of the oolitic series contains throughout the south of England, wherever it is found, numerous bands of shelly limestone, alternating with less shelly bands, all of them partaking more or less of that peculiar granular character which, from its resemblance to the roe or eggs of fish, has been long known as *roe-stone* or *oolite* (eggstone). It is only some of these bands, and those which are least shelly, that afford valuable building stone. The upper members of the Portland series pass into the Purbeck series (which also contains a useful shelly stone, called "Purbeck marble"), and the annexed diagram will illustrate the position of the valuable beds of freestone in the quarry as generally found. There are local differences of some importance, though the alternation of good stone and shelly bands is universal.

Portland stone of fair quality is rather heavy, weighing from 135 to 148 lb. to the cube foot. It absorbs more than one-seventh of its bulk (about 6¾ pints) of pure water per cube foot. It is generally composed of more than 95 per cent. carbonate of lime, with rather more than 1 per cent. of silica and carbonate of magnesia. It can be obtained in blocks of any required size, and can be worked either by the chisel or the plate saw without difficulty. It is, however, expensive. It is said to bear a pressure of 3,279 lb. without crushing.

Fig. 11.

[*Reference to diagram.*—(1) Freshwater limestones and (2) *dirt-bed*, or bed of vegetable mould, with fossilized remains of ancient trees; both these belong to the Purbeck series. (3) *Top-cap*, a white, hard, compacted limestome, 8 to 7 feet thick. (4) *Skull-cap*, a compact but irregular stone, with cherty nodules. (5 to 9) *Roach-beds*. At top (5) are oyster beds and irregular flinty bands in a limestone full of cavities where shells have once been. At a variable depth below this is the *top-bed* (6), the best stone of the quarries; it is fine-grained, free from shells, and without hard veins. The stone is from 3 to 8 feet thick, with occasional bands of impure stone containing casts of shells. (7) *Roach*. (8) The *Curf-bed*, not always present; a middle stone of fair quality. (9) The bottom-bed, inferior stone.]

Although the heavier beds are the most durable for house architecture, the upper beds, or roach, are not unfrequently preferred for some purposes, especially docks, piers, and other hydraulic works. The roach is lighter than the compact stone, chiefly because of the number of empty spaces left in it from shells that have been removed by decay, and have not been replaced by crystalline carbonate of lime or by other minerals. It is also less oolitic, and its cementing medium more perfectly crystallized. It thus resists better than the rest alternations of dryness and moisture. But it is far less sightly, and could not be trusted in exposed situations in the air. The best quarries of Portland stone are on the eastern side and near the extremity of the island; those on the western side, occasionally used for London work, have generally failed to yield a durable material.

The Bath stones may be considered as next in importance to the Portland, because, although in durability far inferior, their cheapness, facility of working, abundance, and pleasing appearance, have caused them to be very largely adopted all through the south of England, and wherever they could be conveyed at small cost. There are numerous quarries, and the qualities differ a good deal. They occur at intervals in a series whose total thickness is from 60 to 120 feet. It is shown in natural sections at various places around Bath, and consists of the following subdivisions, all belonging to the Great oolite and resting on the Inferior oolite, which is developed generally to great thickness below :—

1. Upper rag stones ....thickness 25 to 50 feet.
2. Fine freestones or building bed „ 10 „ 30 „
3. Lower rag stones .... „ 25 „ 80 „

Bath stone is of a rich cream colour, and is so soft that it can readily be cut with a tooth saw. It is lighter than Portland, weighing only about 123 lb. to the cube foot. It is also much more absorbent, taking up nearly 8½ pints of water to the cubic foot, or more than one-sixth of its bulk. It bears a crushing weight of from 1,800 to 2,000 lb. per square inch of surface.

The upper ragstone consists in the upper part of coarse, shelly, and irregularly-bedded limestones, with a few underlying beds of white fine-grained stone, highly oolitic, and consisting of comminuted shells. Below these are tough argillaceous bands of pale brown colour and smooth texture. There are no workable beds in this series, but immediately below it are the fine-grained building beds, varying in number and thickness, and distinguished from each other by structural condition, by the size of the oolitic grains, and by the presence of siliceous particles to a greater or less extent. Sometimes the beds are earthy, close-grained, and of smoother texture than usual.

The lower ragstone is very persistent, and includes numerous well-defined shelly beds with frequent false bedding, resting on the fuller's earth. The importance of determining the geological limits of the valuable freestone beds renders this sharp identification of the lower and upper ragstone peculiarly momentous. The lower beds, though not commercially valuable, have the appearance of fine-textured oolitic limestones, but they are singularly liable to injury from exposure. At the celebrated Box and Corsham quarries, these beds are upwards of 40 feet thick, but they cannot be worked for any but the commonest purposes.

Bath stone, removed from the quarry and exposed to the atmosphere of large towns without precautions, is almost certain to decay very rapidly. By first weathering the dressed stones in the quarry, and thus allowing the surface to harden, they are much improved, but nothing can prevent absorption and the action of frost, which must soon tell upon them, especially when much chiselled for ornamental work. The restoration of Henry the Seventh's Chapel, in Westminster Abbey, is an example of the mistake of using a material of this kind in London without selection and preparation. The consumption of Bath stone at the present time is estimated to exceed 100,000 tons annually.

Caen stone somewhat resembles Bath stone in its great beauty of colour and texture, facility of working, and other qualities. It is even lighter than Bath, weighing only 120 lb. to the foot cube, and its resistance to crushing weights is rather superior. It is distinctly harder and somewhat less absorbent. It is obtained from many quarries near Caen, some of which have been open eight or ten centuries. Besides the best stone from the Allemagne and other quarries near Caen, many other stones from the neighbourhood, but of inferior quality, reach London, and are extensively used. Others of superior quality, for special purposes, are less known. Only small blocks of the best qualities can be obtained, while the other quarries yield stones of any required dimensions.

The Aubigny stone is one of those that have been largely, but not very successfully, introduced. Buckingham Palace and several London mansions were built of poor Caen stones, and have proved great failures, but there are many good materials that might be imported with advantage. It may be remarked of all these stones that they are remarkably pure and not very shelly. The carbonate of lime is often sub-crystalline, and threads of calc spar traverse the stone at intervals. This is the case, however, very generally with the oolitic limestones. The Inferior oolites, as well as the Great oolite, yield good building stones in the west of England, but they are not superior to Bath stone, and are all liable to injury from exposure to the acid vapours present in the atmosphere of London and other large towns in England.

Barnack, in Northamptonshire, Ketton, in Rutlandshire, and Ancaster, in Lincolnshire, are midland oolites that have a somewhat wide reputation; the first named is now replaced by stone from the Casterton quarries. This stone is of a lightish brown colour and compact oolitic structure, and is made up chiefly of fragments of shells and corals. It is a somewhat heavy oolite, weighing more than 130 lb. to the foot cube. Its resistance to crushing weights is not more than 1,500 lb. The Barnack stone has been used with great success in nearly all the mediæval buildings of Cambridge, both the University and county, and also in the north of Suffolk. The Casterton is believed to be equally good. Ketton stone has been chiefly used in Northamptonshire, but is brought to London, and some modern buildings of it seem to stand well. Its colour is rather superior to that of Barnack, being a warm cream tint. It is of lower specific gravity than Barnack, and rather superior in resistance to crushing weights. Ancaster is somewhat superior to Ketton in all respects, and seems to be equally durable, but it has not been very much used in London in important works. All these stones are absorbent, taking up about one-sixth of their bulk of water. They are somewhat expensive to work compared with Bath stone, but considerably cheaper than Portland.

Very excellent building stones, of bluish tint and fine grain, belonging to the "great oolite," are found and worked in Yorkshire. They contain no fossils, and are especially valuable for engineering works.

It is not very easy to ascertain the precise relative value of the midland oolites. Left in the quarry, or used in the immediate neighbourhood, they all wear well, and many buildings from three to five centuries old attest their excellence; but removed, and used carelessly, they are found to resist frost very badly. The number of quarries of each kind is large, but the stones from adjacent quarries are by no means of the same quality. Very careful selection is therefore necessary, and this selection must be made with a knowledge of the peculiar properties of the stone and its tendency to decay. Thus some very coarse stones absorb but little water, while others, far superior in texture and appearance, suck in water like a sponge, and soon decay in an atmosphere such as that which characterises our country. The Heddington stone, near Oxford, used for the public buildings of that University, is an example of a very inferior stone whose first appearance is promising enough.

In quarrying the oolites, it is by no means unusual to run in levels or drifts to the rock, and thus carry on operations almost exactly in the same way as that required for ordinary mining. As, however, large blocks are the most valuable, some difficulties arise which do not occur in mining. In working for stone, the first question to determine is, whether the stone is to be reached by drifts and tunnels, or by open cuttings. If there is a thick covering of upper hard beds, open quarrying is impossible, and as this is likely to be the case in most places where the stone is being got in the Bath district, the work is there almost entirely carried on by tunnels; elsewhere, open quarries are common enough, but in them there is always a large quantity of waste material—either a head of rubbish or bands of useless stone—whose removal is a matter of serious consideration before opening a quarry.

In the Bath district, the workings are carried due west, in a direct line towards the escarpment, commencing from near the entrance of the Box tunnel, on the north side of the Great Western Railway. The distance is nearly two miles on the rise of the stone, the incline being one in forty. The works always keep on the floor of the workable beds.

In getting the stone in these mines, the quarryman commences operations at the roof of the stone, picking out the roof by wedge-shaped picks, on the heads of which longer handles are inserted as the work proceeds, so that the men drive a distance of six or seven feet back into the rock. The width of the stalls must depend on the nature of the stone. When this preliminary work is done the stone is cut with a saw, and removed with great care.

Besides the absorbent oolitic limestones, which are widely used for building purposes, there are also, in the rocks of the same formation, several bands of more compact stone of local value for roofing and paving. These flags are inferior to those found in Yorkshire, and to the slates from Cumberland and Wales; but where these cannot readily be obtained they are employed with advantage. The Stonesfield slate is one of them, but it is more remarkable for the singular fossils it yields than for its building or other constructive qualities. The Colley Weston slate is another. Of both these the evenly splitting flaggy structure is the only important fact in an economic sense.

Although employed for purposes very different from construction, it would not be right to quit the oolites without alluding to the remarkable and valuable beds of lithographic stone they sometimes contain. The best qualities of lithographic stone are worked in large quarries, in the north of Bavaria, near the towns of Solenhofen, Pappenheim, and some others. They are fissile, but in thick beds, and are remarkable for the extraordinary smoothness and fineness of grain of the surface, and its delicate cream colour. They belong to the upper division of the oolites. Other lithographic stones of inferior excellence are obtained from liassic limestones.

Limestones of the tertiary period are not met with in England, but very excellent qualities are worked in various parts of the Continent. Thus, in and around Paris the deposits of the older tertiaries are very useful in this respect, and are opened in extensive quarries, from which the capital is supplied. They are not often exported. They are of good colour, even texture, and easily and cheaply worked, but they do not resist perfectly even the comparatively pure and dry atmosphere of Paris.

The chalk, always soft in England, becomes hard and well adapted for building purposes in the south of France, and hard white limestones of very various degrees of goodness are found throughout the middle and south of Europe, available for construction. Many of these are compact and very durable, and consist of nearly pure carbonate of lime. They occasionally pass into marble, but this is chiefly in veins.

The compact carbonates of lime in England are chiefly members of the carboniferous series, and then also pass into marbles. The building stones of the mountain limestone are not very numerous or celebrated. The Lias supplies compact material, but it is usually argillaceous. The middle beds of lias, forming the "marlstone" of geologists, yield a purer limestone, used locally, but not valuable enough to bear removal. None of these stones, though compact, are in any sense crystalline. They are all absorbent, though not fissile, and they are rapidly injured by exposure to moist air in changing temperatures, and especially when there is frost. Few of them are known beyond the districts in which they are found, except, indeed, that some of them make excellent hydraulic lime when burnt.

Magnesian limestones occur in various parts of the middle and north-east of England. They may be described as consisting of a variable proportion of carbonate of lime and carbonate of magnesia, and as stones of this composition have been extensively used in some recent important buildings in London, I may be expected to give a more particular notice of them than would otherwise be necessary. The colour of the best of them is a good light brown, of warm and somewhat irony tint; their density is greater than that of the oolites; the labour on them is intermediate between that on the gritstones and Portland, and they can be obtained of any required size. They are also four times stronger than Portland. Bolsover in Derbyshire, Anston, and other places, both in Nottinghamshire and Yorkshire, all in the same district, yield abundantly this kind of stone, which appears to possess every desirable quality, and, indeed, when careful inquiry was made concerning buildings of great age in the neighbourhood constructed of it, there was every reason to presume that it was a durable material. Under these circumstances it can hardly excite wonder that the Commissioners for selecting stone for the New Houses of Parliament agreed to recommend it. It was used for that building, and for some others in London constructed about the same time, and among these was the Museum of Economic Geology, in Jermyn Street. The stone in the latter building is extremely good. With regard to the former, it is well known how great a failure has resulted. Whether this has arisen from want of care in selecting the stone, from the more trying exposure, or from the quarry ultimately selected not yielding such good quality of stone as the specimens examined, it is now too late to discuss, but the result should be a warning not to trust to local indications, and not to risk a building of importance to an experimental material, or one of which so little was known in the exact kind of exposure to which it was to be subjected.

The best varieties of magnesian limestone are those in which there is at least 40 per cent. of carbonate of magnesia and 4 or 5 per cent. of silica. But the composition alone is of comparatively small importance, for there is no doubt that the state of crystallisation is the point of chief importance. Where this is complete the stone resists attack, but it is an unfortunate peculiarity of the admixtures of carbonates of lime with carbonates of magnesia that they are rarely the same for many yards together, even in the same quarry. It is not likely that these stones, which at one time enjoyed a high reputation, will again be favourably regarded in the London market, nor is it fit that they should be so.

It is most desirable, but by no means easy, to obtain a test of the relative value of stones to be used for building purposes. An attempt was made by an eminent French chemist, M. Brard, to determine the relative durability of limestones and sandstones having calcareous cements. His method consists of boiling small cubes in a saturated solution of Glauber's salts (sulphate of soda), and then exposing the cubes in the air. It was believed that the effect of expansion by the efflorescence of the salts, as the water evaporated, tested by weighing the amount of material removed from the stone in a given time, would represent and measure the effect of frost. To a certain extent this is the case, but it has not been found that the result can be depended on for practical purposes on a large scale. It is now seldom resorted to.

SLATES.

Slates are too important to be omitted in any notice, however brief, of materials used in construction and for economic purposes. Belonging strictly to argillaceous minerals, and being so completely metamorphosed as to have lost, in most cases, the external marks of their mechanical origin, they have in the place of bedding, and over-riding all appearances of true stratification, that peculiar structure called *cleavage*. In other words, they split into plates of any degree of thinness, in planes parallel to each other, but altogether independent of their original stratification. Those that split into the thinnest plates are chiefly used for roofing purposes, and those which yield large thick slabs for paving and occasionally for walls.

Slates of good quality are not very common, and unless they are readily accessible by sea, and there are means of getting rid of the vast accumulations of rubbish that result from the workings, they cannot be quarried with profit. Generally good slates are obtained only from certain veins or limited bands of rock. These are of comparatively small dimensions, and occur in the midst of a considerable mass of schistose rock and of other slates, too much broken or too badly cleaved to be of use. Most of the slates largely quarried are from rocks of very ancient geological date, but it is certain that this is not necessary, and that excellent material may exist in secondary rocks, though always in mountain districts. The best slates in the London market are obtained either from North Wales, where there are some magnificent quarries near the coast, from Delabole, Tintagel, and other parts on the north coast of Cornwall, from the west coast of Scotland, and from Valentia, on the south-west coast of Ireland. Very good sorts are found in France, near Angers, and in Brittany; in the Ardennes in Belgium; in Western Germany, and in various places in the east of Europe. America also yields sufficient supplies.

It is not easy to judge with certainty of the condition of a vein of slate from its appearance at the surface, after exposure to weather; and much knowledge of rocks is needed to justify the expression of an opinion. Varieties occur both of the purple and green kinds, and there are some well enough adapted for roofing that have a peculiar grey tint. All these exhibit different modes of weathering. To make a good slate there must be great hardness, a perfect facility of splitting, and a very fine grain. The larger the size of the slabs or slates that can be cut, the greater is the value of the quarry. Slates are known by certain names, as queens, duchesses, &c., according to their size.

Quarries of slate are always open to the day, and they are among the most picturesque and largest of all quarries. The great Penrhyn quarry has been opened nearly a century, and is worked in twelve galleries, one above another. These galleries, or terraces, are of horseshoe form; each is 40 feet above the one below, and the highest 500 feet above the lowest. The works are kept constantly advancing in each terrace. Some terraces yield slates very superior to the rest, and it is found generally that those nearest the top are of the poorest quality. The Delabole quarries, in Cornwall, and the Ballahulish, in Scotland, are less extensive, but also very gigantic. Some of the Westmoreland slates are very beautiful, but they are costly.

Slate hardly shows much injury from weathering when placed horizontally, unless it be exposed to incessant foot-wear. It then tends to become worked up again into its original mud. In the better qualities of slate there is little or no pyrites, and the veins and joints are so arranged as to assist in the working. The annual produce of slates from the Ballahulish quarries, many years ago, amounted to six or seven millions, weighing 10,000 tons; and this involved the removal of at least 60,000 tons of rubbish. This quantity, large as it may seem, represents a very small part of the whole trade. The Penrhyn quarries are far more productive than any in Scotland,

and the Cornish and Cumberland quarries, and many of great importance in Wales, besides the Penrhyn, are at least as important. Under favourable circumstances, slate quarries are not only extremely valuable but highly interesting, and are especially useful in illustrating the extent of change and mechanical compression the rocks have undergone. It is generally found that the best slates are obtained from some depth within the quarry, and from valleys rather than on hills. The exposed and weathered slates are more brittle and harder, and seem in some cases to have lost much of their fissile properties. The discovery and opening of a valuable slate quarry is scarcely less costly, and may be even more profitable than the working of a rich mine of lead or copper.

DECAY AND PRESERVATION OF STONES.

Stones of all kinds are more or less injured by long exposure to the vicissitudes of the weather; and in considering the causes of decay, and the best method of keeping back decay as long as possible, the chemical composition and state of mechanical aggregation of the rock must always enter into the calculation. In merely estimating the general value of a particular stone for practical purposes, a knowledge of these is essential, as they teach us at once the direction in which to look for the cause of the injury, and may point to a possible remedy.

It is certain that the causes of decay are partly chemical and partly mechanical, and of these the latter include, (1) the action of rain-water, either in rubbing away by friction or in dissolving parts of the stone; (2) the expansion of the moisture, and consequent disintegration of the stone by the action of frost. The former include, (*a*) the decomposition produced by acids, and the chemical reactions that take place in stones exposed to the air, after being long in the earth; (*b*) the efflorescence produced by the action of acids or alkalies in the air, on certain ingredients of the stone. All these deserve careful consideration, and all depend on the essentially porous and absorbent nature of all stones, which is proved by experiment, and which varies in every kind of material, and, indeed, in almost every hand specimen of similar material that is examined.

It is chiefly, if not entirely, by capillary attraction that water is sucked into the substance of stones, and there are, of course, definite limits to this attraction, though they are not much affected by the mechanical position of the stones. Thus, in a stone, of whatever kind, without distinguishable grain, or any laminated structure that one can detect, water would enter almost as rapidly and as far from below upwards, or from an exposed vertical face inwards, as from above downwards. Together with the water the substances contained in it might also enter, although these would be left behind near the surface. But when afterwards evaporation takes place from the surface, or in other words, when the stone dries after being wetted, it is only the pure water that passes off. Thus the foreign substances are left behind, and produce their due effect in time.

Rain-water, especially in towns, contains both carbonic acid gas and ammonia, and, however small the proportion may be, it is certain that every material liable to attack from these substances will ultimately yield more or less to their action. Thus, even in granite, especially when the felspar contains soda instead of potash, the silicates become ultimately decomposed and the felspar destroyed by the constant action of rain-water. It is clear that when the felspar is gone the rock will soon become rotten and disintegrated. In certain granite districts it is not unusual to find at the surface, covering the compact rock, a great thickness of quartzy fragments. These may be used in the neighbourhood as gravel, and as they apparently form a distinct bed on the surface of the granite, they are called gravels, though they are nothing more than the rock *in situ* acted on by the rain. Such is the case in the islands of Alderney and Jersey, in the British Channel, where the depth of this gravel is in some places twenty or thirty feet. Such is the case also in Cornwall, even near some quarries extensively worked. But if granite is thus destroyed, much more so are sandstones with calcareous cements and limestones.

Nor does a London atmosphere contain only carbonic acid gas and ammonia. Owing to the quantity of coal burnt, and the impurity of the coal, there is always a certain proportion of sulphurous acid in the air, and this becomes dissolved in the rain as it falls, and is extremely active, rapidly affecting the carbonates of lime, especially those varieties that are not crystalline. When, then, we consider the effect of the action of carbonic acid on the moistened carbonates, assisted by the occasional dilute sulphuric acid, and remember that this action is going on almost every day, with every change of weather, it is no wonder that the surface of the stone, freshly bruised by the action of the tool in bringing it to a face, and deprived of the only protection nature is able to give, should very soon show signs of injury, and that a rapid disintegration and destruction should take place. The less homogeneous the stone the more injured is it by this kind of action; for in mixed compositions the whole effect of the absorbed acids is concentrated on the parts that are most destructible, and the durability of a stone, like the strength of a chain, is that of its weakest part.

The mere disintegration of a stone by the action of acid vapours would, however, be slow, except in certain cases, were it not for the combined action of heat and cold, and the consequent alternate expansion and contraction of the moisture contained in it. And this result is obtained in its maximum when the stone is so placed that the moisture following the planes of stratification is concentrated nearest the surface, which will happen when the stone is placed, not in the way in which it lies in the bed, but at right angles to this natural direction. As all stones, except granites, have some planes of stratification or cleavage, and even granites and basalts occasionally peel in concentric layers, it is clear that great care should be taken by the builder to place all stones as nearly as possible in their proper position. In this matter, however, nature is far more acute than the eye; and even when there is no discoverable bedding in the freshly-chiselled material, weathering will soon make it appear if it is badly placed. It is far more difficult than is sometimes thought to discover the bedding of the stone before placing it, and even a practised and educated eye may easily be deceived in this matter.

When stones have been properly placed, the effect of weather may still be seen, but it is only distinguished by the gradual removal of the softer material and the part of the stone most easily acted on. This may, or may not, end in the final disintegration of the material, for some stones hold together soundly enough long after they are pierced through with holes and have lost all chiselled and projecting portions. Too much attention, then, cannot be paid to the mode in which stones are laid; and this remark applies to the whole group of freestones, but especially to the sandstones and limestones employed in the main walls of buildings, and most especially to those selected for ornamental work of any kind. So important is it to attend to the action of the weather on these parts that it has been found to repay the cost to shelter the upper surface of such stones by lead or slates where it is possible, so as to prevent water from resting upon them. As, however, a south-west exposure in our climate involves the constant beating of rain on the surface of stones thus placed, it is impossible to shelter the whole, and we are sure to find out in time the weak parts, by watching the change produced by the action of weather. It is also chiefly under such circumstances that mechanical abrasion takes place; and this also, though small at first and hardly observable for some time in a newly-worked stone, becomes gradually more serious as the weathering decomposes the surface.

The injuries that take place in absorbent stones from chemical reactions, are not so easily traced as the foregoing, but are not for that reason less real than those occasioned by the solvent and mechanical action of water and acids. Thus the various substances accidentally present in stones—those, namely, that are not essential to its composition—may become changed by the chemical action of salt contained in the absorbed water, and in consequence of this may injure the stone and increase its tendency to decay. Perhaps there is no cause of injury of this kind so great as that produced by an efflorescence of crystals, generally nitrates of potash and soda, the consequence in some measure of the organic contents of the stone. Whatever the cause may be, it is certain that many stones suffer from this efflorescence, especially those forming walls constantly damp and shaded from the sun. Loamy clays, places where sea sand has been used, or where salt can in any way have been absorbed, and stones in which an unusual quantity of organic matter is present, are liable to this cause of mischief. It shows itself more generally in the interior than in the exterior walls, and particularly where the walls have been painted or otherwise rendered impervious to the air. Efflorescence from whatever cause is certain to bring away detached fragments of the stone loosened by weathering.

Whatever be the immediate cause of the destruction or disintegration of stones, it may generally be traced to the absorption of moisture, and thus any contrivance that will check the admission of water by removing it from contact with the undefended sides of the stone, will be the most likely to succeed in preserving the material from decay. Many such contrivances have been proposed, all of which may be considered to involve some one of the following principles: (1) the covering up the surface of the stone by means of some animal, vegetable, or mineral oil plastered upon it; (2) the coating of the face of the stone by some insoluble mineral substance deposited upon it; (3) the defending the pores of the stone by causing them to absorb a chemical solution, which, on the application of another solution, becomes decomposed and deposits within the stone an insoluble coat.

A coat of paint on stone, by preventing the absorption of water at the surface, preserves stone so long as the paint remains undecomposed. Not only is this very unsightly, but it can only last a very short time. In London the time hardly amounts to three years, even under favourable circumstances. After that the paint peels and must be renewed. The injection of oily and fatty matters acts in the same way and lasts only a little longer. There is, however, no doubt that in some cases, where the exposure is not severe and the treatment has been adopted before the smallest commencement of decay or the least absorption of moisture had taken place, the result has been such as to secure the stone for so long a time that the result was thought to be permanent. For important buildings, intended to last for centuries, such treatment is, however, certainly useless, as it can only stave off the evil day for a time comparatively very short. Of oily matters, innumerable varieties have been tried, and a vast number have been patented. Perhaps those least liable to destruction are preparations of the mineral oils, but these generally become discoloured if they are not (like tar) already black. Besides true oils, various organic substances, as blood, glue, gum, wax, flour, cheesy matter, and many others, have been suggested. All these are palliatives, checking the absorption of moisture from the air, or neutralizing for a time the action of the acids that would otherwise act on the stone. It is certain, however, from the nature of the case, that the only permanent benefit resulting from them is confined to the hardening and settling that takes place on the surface of stone, when it is exposed for some time to the air without being weathered. This is seen by the difference in the stone of a building that has been protected or sheltered, when compared with the parts against which rain has been constantly beating. Stones hardened before removal from the quarry are known to stand better than those placed immediately in the building for which they are prepared, and thus those that are defended for a time may become more able to resist the action of the weather than before, when the temporary defence has been worn away.

About twenty years ago, a German chemist, Professor Kuhlmann, applied fluid silicate of potash, obtained by dissolving flints in caustic alkali with the aid of water at a very high temperature, to harden chalk and porous stone. He observed that on soaking chalk with this fluid silicate, a change took place, part of the chalk, combining with the silicic acid of the silicate of potash, becoming converted into silico-carbonate of lime. The carbonic acid, thus set free, combined with the potash. In time, particularly when assisted by heat and dry air, the coating of silico-carbonate was found to pass into a true compact deposit of silica, hard enough to scratch glass. The solution of silicate of potash could be applied dilute, either with a brush or a syringe, the surface being first cleaned and scraped. Three applications were considered sufficient. Although successful in the laboratory, this method failed when applied to buildings, because a dry atmosphere is needed during the whole period of hardening.

Not long after this suggestion had been made in Germany, Mr. Frederick Ransome, of Ipswich, while manufacturing fluid silicate of soda on a large scale, repeated Professor Kuhlmann's experiments, and observing the cause of failure, attempted to fix the solution when absorbed into the stone, by inducing it to absorb another solution, which should act by double decomposition, thus leaving an insoluble deposit within the substance of the absorbent stones.

on which it was desired to act. He found that by a weak acid solution he could set free the silica, but in that state the deposited mineral had no cohesion. Following up, however, the application of the fluid silicate by a dose of chloride of calcium (muriate of lime—a waste product in chemical works), it resulted that the chlorine parting from the calcium attacked the soda of the silicate, forming common salt, which is easily dissolved away; while the silicic acid set free and combining with the lime formed with it silicate of lime. This mineral is nearly insoluble, very hard, and adheres with great tenacity to foreign substances, as is illustrated in common mortar. Silicate of lime thus formed resists carbonic acid and dilute sulphuric acid, and is little affected by any of the common alkalies or ammonia.

The effect of this treatment on stones that have not already been inserted into buildings has been very favourable, and they appear to have stood without decay under exposures sufficient to produce much injury on the same stone unprotected. Applied on a large scale to buildings that have already shown symptoms of decay, the result is less satisfactory, but years must elapse before a very decided opinion can be given on the process. Portions of the decaying magnesian limestone of the Houses of Parliament, and parts also of Westminster Abbey, have been subjected to the process, besides many buildings in London and elsewhere. The state of these will enable us after a time to know the real value of Mr. Ransome's discovery.

A combination of Kuhlmann's process with a temporary wash of some bituminous substance has been tried on a large scale in the Speaker's Court of the Houses of Parliament, and elsewhere in London, by M. Szerelmy. It remains to be seen whether this result will be more satisfactory than that of Mr. Ransome.

As a further recommendation in reference to this subject, I may remark that whatever be the stone selected for the main walls of a building, the greatest care should be taken in reference to those parts near the foundation, "between wind and water," and also to copings, parapets, window-sills, battlements, and other places where water can lodge. Care should also be taken to avoid the use of mortar made with sea-sand. Wherever it is possible, the stones used for the foundation should be non-absorbent; and effective drainage all round a building will often do more to preserve stone than any amount of care and treatment.

When for reasons of economy it is necessary to make use of local stones of poor quality, they should, if possible, be treated by some process such as that introduced by Mr. Ransome, before being put into the building, and every precaution should be taken to ensure the stones being laid in their natural position. Stones should be preferred whose component parts are at least compactly cemented together, if they are not crystalline, and the cementing medium should be as little liable to destruction by weather as circumstances admit. Ordinary experiments to determine the quality of stones are valuable in their way, but must not be implicitly depended upon, as experience still remains the most useful guide. In the actual selection of the blocks, after the kind of stone has been decided on, it is very essential that there should be careful supervision, and there is no better proof of this than the fact already cited, that in the Museum of Economic Geology and the Houses of Parliament the same material was employed; but in the one there is hardly a piece injured by weather, in the other half the stones have decayed.

FULLER'S EARTH.

Besides stony minerals used in construction, the earth contains many others of great value, to obtain which methods analogous to quarrying must be resorted to, while to discover them geological knowledge is required. These are of various kinds and belong, some to the clayey and some to the stony group of minerals; of the former I may say a few words in reference to fuller's earth; of the latter, salt deposits and bituminous shales are perhaps the best representatives.

Fuller's earth is a greenish or bluish earthy mineral, containing about 50 per cent. of silica, 20 per cent. of alumina, and 25 per cent. of water, with a little iron oxide. It is soft, tenacious, and falls to pieces when immersed in water. It absorbs very greedily all oily and greasy substances, and for this reason is extensively used in the fulling of cloth. It is generally found in segregated bands in clay.

Large quantities of fuller's earth have been found near Nutfield, Reigate, and Blechingley, to the south of the range of the North Downs; and other deposits, but of inferior quality, exist near Sutton and Croydon, to the north of these hills. The most considerable pits are near Nutfield, between which place and Reigate the fuller's earth lies so near the surface as to be turned up by the wheels of the waggons. It is not known how long this earth has been wrought in Surrey; the oldest pit now wrought is said to have lasted between seventy and eighty years, but is fast wearing out. The seam of fuller's earth dips in different directions. There are two kinds of it, the blue and the yellow, the former, on the eastern side of the pit, between Redhill and Nutfield, is frequently within a yard of the surface, being covered merely with the soil, a tough, wet, clayey loam. A few yards to the west, the blue kind appears, with an irony sandstone, of nearly two yards in thickness, between it and the soil. The blue earth in this pit is nearly sixteen feet deep. In some places the yellow kind is found lying on the blue. There does not appear to be any regularity either in the position or inclination of the bands where the fuller's earth is found, nor any mark by which its presence could be detected. It seems rather collected in patches than in any continued or regular vein. In the midst of the fuller's earth are found large masses of mineral, translucent and remarkably heavy; these consist of sulphate of barytes, encrusted with quartzose crystals. They are carefully removed from the fuller's earth, as the workmen say they often spoil many tons of it which lie about them. There is also found, with the yellow fuller's earth, a dark brown crust which the workmen consider injurious. The mineral when got out is carried from the pits on tram-roads, along which it is taken to the banks of the Thames, where it is sold, and whence it is shipped off either to the north or west of England.

Other supplies of fuller's earth are obtained from one of the beds of the great oolite developed in the west of England.

SALT.

Salt is a mineral so important, and obtained in such large quantities from the earth, chiefly from a very limited group of geological localities, and it occupies so marked a position in the mineral statistics of our own country, that it must not be omitted in speaking of minerals from stratified deposits. The Cheshire salt mines and the Worcestershire brine pits, both derived from the same part of the new red sandstone formation, not only supply salt for the consumption of almost all England, but export annually nearly a million of tons to all parts of the world. Other deposits are found at Halle, in the Tyrol; among the Carpathian mountains, in Poland; on the Spanish side of the Pyrenees; not far from Barcelona, in Spain; in the Kirghis steppes of Russia, and in North America. Most of these are of tertiary origin. Although some deposits are less accessible than others, the extent of the supply is practically unlimited.

Salt occurs generally as a mineral in a purer state and less mixed with magnesian salts than is the case with the salt dissolved in the ocean ; but in most places, especially in the English salt-mines, the crystalline mineral is associated with marl and clay, even the surface of the crystals being coated and plastered with a muddy deposit that altogether disfigures them, and renders it difficult to distinguish at first between the salt crystals and the rubbish enclosing them. The marls are red or pale green in colour, and the crystals of salt are of a dull red tint, owing to the presence of iron. In Cheshire, the salt-beds are in several bands, often at a depth of from 50 to 150 yards below the surface. The number of beds is five, the thinnest being only six inches, while the thickest is 40 feet thick. The marls alternating with these beds are also salt. Much water exists in the sands alternating with the marls and salt-beds, and this becomes saturated with salt in passing through the beds, yielding the brinish springs, which for a long time were the only sources of supply in Worcestershire, and which are still the means by which salt is obtained in many important districts.

The great deposit of salt in the valley of Cardona, in the Pyrenees, is one of the most remarkable of which we have any account, though some of the Carpathian and Polish beds are not inferior. At Cardona, two thick masses of rock-salt, apparently united at their bases, appear on the slope of a hill. One of the masses has been worked. It measures about 250 yards by 13, but its thickness has not been ascertained. The salt is in a laminated condition, with confined crystallization. The part exposed consists of eight horizontal beds, separated by red and variegated gypsum and marls. Its thickness is 15 feet. A second mass that does not exhibit stratification has been weathered, and is steeply scarped, resembling a glacier in appearance.

Rock-salt is by no means confined to any particular geological age, nor are the rocks that sometimes contain this mineral always saliferous. But a certain kind of grouping of gypsum with marls and sandstones seems so usual as to be almost natural. A very remarkable instance of the formation of beds of salt, by evaporation from a salt lake originally connected with the ocean, seems to exist in the Dead Sea, and in the waters of that sea there is now a remarkable excess of the salts of magnesia. Judging from the composition of the water of this lake, there must be at the bottom enormous deposits of common salt (chloride of sodium), with gypsum and some carbonate of lime, while very much more than the usual proportion of magnesian salts is contained in the mother liquor, now forming the supernatant fluid.

BITUMINOUS SHALES.

Besides the varieties of schist and slates used in construction, there are, in most countries, hardened clays, more or less fissile, called shale. Some of these are loaded with hydro-carbons to so great an extent that the rock will take fire on being exposed to heat and flame. Once set fire to, it will continue to burn for some time, with much light and smoke, and when burnt will yield an ash exactly identical in form with the original stone, and not much altered in colour. Such rocks are generally called *bituminous shales*, a name not very accurate or satisfactory, but understood and recognized. Shales of this kind occur in rocks of all ages, sometimes associated with animal remains, sometimes with plants. They are of various thickness, and exist under very different conditions, but in a general way they may be regarded as clay bands in sandstone rocks, into which a large infiltration of hydro-carbons, and occasionally much iron, has taken place subsequent to the deposit of the rock, though not unconnected with the circumstances of the deposit. Till lately these shales have been of little value, and have therefore attracted no attention for commercial purposes, only those being valued in which the percentage of iron was sufficient to enable them to be used as ores of iron. Since the manufacture of illuminating and lubricating oils from mineral hydrocarbons has been carried on largely, they have been more looked for than formerly; and at present such shales as yield a sufficient percentage of oils on distillation to be worth working (from 10 to 60 per cent, or more, according to circumstances and localities), are regarded as part of the mineral wealth of the district in which they occur.

Bituminous shales are found in rocks of almost all geological dates. From the tertiary rocks we have the thin, hard, flaky mineral called *paper-coal*, of which there are considerable quantities on the banks of the Rhine, near Bonn. This has been used for distillation in some works nearly opposite Bonn, and, though poor, was found at one time to pay for distillation. From the cretaceous beds in some parts of the Continent other shales have been worked, though to no great extent. The oolites are richer in bituminous strata. In the Kimmeridge clay, in Dorsetshire, near Weymouth, there is a band of highly bituminous shale, of dark brown colour, and without lustre, burning readily with a yellowish, smoky, heavy flame. Part of it has been used for making pottery, and is called "Kimmeridge coal." This material has been distilled from time to time, but without much success. It is difficult to purify, and is not very rich in valuable products. The lias is much richer in shales of the kind I am now describing than the upper members of the secondary series of rocks. The "Posidonia schist" is a bed of the liassic series that has been brought into use for distilling near Tübingen, in Würtemberg. Good specimens might easily be found from the lias in many parts of Northern Germany, well enough adapted for distillation.

It is, however, chiefly from rocks of the carboniferous series, especially those of the coal measures, that the most valuable and the richest of these deposits have been procured. In the British islands, and especially in Scotland, near Edinburgh, there exist varieties of coal that pass so nearly into shales, and various shales that so accurately put on the characters of coal, in some parts of a continuous stratum, that it becomes practically very difficult, and theoretically impossible, to distinguish between them. The well-known Boghead coal, and the Torbane Hill mineral are examples. These are either shales or coals, according to the line that may artificially be drawn between coal and shale. They are, however, almost exceptionally rich in products given off by distillation at a low heat, and are certainly ill adapted for fuel. Many other minerals, departing very widely from coals in appearance, are called in Scotland *parrots*, or crackling coals, and in England *cannels*. When once set on fire they burn freely, with a bright flame and much smoke. They alternate with coals, but are easily distinguished from them, and in many cases they have been carefully separated from coals to render the coals more saleable. Some of the stones thus rejected have since been found more valuable for distilling than the coals themselves. In the coal fields of Lancashire, North Wales, and the Potteries in North Staffordshire, many such bands of shale, fit for distilling, have been recognized. Some of them are rich also in iron, and many of the iron stones of these and other coal fields, including the celebrated "black band," are highly bituminous. The bituminous shales hitherto made use of in England are almost entirely from these black and brown bands, among the coal itself, but this is not the case elsewhere. In the east of France, near Autun, not far from Dijon, there has long been a large manufacture of oils distilled from schists, which exist there in the coal measures, but are quite independent of the coal. The bands of shale are four in number, and they are perfectly regular and continuous, always occupying the same position in relation to the coal. They have no resemblance whatever to coal in appearance, but one of them, locally called "Autun Boghead," resembles the Scotch Boghead in some striking peculiarities. Other cases exist in the west of France, where similar shales have been distilled, but there, as at Autun, they do not enough resemble coal to admit of any difficulty in drawing a line between the two minerals. As a general rule, the lighter the bituminous shales the richer are they likely to be on distillation, and those of a pale brown colour are often much more valuable than the intensely black, indurated, or coal-like varieties. Good bituminous shales, adapted for distillation, rarely soil the fingers; they have a brown appearance when scratched with a sharp point, and they break up with an irregular fracture. They are usually tough, and sometimes fissile.

Lecture the Fifth.

MINERALS FROM STRATIFIED DEPOSITS, CONTINUED.

Ironstone and Coal.

IRON and coal, more than any other mineral substances that exist, are the sources of material wealth to an intelligent and active people; and I need not inform you that none possess natural wealth of this kind more conveniently than ourselves—few possess it so abundantly, in proportion to the area of their country, as the inhabitants of Great Britain. The circumstances under which the ores of iron and the deposits of mineral fuel are found in the earth, the magnitude and extent of the deposits, the mode of discovering them, and the way in which they may best be obtained,—these are the subjects of practical geology to which I have to direct your attention on this occasion, and I need not say they will supply ample material for consideration.

Iron is very widely disseminated on the surface of the earth, and it forms part of almost every substance, animal, vegetable, or mineral, with which we have to do. Few rocks, and probably no soils, are without it. It is present in water and even in the air. It is associated with various elements in definite proportions, and is recognized in others by some of its properties, among which the colour of its oxide is not the least striking. Abundant as the metal is in a manufactured state, there are hardly any specimens of native iron known, except, indeed, those that have fallen through the atmosphere from wandering fragments of matter coming within the sphere of the earth's attraction.

But although iron is thus common, the ores from which it may conveniently be obtained are not universal. Almost all exhibit iron in combination with oxygen, and there are two or three well-marked groups of such ores. The first comprises the mixed protoxides and peroxides, or *magnetic iron ores.* The second, various peroxides of iron, some without water, known as *specular iron ore*, *red hæmatite*, and *micaceous iron;* and numerous hydrates, or ores with water, which may conveniently be called *brown hæmatites.* The third includes the carbonates, called *spathic iron* and *brown spar*, when crystalline, and *clay ironstone* when in the impure and earthy state. Besides these, the silicates and phosphates of iron are sometimes used, but not much in England, and with doubtful advantage. Of the whole number the richest ores are the protoxides; the next the peroxides; and the least rich, but most abundant, the carbonates, or rather the carbonates of the oxide. The phosphates are sometimes rich in iron, and the silicates also. The former are chiefly worked in Canada; the latter near St. Maurice, and in the Canton of the Valais, in Switzerland. The sulphates are sometimes used as ores. The sulphides are valued chiefly for the sulphur they contain.

It will not be necessary that I should refer to such of these latter ores as are rarely and exceptionally smelted. We shall have quite enough to do to consider the facts with reference to the oxides and carbonates. Neither is it necessary that I should speak of the sulphates of iron or of iron pyrites. Indeed, the latter mineral is found generally in mineral veins, and not in beds. For the sake of convenience, and to avoid repetition, I propose to include in the present account the crystalline oxides, the red hæmatites, and the sparry carbonates, as well as the clay ironstones which are the chief stratified deposits of iron ore.

Magnetic iron ore is a rare mineral in England. It is very generally diffused indeed in the old rocks, but is not abundant enough to be worked as an ore. It exists occasionally in iron sands; sometimes in large quantity and with titanium, but more generally in a crystalline state in veins. The chief supplies are obtained from Norway, Sweden, and Russia, where it is the principal ore, and where it is largely used (smelted with charcoal) for the preparation of the finest iron fit for the manufacture of steel. The central portion of a vast and very remarkable mass of ore in the island of Elba is of this material. Important veins of it exist and are worked in India and the East, in North America, in various places in Mexico, and in Brazil. It is sometimes combined with zinc, and in this state forms a valuable ore in the state of New Jersey, in North America. Pure magnetic oxide contains 72 per cent. of iron.

The hæmatites are much more common in England than magnetic ore, though not the most abundant of our ores. They are important from their richness in iron, but it is found more convenient and profitable to mix them with the carbonates and poorer ores than to use them alone. I have mentioned that there are two kinds. One of them yields, when pure, about 69¼ per cent. of iron, and the other about 56 per cent. Practically these per-centages are not obtained, as the ores are rarely quite free from foreign substances. Besides the division into richer and poorer, owing to the presence of combined water in the latter ores, there is a further division into metalloid and earthy. The former occur chiefly in veins, and are very brilliant. The common Elba ores are of this kind, but they are rare in England. They are either specular ores, with brilliant metallic lustre; micaceous ores, composed of flat spangles, soiling the fingers; or oligist. The earthy ores are opaque and often of blood-red colour, whence the name *Hæmatite*, or blood-stone; but when containing water, this colour passes into brown. These ores are very valuable for smelting, but they are also used in a state of fine powder for polishing; and some varieties called red and yellow ochre, and umber, are employed as pigments.

Lastly, the carbonates of iron, yielding from 20 to 45 per cent. of metallic iron, and very variable percentages of carbonaceous and earthy matter, are sometimes crystalline, as in spathose or sparry iron, and brown spar, but more often earthy, as in the common ores of most parts of England. In the latter state they are combined with clay and carbon, and form the group of clay ironstones. The sparry ores are not common in England, though they are not unworked in the northern counties.

The source of the hæmatite ores used in England is the carboniferous or mountain limestone, coming out from under the coal measures in the northern counties; and the chief mines are at Ulverston and the neighbourhood of Whitehaven, at the bottom of the limestone, almost in contact with the slate that underlies that formation. A section of the beds containing the ore is exhibited at a place called Todholes, near Cleator, where an open work is in operation that illustrates the fact. The red iron ore is there worked as a quarry. The floor of the deposit is a white and red mottled shale of the limestone series, almost a fireclay. It is at least 40 feet thick. The surface of the shale is uneven and is covered by a conglomerate of white quartz pebbles about eight inches thick. Then comes a magnificent bed of hæmatite, from 15 to 30 feet thick (sometimes as much as 60 feet). This is, for the most part, a dense mass of red ore subdivided by irregular and nearly vertical joints. There are numerous small cavities near, which contain a peculiar form of the mineral called kidney ore. In these parts rock crystals are found, and calc-spar has crystallized in the hollows. Over the hæmatite is an impure limestone forming a roof.

In this deposit two or three bands of greenish-black shale are interstratified with the ore and complete the appearance of bedding of the whole mass. Similar appearances, though hardly so perfect, occur in some lead deposits where the mineral found is galena. It is difficult to say whether and in what sense the ore is a contemporaneous deposit, but more than one such stratum or mass of the ore have been found. The ore is extracted very much in the manner adopted in the case of coal, and the quantity removed is very large. Ten years ago, nearly a quarter of a million of tons of hæmatite per annum were removed. Besides these mines at Cleator in which the hæmatite is bedded, the same ore has long been worked from the carboniferous limestone of Low Furness, in a deposit more resembling a chasm or vein in the rock, and again at and near Dalton, apparently under similar circumstances. The ore is only a true hæmatite, and fit for smelting, adjacent to one wall of the chasm; the rest of it is micaceous, and fetches a high price from its utility in the process of puddling.

Very curious dish-shaped deposits of hæmatite exist also in the same neighbourhood, a little to the north of Dalton. Some of these, whose boundaries have been determined, run from fifty to sixty yards in width, and are fifteen to twenty yards deep. The contents are irregular, and the hollows they occupy in the limestone seem to have been eroded. In this case the ore is only covered by drift. A little to the west is another very remarkable deposit apparently occupying two slightly connected basins. The ore is fine and crystalline. From one point you may proceed 400 to 500 feet in either direction in one solid mass of this valuable substance, and its bottom has not been reached. It is covered only by sea-sand or boulder clay.

Other hæmatites are obtained from Derbyshire ; and others, again, from the Forest of Dean, Somersetshire, and South Wales. Those of the Forest of Dean are especially remarkable, and seem to be almost inexhaustible. There is thus an ample supply of this ore of iron in England, and, being found in various localities, it is likely to remain available.

While the carboniferous limestones are remarkable for their hæmatite, the coal measures are equally rich in iron ores, but these are almost exclusively clayey ores and carbonates. They are rarely pure carbonates, though spathose iron is known and worked. By far the greater part are impure, earthy, and carbonaceous minerals, among which iron oxide is occasionally present to so large an extent as to be worth reducing. Other similar minerals less rich in iron are not called ores, though differing only from the clay ironstones in the proportion of the metal.

The clay ironstones are generally black, blackish-brown, yellowish-brown, pale yellow, or drab in colour. They are not often in regular bands, but rather consist of groups of nodules alternating with coal-bearing deposits ; but there are marked exceptions to this rule. Thus, in Yorkshire, in the Bradford districts, there are three groups of bands near the bottom of the coal measures : the upper group contains five bands, and the middle six. The upper beds only are worked. These bands are very valuable though not remarkably pure. They contain 36 per cent. iron oxide and 25 per cent. carbonic acid, besides nearly 20 per cent. of silica. In another district they are much more closely connected with the coal seams, occurring in these bands between important coals throughout the whole thickness of the series. These are rather richer, containing 43½ per cent. iron oxide, and 31 per cent. carbonic acid, yielding 33 per cent. of metallic iron; but, in this case, the ironstones are nodular. Some of these bands yield from two to three thousand tons per acre.

In Derbyshire the ironstones are called "Rakes," and they are very numerous, their yield ranging from two to six thousand tons per acre. The most remarkable of the Derbyshire series is the "black shale," or "striped rake," worked for the Stavely iron furnaces, near Chesterfield. It consists of two groups: the upper containing nine, the lower twelve seams, none of them very thick, and some only half an inch, an inch, or an inch and a half in thickness. Some of these thin seams are grey stones, very compact and much cracked, the cracks containing crystals of zinc blende and galena, with copper and iron pyrites.

The Shropshire and North Staffordshire coal-fields yield bands of the common varieties of ironstone in the lower part of the series. They include some excellent qualities of ore, adapted for making the best kinds of iron, but the quantity per acre is not large, nor are the ironstones very rich; one of the best contains scarcely 38 per cent. of iron, about 33 per cent. carbonic acid, and 14 per cent. of silica, alumina, and lime. The ironstone concretions abound with vegetable remains, an exception to the usual condition. In the Potteries coal-field it is chiefly in the upper part of the field that the ironstone bands occur. This offers a marked exception to the northern ironstone deposits. In this and some other points the Potteries iron-field agrees with those of South Staffordshire and North Wales, where, also, the ironstone bands have great value, and include the richly carbonaceous and bituminous *black-bands,* originally worked in Scotland, but now generally recognized.

In South Wales, the coal measures form two series separated by a great thickness of siliceous rock, and of these the lower series is sometimes called the iron-bearing measures, since the great bulk of the iron bands is found there. These lower beds of ironstone may be followed across the Bristol Channel to Ireland, but they are there much poorer than in Wales, yielding an average of less than 20 per cent. There are only two somewhat irregular bands of iron ore in the upper coal series. The ores are moderately rich, but they are improved by admixture with hæmatites, large quantities of which are imported into South Wales for that purpose. Scotland is exceedingly rich in similar ores, and in both districts "*black-band*" is known and worked to great advantage. The original black-band of Lanarkshire was from 14 to 18 inches thick, and yielded after roasting from 60 to 70 per cent. of iron oxide.

The pure carbonates of iron in a crystalline state, though not common in the British islands, abound in some parts of Europe. Near the right bank of the

Rhine, in the Duchy of Nassau, there are numerous thick masses of spathose iron, and there are others much more extensive in Styria. A kind of steel is readily made from these ores without passing through the process of cementation, and they are sometimes called for this reason *Stahlstein*, or steel-stone, by the Germans.

Within a few years enormous deposits of iron ore have been obtained from the lias of the Cleveland Hills, in the east of Yorkshire. On the coast line, and also at a small elevation from Redcar to Middlesborough-on-Tees, there crops out to the surface a thickness of no less than fifteen feet of ironstone, containing an average of 30 per cent. of metallic iron, but so unlike an ore, that it had remained till lately unnoticed. It resembles an irony sandstone, the surface being rusted by the peroxidation of part of the iron, and it occupies the position of the marlstone in the middle of the lias formation. It is very fossiliferous. This singular deposit extends over a region of some hundreds of square miles. It is best developed near Middlesborough, and for some miles to the southward, but extends in an unbroken area for a long distance, thinning out towards the south. Its magnitude is so vast, that the supply must be regarded as practically indefinite, and the ore is obtained with extreme facility. The yield at one point near Exton, has averaged 50,000 tons per acre, and even where the thickness is greatly reduced, as at Whitby, as much as 20,000 tons per acre have been obtained. Estimating the average thickness at only four yards, and assuming that one-fifth of the ore is left behind, the available ore would average 40,000 tons per acre. From this quantity 10,000 tons of metallic iron may be manufactured. Each square mile, therefore, of this bed, is capable of yielding six millions of tons of iron, a quantity equivalent to eighteen months' supply for the whole of Great Britain. The several hundred square miles to which the Cleveland iron-field alone is known to extend, would then be sufficient to feed all the furnaces of England for many centuries. Similar though not equally rich deposits occur in Lincolnshire, Rutland, and Northamptonshire. In these counties, and indeed in Yorkshire, the lower beds of the oolitic series are also extremely remarkable for the ores of iron they contain. The general conditions are very similar throughout, and there is little in the appearance of the deposit to indicate the fact that it consists of more than one-third part of iron oxide, and is well adapted for use in the furnace.

Nor is England the only country containing inexhaustible mines of this mineral wealth. In France, in certain districts, the oolitic rocks are partly made up of rich ore, and ores of iron have already been found in a workable state over sixty departments. Here, as in England, the ores are earthy and cannot be said to be recognizable, except by those whose eye is already accustomed to the variety, or who trust to analysis instead of appearance. Most of the ores are stratified and consist of grains, kidney-shaped concretions, and hollow lumps. They are often superficial deposits due to the removal by water of ferruginous beds in the adjacent oolitic rocks, and the separation of the ironstones has been owing to their greater specific gravity. The yield of such ores is about equal to that of the English oolitic ores, the general average being about 30 per cent. The most remarkable beds of ore in the oolites are in the centre of France, not far from some remarkably thick beds of coal. The superficial ores are found chiefly in the northern departments.

Belgium and Germany are not less rich in valuable iron ores than France; and, indeed, throughout northern Europe it would be difficult to name any important district that does not contain some of them. They are not always available for the manufacture of iron, as, without accompanying fuel, either wood or coal, the richest iron ores are of little more value than the stones of flint and gravel that abound in the fields. The value of ironstone does not solely depend either on the quantity or quality of the raw material, or the facility of getting it from the earth, but quite as much on the supply of fuel at hand, a matter with which it might seem to have little relation. It is for this reason that the ironstones of the coal measures, though not rich, are so important: while it is only from the accident that the oolitic and liassic ores and those from the carboniferous limestone are for the most part found and worked near coal-fields, or in localities from which there is easy and cheap transport, that they possess the great value now attributed to them. In the north of Europe, where there are still extensive forests, and labour is cheap, charcoal iron can be made from the pure ores of these countries; and in India, owing to the low price of labour, smelting can still be carried on to advantage in small furnaces; but these are exceptional conditions, and ultimately it will be found necessary to depend for iron, on those places where the ore and the fuel are equally abundant and equally cheap. In these matters, at present, England retains pre-eminence, and though labour is dear, the raw materials known and worked are at the present time more abundant and more available than at any previous epoch of our history.

The methods of obtaining iron ore vary according to the position the ore occupies in the earth, the magnitude of the deposit, and the presence or absence of other useful minerals. In the lias and oolites the ores are removed by digging from the surface, or are quarried. In the coal measures they are got with the coal by mining. But both here and in the carboniferous limestones, there are some peculiar methods that deserve notice. Thus, the system of bell-pits is adopted where the ironstone nodules of the lower coal measures come close to the surface. These are small shafts arranged in great numbers on the line of strike at a distance of a few yards from each other, leaving, when the ores are got, long lines of irregular holes and pits. The land is thus unfitted for agriculture, but belts of trees may be planted. Thus, even at a distance, the old works once carried on in the neighbourhood may be distinguished by the eye, and the general line of strike of the deposits accurately determined. In the Forest of Dean, where the ore lies in open spaces in the limestone, called "churns," or "pockets," the ore is cut away, leaving natural pillars and arches of limestone to support the roof. The contents of the deposits vary a good deal, both in quality and quantity, and the result, when the ore is removed, is a picturesque irregularity in the mine, strongly contrasting with the long lines of monotonous galleries characteristic of coal mines.

To utilise the poorer and more impure ores of iron a certain admixture of other mineral is needed in the furnace. This is called a flux, and according to the nature of the ore must be the nature and amount of flux added. With the common clay iron ores limestone is the flux required, and in most parts of England this rock is at hand in abundance. The richer ores of iron can be reduced at once with charcoal, but only in comparatively small quantities, and the great operations of iron-smelting are confined to those countries where the clay ironstones and limestone abound, and where there is also an abundant and cheap supply of mineral fuel.

Everything thus resolves itself into a question of coal. Where there is coal there are always the other things at hand that are required to render a country rich and great. When coal is absent, on the other hand, all other mineral wealth is comparatively useless. Too much attention cannot be given to the whole history of the deposits of mineral fuel in order that we may learn where to expect them and how to obtain them when they are known to be present in the earth. For this purpose it is necessary that I should describe:—(1) the nature of mineral fuel; (2) the varieties of its composition; (3) the geological age and position of the beds with which it is found; and (4) the various modes by which it can be economically worked.

There are many varieties of mineral fuel, all more or less available, but differing extremely in their properties and in the circumstances of their occurrence. I do not propose to include among coal those shales rich in hydro-carbons, which simulate the coals and are even sometimes described as belonging to them. These I have already alluded to. I refer only to the coals strictly so called. Under this name I include anthracitic and bituminous varieties, and lignites or brown coal. Some of the varieties have no value for commercial purposes, but their carbon contents are all strongly marked, and these afford the best measure of their relative practical utility.

Lignites are in most countries very inferior to coals. They are found rather irregularly distributed in sand and other rocks of the tertiary period. They are usually so far altered in their texture as to have a mineral aspect, but they retain something of a woody character. They exist sometimes in accumulated masses of enormous dimensions, but not often in regular beds. They are rarely of the same thickness and general appearance in different parts of the same field. In England lignites may be said to have no value for economic purposes. They are not extensively developed, and can never enter into competition with the regular coals. In Germany, on the right bank of the Rhine, they are important deposits, very thick and tolerably uniform. In the Alps, and in Italy and Switzerland they afford a poor fuel. But in Styria, in Austria, near Vienna, and at various places on the banks of the Danube, there are beds of greater importance, more uniform in character, and traceable for long distances. But this kind of fuel labours under a great disadvantage. It always contains water (generally more than 10 per cent.), some of which may be got rid of by drying in the air, but a considerable part of this water cannot be evaporated till the fuel is actually consumed. Lignites also contain much ash (rarely less than 10 per cent.). Thus, when used for economical purposes, a certain proportion of the heat obtained by combustion is neutralized, and lost in the conversion of the contained water into steam; and this alone is sufficient to render a good lignite less valuable than many very inferior coals; part also of the heat is wasted on the ash. Notwithstanding these sources of weakness, lignites are not to be despised as fuel. They have even been found available for manufacturing purposes, as for iron smelting and for railways and steam-boats. The magnitude of the deposits in some places is so large that this alone would render them important. In the valley of the Rhine, on the shores of the Baltic, and in Styria, are the largest and thickest of these deposits. Some of them approach 200 feet in thickness. In most of them there are partings or alternating layers of marl of no great thickness, and there is often among them a certain amount of woody matter so little altered that, after removal from the mine and drying, it splits, like wood. In drying in this way it is almost sure to fall to pieces.

Even the very best qualities of lignite, including such as are adapted to raise steam, and are not distinguishable from coal to the eye, may be detected by exposure. After a very short time they begin to change, and after being above ground for a few months, although thoroughly sheltered from weather, they fall to powder and lose their value. It is thus quite impossible to store them, and they must be brought into use immediately after coming out of the mine. In some cases they may be roasted with advantage, but the best qualities can be used at once.

It is not easy to understand why almost all the principal deposits of lignite cover a small area, and are not continuous and of uniform thickness to any distance in any direction. Even those that are most continuous are apt to die out and re-appear at no great distance. The excellent lignites of the valley of the Danube, worked near Gran, between Vienna and Pesth, are examples of this. Those of Oedenberg, to the south-east of Vienna, are of the same kind. They are worked extensively, and were formerly more used than they are now, having been replaced by the coal of Fünfkirchen. From Gran are still raised more than 14,000 tons per annum, and from Oedenberg nearly as much. The thickness is uniform, and over areas ot many square miles of tertiary sandy marls there are comparatively few parts where these deposits may not be found by boring. Besides the comparative inefficiency of the lignites as fuel, the want of continuity in a promising stratum greatly takes from the value of deposits even where they are of the best quality. Lignite exists, in fact, in lenticular masses, and not in beds.

I have mentioned that there is a marked economical difference between lignites and coals. I may add that many of the secondary and almost all the tertiary deposits of mineral fuel belong to the former group. The exact reason of this is not clear. It was long regarded as an axiom in geology, that no coals were deserving of the name but those of the carboniferous period; and even when it was admitted that coal seams existed in a workable state in secondary rocks, it was thought that in the tertiaries, at any rate, they were impossible. That this is not the case is proved, if only by the contents of a remarkable coal-field in the valley of the Zsil, in Transylvania, which I had the opportunity of visiting in 1862. There, in tertiary sands containing fossil shells, whose nature cannot be mistaken (among them is a known species of *Cerithia*), are regular seams of excellent coal, some of them very thick, and all standing every test that can be imagined in proof of their true coal nature, as distinguished from lignite. The coal of the Zsil agrees in colour, brittleness, streak when scratched, texture, style of burning, both with and without a blast, character of ash, and capacity of being stored for a long time without injury, with the coals of good quality from the best English coal-fields. It is regularly bedded, and the beds are continuous, so far as they have been traced, round the whole line of outcrop of the coal-measures in the valley. Now that one good specimen of tertiary coal (not lignite) has been found, it is likely that others may be met with under similar circumstances elsewhere. Associated with the Zsil coal are shales, ironstones, and grits. One of the seams opened in the Zsil valley is fully sixty feet in thickness, and of good quality throughout.

There are some places where coal of the cretaceous period is worked. It is associated with shales, and is of poor quality, but quite capable of being burnt. One of these little coal-fields is also in Hungary, and not very far from that of the Zsil valley. In the chalk, and again in the Wealden deposits of England, fragments of fossil wood and vegetable remains have long been known to exist, but workable seams of coal are absent; and this is not extraordinary, since true chalk is not only of marine origin, but is believed to have been deposited in a deep sea. Contemporaneous deposits not identical with the chalk in mineral composition are rare in Europe.

The oolites and lias also contain coal. In England there are several beds of the middle and older secondary period that are thus provided; the Kimmeridge clay, the Brora beds, and an interesting coal-bearing group of strata near Whitby, in Yorkshire, are the chief. The Kimmeridge is a rich bituminous shale. The Brora field is more important, possessing two seams of coal, worked by pits sunk

80 or 100 yards. The coal is bituminous, and burns to a white ash. One pit alone yielded 70,000 tons between the years 1814 and 1826, but it is now less worked. The main coal is a 4-foot seam. The Whitby coal is much more valuable than the Brora, and it was worked a century ago. Some of it is of fair quality, though its use has generally been confined to the immediate vicinity of the mines. Bands of inferior coal or lignite are sometimes met with in the other beds of oolite in England, but none are of value. Thus the oolites are with us of no importance as a coal-bearing series, and it was long the custom to regard oolitic coal as little more than useless rubbish. This is not the case now, for in many parts of the world there are large deposits of excellent mineral fuel from beds of this age, adapted to all the purposes for which coal is needed.

In Europe there is excellent secondary coal on the Danube. There are two deposits in actual work, both of which are from the lower beds, corresponding with our lias. The coal exists in several seams, alternating with shales and sandstones. One of these is at Fünfkirchen, not very far from Pesth. The beds crop out on the road and hill-side, and are worked by deep pits. The dip or inclination of the strata is considerable. Though very poor in appearance, and sometimes mixed up with a great deal of rubbish, and falling easily into powder, this coal burns well, with flame and much heat, and without an excessive proportion of ash. It has driven other Danube coals out of the market. There are in all twenty-five seams, having a total thickness of 140 feet of coal. The production in 1860 was about 140,000 tons per annum, and increasing. This coal-field is the only source of supply for the steamboats of the Danube Steam Navigation Company, and a railroad is contemplated to pass through the coal district and connect the Middle Danube with the Vienna and Trieste railroad.

The Oravicza coal is inferior to the Fünfkirchen. It supplies the railroad, of which there is a branch from Basiasch to Oravicza. There is a fair supply of coal actively worked at Oravicza, upwards of 60,000 tons of coal being raised in the year. Besides these oolitic coal-fields, there is reason to believe that others exist still further to the east. Impure coal, resembling lignite, is obtained from the Jurassic rocks in various parts of Europe.

Asiatic coals, of which there are now a great variety well known in the Indian market, and others coming into use, are chiefly from oolitic rocks. There are five districts yielding this valuable mineral,—three in Northern India, one in Cutch, and the fifth on the coast of the Burman empire. The former are in the district lying between the valley of the Ganges and the first mountain chain to the south. The coal is associated with, and overlies limestones, which are often poor and argillaceous. There are also clays and ironstone bands.

The Burdwan coal district, near Calcutta, has been long known and much worked. It contains workable beds, seven and nine feet thick respectively, associated with ironstone, shales, and grits; the coal is of poor quality. The same kind of coal, if not the same beds, reappears at Palamon and on the Saone river, about 109 miles above its confluence with the Ganges. They are traced also westwards for more than 150 miles. Throughout this long line the coal seems to improve towards the west and south-west, and a very extensive coal-field is indicated, though hitherto it has not been extensively opened. It is not to be supposed that the outcrop is continuous, and it is far more probable that a number of detached basins will ultimately be recognised; but that there is in this part of Asia a large development of valuable mineral fuel there can be no doubt.

The Nerbudda district contains coal of great value in extremely thick beds, said to be 20, 25½, and 40 feet respectively, besides others of more moderate dimensions. This coal-field is about 350 miles from Bombay, and there appear to be several deposits, some of which have been opened with advantage. The quality is considered to be the best in India. East of Calcutta there are several deposits of great thickness and value. Assam also contains several coal-fields, the coal being associated with clay ironstones, but the coal is sometimes described as lignite. Without detaining you with the details of these deposits, which are, indeed, still but imperfectly known; it is enough to point out that if, as is supposed, these beds belong to the oolitic or some newer rocks, it is evident that coal-fields of the most complete character and greatest value are totally independent of those limits of age once thought essential. I may add that some at least of the South African coal from Natal is from rocks of the same age.

A large tract in Eastern Virginia, in the Confederate States of America, contains valuable oolitic coal, highly bituminous. This coal has been largely worked near the city of Richmond. There are three seams, one of them occasionally 30 or 40 feet thick, but the total thickness of the three seams averages 30 feet. The quality of the coal is good, and well adapted to the manufacture of gas, but it varies a good deal in different parts of the field. It is generally extremely similar to that of beds in the other coal measures of America, belonging to the carboniferous period. The beds are highly inclined, and the pits to work it are already deep. The floor is very irregular, and the coal is divided by partings of earthy matter.

There are thus in various parts of the world, out of England, numerous deposits of coal, many of them largely worked, and fully available for all purposes of mineral fuel, but belonging to rocks of various geological age; both secondary and tertiary. And these are all true coals, without any injurious quantity of water, with moderate ash, and capable of being kept and stored for a long period without loss of value. I have been the more anxious to impress upon you the extent and variety of these stores, because I am aware that even now there is a general feeling among those who have not carefully examined modern progress in practical geology, that no valuable coal is to be found out of the carboniferous system.

This feeling arises from the limited experience of English miners, and has no foundation in fact.

It is true, however, that the great coal-fields of England, of Belgium, of Spain, of France, and of North America, besides those of Bohemia, Moravia, and the Rhine, of Russia and China, and probably of Australia, belong to the oldest, or Palæozoic rocks, and that for some reason that may perhaps be better understood at a future time than it now is, these deposits are more regular, more uniform over large areas, and in that sense more to be depended upon, than those of newer date. We must take facts as they are presented to us by Nature, and my business is to state them, and make the knowledge of them useful.

The extraction of saleable coal from British mines approaches a hundred million of tons per annum, and the waste of coal involved in getting this quantity is probably more than one-fourth part more.

Coal weighs rather less than a ton to the cubic yard, and we are therefore removing and using, or destroying, from the portion of our own small island to which coals are limited, 125,000,000 of cubic yards every year of one of the most valuable substances in existence. Assuming a coal seam to have an average thickness of two yards, it would take twenty square miles of such a seam to supply one year's consumption. It behoves us, then, to look around, and consider the resources we possess, whether we can afford to expend this portion of the capital stock of our national wealth, and what chance there may be of this stock becoming exhausted.

The coal-fields of Great Britain are numerous and widely distributed. They range at intervals from Somersetshire and South Wales, in the south, to Ayrshire, Lanarkshire, and Fifeshire, in Scotland, in the north. They are limited to the western side of England in the south, and do not reach the south coast. Advancing northwards, they first reach the midland counties, then expand on the flanks of the Derbyshire limestone hills, and in Yorkshire they approach the eastern shores of our island. Extending through Durham and Northumberland on the east, they are found at Whitehaven and in the Lothians, on the west. There are four principal groups of deposits, distinguished as the Northern, Eastern, Western, and Southern. These again are subdivided, and we have, in a different order, the following coal-fields :—(1) the Newcastle coal-field, (2) the Cumberland and Westmoreland coal-fields, (3) those in the West Riding of York, (4) the South Lancashire coal-field, (5) the Flintshire coal-field, (6) the great Yorkshire and Derbyshire coal-fields, (7) the North Staffordshire, (8) the Coalbrook Dale and other Shropshire coal-fields, (9) the Worcestershire coal-fields, (10) the Leicestershire, (11) the Warwickshire, (12) the South Staffordshire, (13) the Forest of Dean, (14) the Bristol and Gloucestershire group, (15) the South Welsh coal-field. In Scotland, in the valley extending from the Firth of Forth to the Firth of Clyde, we have (16) the Clyde Basin, (17) the Ayrshire coal-field, (18) the Lesmahago Basin, (19) the Clackmannan coal-field, (20) the Fifeshire, (21) the Lothians, and (22) the Dumfries.

All these agree in supplying bituminous coal of the ordinary kind. Some also yield cannel coal, steam coal, or anthracite. These varieties are useful for special purposes, and I must occupy a few moments in pointing out their nature and properties, and something of their history. I may say, however, that while all the coal-fields yield beds of mineral fuel that may be designated "coal" in the ordinary sense of the word, the quality of coal differs, not only very much in each district, but in every seam. The number and thickness of the beds of coal are equally variable, and often in the same coal-field, a seam of coal that may be followed by actual workings passes from one condition to another in different parts of the field, becoming more or less anthracitic, more or less bituminous, thicker and thinner, according to circumstances that are by no means easy to trace. Still, those familiar with a coal-field are enabled to identify the coals of each seam, and their general peculiarities are tolerably constant.

I may also remark, at this point, that all the coal-fields of England, and all parts of them, are singularly liable to those disturbances of strata called faults. There are faults of all degrees of magnitude, and offering every variety of condition: main faults, throwing the coals several hundred fathoms from the continuation of the same seam; ordinary faults, varying from a few fathoms to a hundred fathoms; and an infinitude of smaller disturbances called slips, throws, or slides, separating beds a few inches, a few feet, or a yard or two. So also the faults are sometimes mere interruptions of continuity, but sometimes wide gaps filled with stones or rubbish.

It must not be supposed that because faults are the rule in English and Scotch coal-fields, they are in any way essential to the existence of a coal-field. Other countries, where the coal has been deposited in equally thick and continuous beds, exhibit few faults, and nothing of the complicated systems of disturbances characteristic of the British coal-fields. It is necessary to bear in mind this fact, in estimating the relative value of coal-fields and the probable cost in getting the coal. The irregularity of bedding is universal, though exhibited in various ways. Sometimes the coal in a seam apparently very regular will suddenly come to an end, and be replaced by sand or gravelly material. After lasting for a time, this will once more give way to coal. Such a phenomenon is called technically a "horse."

Coals generally rest in England on beds of shale, containing black markings, that appear to be matted roots. The shale, or clay, is called *under-clay*, and it is particularly valuable for working up into materials that will stand exposure to a strong heat without melting. Under-clays appear to replace or represent the remains of the soil whereon grew the vegetation now converted into coal, but they are now singularly pure beds of clay. They are not always present under the coal, and it is supposed that when absent the coal has not grown on the spot, but has drifted from some adjacent land.

Though exhibiting little structure, there is no doubt of the vegetable origin of all coal. In some cases, shells and remains of insects, fishes, and even small reptiles, have been found embedded with coal, but there are no appearances of aqueous deposits of this kind in the substance of the mineral. Evidence of the mode of accumulation may no doubt be detected, not only in the position of the innumerable leaves, twigs, and stems of plants, in the neighbouring clays and sandstones, but in the substance of the coal itself. But all kinds of coal have been so greatly altered in their conversion, they have lost so much of various substances commonly present in plants, in addition to carbon; they have become so compacted and are reduced so thoroughly to the condition of a simple mineral, that the absence of vegetable structure cannot be wondered at. It still remains a mystery how coal was formed, or what combinations were necessary to produce it. In most cases, especially in thick beds, it represents a mass of vegetation that must have taken many years, or a large area, to accumulate, but yet in some instances there is proof that it must have been accumulated rapidly. That it is generally associated with certain shales, with ironstones, either in nodules or bands, and with sandstones more or less compact, and that in most cases, though not all, it seems to have been accumulated near the mouths of large rivers or low swampy flats, and in estuaries, are facts and inferences that include the results of recent discoveries and investigations in this matter.

The following analyses of some of the principal varieties of coal from the British Islands and other countries will be found useful for reference. They include the most common kinds in each country, and may be considered as representing the average qualities.

COMPOSITION OF DIFFERENT VARIETIES OF BITUMINOUS COAL AND ANTHRACITE.

	Welsh.		Scotch.	English.		French	Westphalian	American	
	Anthracite.	Ebbw Vale Coal.	Grangemouth Coal.	Newcastle Caking Coal	Forest Dean Coal.	Coal.	Anthracite.	MauchChunk Anthracite.	Pomeroys' Virginia.
Carbon	92·56	89·78	79·85	83·59	73·52	76·48	96·02	84·98	76·70
Hydrogen	3·33	5·15	5·28	5·15	5·69	5·73	0·44	2·45	5·67
Nitrogen		2·16	1·35		2·04			1·22	1.71
Sulphur	2·53	1·02	1·42	8·74	2.27	16·01		..	..
Oxygen		0.39	8·58		6·48		2·94	1·15	11·32
Ash	1·58	1·50	3·52	2·52	10·00	2·28	0·60	10·20	4·60
	100·00	100·00	100·00	100·00	100·00	100·00	100·00	100·00	100·00

Bituminous coal is moderately hard, brittle, burns readily with much flame and smoke, and gives off much gas on dry distillation above a red heat. *Caking coal* is a variety common in the Newcastle coal-field, which runs together in the fire. Bituminous coal contains from 10 to 30 per cent. of volatile substances; and when these are removed, there remains a beautiful semi-crystalline coke. *Cannel coal* is compact, does not soil the fingers, and can be sculptured like wood. It is tougher than common coal. In Scotland it is called *parrot.* When exposed to heat, it takes fire and burns like a torch or *candle,* with much light and smoke. It contains from 40 to 60 per cent. of volatile substances. *Steam coal* is a hard semi-bituminous coal, with little volatile matter, but burning freely with flame and much heat. *Anthracite* is nearly free carbon, almost vitreous in its nature, perfectly homogeneous, and showing conchoidal fracture. Some varieties are powdery or flaky; some resemble graphite. None of the true coals contain water in sensible quantity. It occasionally happens that a bituminous coal in one part of a bed passes into a cannel coal, and even into a bituminous shale, in another part, while the same coal-bed, followed some little distance in another direction, is converted into anthracite. It is thus very difficult to draw a well-defined line between the different varieties. As a general rule, however, the three divisions are to be recognised, and a seam of one variety does not alter very much in the same coal-field.

The Newcastle coal-field (1) is that which has been the most extensively worked of any in the world. Till lately it has yielded only bituminous coal and cannel, the latter being rare ; it now also yields excellent steam coal from a part of the field towards the north, recently opened. The coal from this coal-field has long enjoyed a high reputation for household use, and it makes the finest and most crystalline coke. No anthracite has been found here. The extreme length of the coal-field is about fifty miles, including the country covered with other rocks beneath which the coal is proved. Its extreme width is about half that distance, but the area is diamond-shaped rather than square, and cannot contain so much as 700 square miles, even including the parts of the field covered and concealed by the magnesian limestone. It is divided into two districts by a great fault crossing the whole field from east to west, a little north of the Tyne at Newcastle. The strata are lower on the northern side of this fault than on the southern side by as much as ninety fathoms. This is called the main dyke. The strata on the two sides of the fault do not exactly correspond. There are no important bands of ironstone, but the coal lies among shales and sandstones.

There are as many as forty distinct coal-beds in the Newcastle field, but only eighteen are workable. The most valuable is only two yards thick, and none of the others are much more. The total thickness of workable coal is not above eighty feet, and the mean thickness of workable coal over the whole area is not estimated at more than four yards. Some of the best seams are worked out to a considerable depth; and in this district are some of the deepest and most costly pits that have ever been sunk, working in some cases several square miles of coal from a single communication. The depth of one pit exceeds 1,800 feet, and the workings are expensive, owing to the quantity of water that has to be pumped. The supply of coal still remaining in this valuable coal-field has been frequently calculated, and as there is a much wider basis of facts here than in any other case on which to base a conclusion, the result may have some value. Estimating the area at 450,000 acres, the average thickness at four yards, and the weight of the coal at one ton per cubic yard, there would be about eight thousand millions of tons of coal. Of this a part can never be reached, and another part is already used or rendered useless. There remain, perhaps, six thousand millions of tons available, and this, at an annual consumption of twenty millions of tons per annum, would last 300 years.

On the opposite side of England to the Newcastle coal-field is a much smaller area (2), in the neighbourhood of Whitehaven, whence a considerable quantity of valuable coal is extracted. The extent of this area is estimated at 80,000 acres, and, with two other small fields adjacent, the whole amounts to 100,000 acres. There are here seven workable seams, the thickest of which is about eight feet, but most of them are very thin. They are worked under considerable difficulties and at great depth, sometimes beneath the sea. The coal is good and caking. There are two divisions of these coal measures, the upper being the more valuable. There is also a small coal-field in the West Riding of York (3) adjoining these, in which there are some seams of good workable coal.

The South Lancashire coal-field (4) is of extreme importance, as supplying the vast population concerned in the manufactures carried on in that part of the kingdom. The coal occupies an irregular area, reaching from near Liverpool into Yorkshire, and including several of the most important manufacturing towns in the kingdom. The coal is found not only in the true coal measures, but in the underlying millstone grit, and the whole area may include a thousand square miles of coal-bearing strata. Over a great part of this area the coals are thin, and the sections are very unequal in different parts of the field. Thus, in one direction there are 75 beds of coal, each more than one foot thick, distributed through 2,000 yards of measures, but the total thickness of coal is only 150 feet. In another direction there are only 26 seams, though the total thickness of coal is upwards of 90 feet. The thickest bed is 10 feet. The quality of the coal is good—well adapted for all economic purposes. It is chiefly bituminous, but includes some excellent cannel, worked near Wigan and elsewhere. The cannel is particularly valuable for gas. To the geologist the Lancashire coal-field is especially interesting, and to the economist it is not less important. The available coal in the district has been estimated at 4,000,000,000 tons, but the evidence is very imperfect. The sinkings are not generally very deep, and the quantity of water is not excessive. The Flintshire and Denbighshire coal-field (5) is smaller and much worked. There are five workable seams, of which one is nine feet thick. The total thickness of workable coal is said to be nearly forty feet. Among the beds is a very remarkable cannel, called curly cannel, extremely rich in hydrocarbons. There are shales almost equally rich.

The great Yorkshire coal-field (6) supplies Sheffield, Leeds, Bradford, Halifax, and other large towns in the north of England. It occupies an area of more than a thousand square miles, and though the number of workable seams is not large, one of them is ten feet thick, and there is more than thirty feet of workable coal. The quality of the coal is excellent, and it is reached by pits of moderate depth, over a great part of the field. Many varieties of coal are obtained, among which are some excellent cannels. There are also very numerous bands of ironstone. The North Staffordshire or Pottery coal-field (7) occupies an area of 40,000 acres, and contains a number of good seams, also of excellent coal. Here there is nearly forty feet thickness of coal, in twenty-four workable seams, one of which is ten feet thick. With the coals are valuable ironstones, and also some shales, highly bituminous and well adapted for distillation. All are worked together, but some of the seams are already exhausted in some parts of the field.

The Shropshire coal-fields (8) are four in number, the most important being at Coalbrook Dale. The others are near Shrewsbury, at Brown Clee Hill, and at Titterston Clee Hill. Of the three latter, the first-named is the principal. The Coalbrook Dale district has been rich both in coal and iron. It contains seventeen seams, having a total thickness of forty feet, many of the seams affording good coal, very rich in gas; and the iron made in the district is considered to rank among the best in England. The beds are accessible, but unusually faulted. They are very nearly exhausted. It was worked by the Romans. At two places in Worcestershire—Lickey Hill and Bewdley—there are small coal-fields (9) yielding useful coals. The Bewdley is the most important and much the largest. The Ashby coal-field, in Leicestershire (10), is another small but not unimportant district, much worked, and yielding excellent coal, though no ironstone of importance. It probably connects with the Warwickshire coal-field at Nuneaton (11), which occupies about the same area (6,000 acres), and possesses nine seams, one of them fifteen feet thick.

The South Staffordshire (12) is one of those coal-fields which, by their position in reference to the great manufactures of our country, occupies a very important place. It is brought up by main faults through the New Red Sandstone. It is not very extensive, but has one seam whose thickness reaches from twenty to forty feet. This seam, called the "thick coal," or "ten-yard seam," is so exceptional among the English coals, that it is regarded as a very strange phenomenon. Experience in other countries has shown that there are many beds of coal that bear the same proportion to this that the thick coal of Staffordshire does to the six-foot coals of Newcastle. Still, placed as it is close to great centres of manufacture, associated with other coals and with valuable bands of ironstone, and being for the most part of good quality, some of it being cannel coal, it is certainly a matter of great importance, and deserves special notice in any account of English coals. The effective area of the South Staffordshire coal-field has been estimated at a hundred square miles. A considerable proportion of all the coal of this field has been worked out, and an unusual proportion has been injured and wasted by careless working.

The Forest of Dean (13) yields a number of workable coals, cropping out over an area of about thirty-four square miles. It has been less worked than some, but is of considerable importance. Near it, in Gloucestershire, is another small coal-field. Near Bristol there is an extensive and important coal district (14), now much worked, and yielding a large supply of excellent fuel adapted to all purposes. The area is broken up, and the beds are for the most part thin; but they are numerous. The mines are very deep, and the coal measures are covered up by the New Red Sandstone, and in some cases by the lias.

We come now to the great South Welsh coal-field (15), next in importance to the Newcastle in some respects, and superior in others. The whole coal-bearing district includes upwards of 900 square miles. It is divided into three unequal parts; the west anthracitic, the middle steam coal, and the east bituminous. The richer beds lie near the bottom. It is an elongated trough, the beds dipping towards a central axis. With the coals there are numerous bands of ironstone, generally thin, but of good quality. The thickness of the coal-bearing strata has been estimated at 10,000 feet, and the total vertical thickness of the available coal at from seventy to a hundred feet. Although it is not unlikely that the estimates that have been made of the total quantity of coal in this field are much exaggerated, there cannot be a doubt that it is the largest and most important in the British islands, and that its resources may be available long after the smaller coal areas of the North have been either exhausted, or rendered unworkable by the mechanical difficulties attendant on increased depth.

The Scotch coal-fields are both numerous and rich. They are rich in the number of beds of coal, in the ironstone bands associated with the coal, in the quality of the coal, which includes numerous varieties of cannel or *parrot*, and in the usefulness of the coal, and its special adaptability to certain purposes of gas-making and the distillation of oils. Most of the coal is dry, free-burning, but not caking. The various subdivisions, though of some local importance, do not belong to any great natural divisions, for all belong to the lower members of the carboniferous series, and are of greater antiquity than most of the English coals. Geologically, these deposits are interesting from the numerous intrusions of igneous rock, and the occasional breaking off of the coal series by the upheaval of the

Carboniferous Limestone and Old Red Sandstone. The total area is estimated at upwards of 1,600 square miles. Coal has been long and extensively worked in Scotland, and the total quantity raised amounts to 12,000,000 tons. An important part of the Scotch coal has been made use of for distillation at moderate heat, to obtain paraffin oils, for which it was particularly adapted. The large imports of petroleum from America, and the gradual exhaustion of the richer seams, have greatly checked this manufacture in the places where it was first commenced.

Ireland, also, has its coal-fields, both bituminous and anthracitic. The former are small, but the coal is abundant and easily reached; twenty or thirty feet of workable beds are found in Tyrone at a depth of between two and three hundred yards. The anthracitic deposits are more numerous and more worked than the bituminous. The coal of Munster is the most developed. It occupies considerable portions of the counties of Clare, Limerick, Cork, and Kerry. In Tipperary and Leinster there are deposits of anthracite in deep troughs between hills of moderate elevation.

Belgium is extremely rich in coal, as well as iron. Next to England, it is the most important coal-producing country in the world, and the province of Hainault, the western division of the coal-field, is very remarkable. Every variety is found there—from pure anthracite, burning without flame, through the rich bituminous kind called "*Charbon gras,*" making excellent coke, to the flaming coal or cannel called "*Fléau.*" The most valuable of all is called "*Charbon maigre à longue flamme,*" found only in this district, and worth nearly £1 sterling per ton at the pit mouth. All the three principal coal-fields of Belgium are situated in Hainault, and the produce has been rapidly increasing for some years. The following are the qualities of coal and the local names, with the quantities extracted in 1860 :—

1. "*Charbon maigre*" or anthracite, burning almost without flame	682,709 tons.
2. "*Demi-gras*" or dry coal, burning with a short flame ...	792,750 "
3. "*Charbon maigre à longue flamme,*" thin coal, burning with a long flame	1,804,800 "
4. "*Charbon gras,*" bituminous coal, burning with long flame	4,266,786 "
5. "*Maréchale,*" Smith's coal, a bituminous variety	2,063,780 "

Of these coals by far the larger part, except of No. 1, are got from Hainault. The other two coal districts are Namur and Liège. All the Namur coal is a poor variety of No. 1, and the total quantity raised in 1860 was only 200,000 tons. Liège yielded at the same time about 450,000 tons of a better quality of No. 1, about half a million tons of No. 4, and nearly a million tons of No. 5. The rest was from Hainault. The qualities of Belgian coal are inferior to those of British coals, but a very large quantity is exported into France. About three and a half millions of tons were exported in 1860.

France possesses a very large number of small coal-fields. Those in the northern departments are geologically portions of the Belgian coal-fields, and contain the same varieties of coal. In the eastern part of the country, as at Saarebrück, on the Moselle, there are other deposits of the same nature. Upwards of one hundred beds of coal are here recognised, their thickness varying from fifteen inches to as many feet. In the interior of France the most important coal-fields are in and near the basin of the Loire. Of these St. Etienne is the largest. There are here eighteen beds of bituminous coal, and in adjoining basins several deposits of anthracitic coal. The coal was formerly worked in quarries from the outcrop. In central France there are numerous small basins, in some of which, as at Aubin, the thickness of the coal is extraordinary, and the quality very good. At Aubin there are 124 yards of solid coal in eight seams, one of which measures fifty yards at its outcrop. Almost all the French coals are in small depressed basins in granite, and the coal does not rest on under-clay, but on coarse conglomerates. This is especially the case in the coal found in the interior.

In Rhenish Prussia, the basin of the Ruhr, near Düsseldorf, is the seat of important coal-mining operations, and the Saar coal-field extends across the frontier from France into Germany. Saxony also yields coal. The chief German coal-fields are those of Bohemia and Silesia, Moravia and Galicia; but these are only extensively developed in a very few districts. In Bohemia, at Unhoscht, there are two seams worked. One of these measures from 18 to 36 feet thick, and the second 21 feet. From the mines working them nearly 200,000 tons of coal were raised in 1860. At Schlan another seam of 26 feet is worked, yielding nearly 100,000 tons per annum. In Moravia is a seam of 12 to 14 feet, and many others of very good thickness, all worked to some extent. In Galicia are two seams measuring 30 feet, and one seam of 12 feet, besides three others amounting to 21 feet, all worked in the same mine not far from Cracow. Upwards of 40,000 tons per annum are raised from this mine. The quality of all these coals is good, and the works are carried on with some vigour. The total yield of bituminous coal from the Austrian empire in 1860 was about one and a half million tons.

Some of the rivers of Russia, entering the Caspian, and some localities on the shores of the Black Sea, yield good coal of the carboniferous period. A few of them are worked.

The Iberian peninsula is very rich in coal, especially in its north-eastern extremity, where, in the province of the Asturias, there is a coal area of very large dimensions, containing upwards of a hundred workable seams, varying from three to twelve feet in thickness. A few mines have been opened, and the coal is known to be of excellent quality and easily obtained; but the work hitherto done is very small. In the south of Spain, on the flanks of the Sierra Morena; in Portugal, at Coimbra, between Lisbon and Oporto, and elsewhere; and in a small district near Barcelona, there are workable coal seams, all of the palæozoic period. There are beds of coal in the northernmost land of Europe, almost within the arctic circle.

North America contains several coal-areas, compared with which the richest deposits of Europe sink into insignificance. These are the central coal-field of the Alleghanies, including the basin of the Ohio and the coal-field of Illinois, the basin of the Missouri, and the coal-fields of Nova Scotia, New Brunswick, and Cape Breton. Besides these, there are many of smaller magnitude.

The Alleghany or Appalachian coal-field measures 750 miles in length with a mean breadth of 85 miles, and traverses eight principal States, among which are Virginia, Pennsylvania, Ohio, Kentucky, and Alabama. The whole area is not less than 70,000 square miles; but, making a liberal deduction for unproductive portions, denuded strata, and unattainable depths, there probably remain 25,000,000 acres of productive and valuable coal-field. The coal is partly bituminous, partly anthracitic, and the seams are numerous and of convenient thickness. Bituminous coal prevails in the southern portion of the field; and an intermediate quality of steam coal, well adapted for iron-smelting, comes in between: there are also cannel coals. The beds are in some places, among the mountain valleys, very steeply inclined, but elsewhere almost horizontal and very little faulted. Some of the beds of coal measure thirty feet or more in thickness. They are associated with grits and shales, and with occasional bands of iron ore. Within the district are the coals of the Ohio and its tributaries, including important deposits of excellent mineral fuel, in beds of considerable thickness, lying nearly horizontal, cropping out on the banks between which the rivers pass in the mountain districts, or lying in convenient places on the plains. The Illinois field includes four subdivisions; one of these is the Indiana district, where a rich bituminous coal extends over an area of 8,000 square miles. In the State of Illinois itself there are 30,000 square miles of coal country, in many parts of which the coal comes close to the surface, and in adjoining States are large coal-bearing tracts. There is another great coal-field in Missouri.

British America supplies coal in ample quantity in New Brunswick, Nova Scotia, and Cape Breton. The New Brunswick beds are thin, but the coal is bituminous and lies horizontally. Nova Scotia is extremely rich, and contains one seam of considerable thickness, amounting to thirty-four feet of good coal; besides a large number of others of ordinary proportions. Some of the coal is excellent for steam purposes, and other beds more valuable for gas. The Sydney coal of Cape Breton is the best household variety, and of it there are fourteen seams, each more than a yard thick. One of these measures eleven and another nine feet.

South America contains coal supposed to be palæozoic, cropping out on the coast of Brazil, ranging from near Monte Video to a point nearly four hundred miles to the north, and traced several hundred miles into the interior. Several seams of good steam coal have been described.

China and Japan are believed to possess good stores of mineral fuel of the same age as those of England, and these seem to extend at intervals down the eastern side of Australia. where, in the colony of New South Wales, the coal has been long worked. There is evidence that the Chinese coals were worked at least six centuries ago, and they include several kinds, both anthracitic and bituminous. New Zealand contains coal, and in several of the islands of the Eastern Archipelago mines are already somewhat largely opened. Borneo yields the most important supplies.

Thus, over a very large part of the earth's surface deposits of coal are already proved to exist, and in many of them rich and valuable deposits are actually worked. They have been so worked for more than two thousand years. The beds associated with the coal are by no means always the same, but they consist generally of shales or hard laminated clays, and grits or sandstones containing vegetable remains and ironstone bands. The conversion of vegetable matter into true coal, as I have already pointed out, is a process by no means clearly understood; nor do we know the precise circumstances under which such a change could now be effected. We may fairly assume, from the nature of coal, that such materials as sulphur, present in coal but rare in organic bodies, and alkalies, common in plants but absent in coal, have become introduced or separated during the transformation, and have passed away to form fresh combinations; but why the process has been perfected in coal and left half-effected or not commenced in lignites, is still to be explained. That during the carboniferous period the land in those parts of the world where coal is found was low and covered with luxuriant vegetation, there is no doubt; and that the vegetation in different latitudes was much more uniform than at present, seems equally certain; but these conditions may have been due to extreme alterations in the form and position of the land.

While speaking of coal, I must not omit allusion to those marvellous stores of mineral oil that have recently been obtained by boring to some beds in the American coal-fields. The most important springs are to the west of Pennsylvania, not far from Pittsburg. Wells are sunk from 150 to 200 yards, and the mineral or petroleum is found in crevices in the limestones below the coal. The supply has varied greatly within the last few years, owing to the war. In 1861 the yield was about 3,000 tons weight, in 1862 ten times as much, but in 1863 only about 8,000. Large quantities are also obtained from Canada, and it is believed that the supply has not diminished from any exhaustion of the springs. It is stated that the annual value of the oil exported is not less than fifteen millions of pounds sterling. Petroleum is also obtainable from many other parts of the world in large quantities.

I must now direct your attention to the methods adopted to obtain these valuable materials from the earth. Such methods constitute the practice of mining, and vary according to the position of the coal, the thickness of the seam, the nature of the rocks above and below (called respectively roof and floor), the quality of the coal, and the quantity of gas it gives off underground. The quantity of water met with in reaching the coal, and other practical matters, also enter into consideration.

In the diagram No. 12, which may be supposed to represent a section, some miles in length, across a coal country, where seams of coal are workable, and where faults do not interfere with the workings, several of the more simple conditions of coal-mining are illustrated. Thus, if the coal crops out at c c′ on the side

Fig. 12.

of a valley, it can be got readily, and at small expense, by levels or galleries tunnelled into the side of the hill. The coal, however, being rarely horizontal, a gallery, following the dip of the coal, will enter, inclining down-hill on one side and up-hill on the other side of the valley. In the first case, any water that enters will soon escape, but in the other it will accumulate. The coal also can be run out readily in the one, and must be drawn up-hill at some expense in the other case. Thus, it is only when the coal is horizontal, or when the dip is towards the valley, that crop workings can be carried on to any extent or with advantage. In the other case it will be better and cheaper to sink a pit as at *p*, and obtain the coal by running a drift up from the bottom of this pit. The water will then either run away or can conveniently be lifted, and the coal may be run down to the pit bottom, and lifted thence, at small cost, by simple tackle at first, and, as the works become larger, by machinery constructed for the purpose. Crop workings, though apparently applicable whenever the coal comes to the surface, are really limited to a single and not very common case. They are always confined to the early workings on a seam.

But, now and then, coal at its outcrop may be obtained by quarrying. This is still more exceptional, and is confined to cases in which the seam is thick, and retains its quality as a useful fuel after long exposure to the weather. Quarries of coal are not unknown in some countries even now, but in England they have long ceased to have much value. Open workings, indeed, are sometimes dangerous. A few weeks ago (probably it is so still) one of the richly bituminous shales of the Pottery coal-field, in the north of Staffordshire, was burning fiercely, with the prospect of destroying a large amount of valuable property, in consequence of some one carelessly throwing down on the surface of the outcropping bed a quantity of red-hot ashes from a distillery of the shale adjacent. Among the more remarkable of the open workings of coal is that of St. Etienne, near Lyons, in France. Very thick beds are worked in this way in other parts of France, in Austria, and elsewhere. They differ in no respect from ordinary quarries.

When, as is almost always the case, underground works are to be reached by a pit or shaft, it becomes a matter of great importance to know whereabouts, at what depth, and in what state the coal lies. Where the outcrop is known, the dip of the coal regular, and the coal not faulted, this is not a difficult task. The mine surveyor has only to calculate the distance on the line of the dip from the crop to the point where it is proposed to sink, the amount of the dip or the fall of the coal seam per yard, and the difference of level of the two points from a fixed datum. These known, the calculation is simple enough. But the permanent inclination of a coal seam is not always determined accurately by its dip at the outcrop, the dip of a bed not being a very regular phenomenon. Faults also must not be left out of calculation. Some better ground for an opinion than simple calculation is therefore necessary, and it is often worth while to resort to boring, by which we may learn the general relations of the beds and the depth to a known point in the series, after which calculation is easy. In this event, too, three or more borings are necessary where the coal is not already proved, and its outcrop is not clearly known. Several are required when there is reason to expect faulted ground.

When, by a general knowledge of the strata, by a study of the outcrop and general run of the beds, and due inquiry into the probable direction and amount of the disturbances, assisted by a few borings, we have learnt all that can be made out concerning the circumstances under which the coal lies in any given property, the next operation must be to sink a shaft or a pair of shafts to intersect the bed at a certain depth, and in such a part of the estate that the largest possible proportion of the various coal seams of the district may be cut and worked. Great judgment and experience are needed to decide this point. On the one hand, if the pits are placed to reach the coal at too great a depth, unnecessary expense is incurred, not only at first, but afterwards, in getting as well as reaching the coal, and in lifting the water. On the other hand, if they are so placed as not to be able to remove the coal from the extremity of the estate, that portion will be practically lost or left to be pillaged by a neighbour; for after expensive pits have been sunk, and much of the coal got, it may not be worth while to get the rest by a fresh sinking. So with regard to faults, if the pits be sunk without reference to them, great difficulty may be experienced and heavy expenses incurred that might be avoided by better knowledge of the ground.

It is usual in practice, when coal is being got from near the outcrop, to sink shafts with less consideration, and to sink many more of them than when the mine is deep. The conveyance of the coal underground, the expense of keeping in order the main ways, and various economic considerations, decide this question. In large deep mines in an old worked district, few shafts are sunk; the number is limited as much as it can be with safety. The enormous cost of deep shafts in some cases fully justifies this economy, but there are both disadvantages and great dangers in mines that are carried on by a single shaft or by shafts too far apart. In the event of an accident, either to the shaft or in the ventilation, communication may be entirely cut off, and thus a heavy loss of life may result. Thus the determination as to the number and position of the shafts is a matter to be very carefully considered.

In shallow mines, the pits are generally single and of moderate size. In deep mines, they are in pairs, or one very large shaft is divided into three portions. We shall see presently why this is necessary.

A shaft or shafts being decided on, and the details of its probable depth and dimensions arranged, the work of sinking commences. The rocks through which the sinking has to pass will be very different in different places, and even in different parts of the same pit. Hard or soft sandstone rock, tough or soft clay rock, occasionally very hard bands, and occasionally very soft sandy portions, make up the usual series. In all of these there is more or less water, but some of them are water-bearing beds, and would supply strong springs, if that were the object of the sinking. Water, however, in a mine is as undesirable as it is useful at the surface. If water be reached while sinking, it must be shut off and prevented from entering the pit; if it come in at the bottom, it must be pumped out. The only way of shutting it off is by lining the shaft, and this must be done with an iron casing passed down from the top to fit the sinking as it proceeds. In the case of soft, loose strata, that would otherwise fall but that do not carry much water, this *metal tubbing*, as it is called, is not needed; but the shaft must in such strata be timbered or bricked, or lined with cement, according to the circumstances.

The bottom of the shaft is the coal seam which it is intended to remove; and, as much work is to be done there, it is necessary to open out the coal a little to make room, supporting the roof with extreme care, as everything depends on its stability in the future working of the mine. A shaft fallen in at the bottom is hopelessly ruined. In ordinary cases, at moderate depths, when the coal is reached, and there are two pits, these are immediately connected. This is partly for the sake of ventilation, and partly for the convenience of further workings. It is convenient that one pit should be free, or comparatively so, in order that it may serve as a chimney for the purpose of carrying off the air which is injured, either by the breathing of the men at work, or by emanations of gas from the coal; and as the ordinary works of the pit, the lowering and raising of men and stores, and the lifting of the coal when brought to the pit bottom, necessarily choke up a shaft, this chimney is very essential. During the sinking of each pit, if more air is wanted than naturally comes down, the shaft is divided into two portions by a partition, and ventilation is effected by artificial means. If there is a pair of pits close together, they are usually sunk on the line of dip of the beds, so that one shall reach the coal at a greater depth than the other. In this case a natural ventilation sets in, one shaft acting as a chimney to carry heated air up, and the other as a pipe down which the heavier air descends.

When coal is reached, a drift or tunnel is carried in it for some distance in the direction of the strike, and therefore on a horizontal line. In the case of a pair of pits two such drifts are cut, one from each. This preliminary operation enables the field to be laid out conveniently, and reveals the condition of the coal, the state of the roof, and the continuity of the seam. Along these level roads the coal when removed can conveniently be drawn, and one of them is therefore generally made wide and roomy (9 to 12 feet wide and 6 feet high). Rails or a tram must be placed upon it, and in a large mine this main road is adapted for horses. Along the lower drift, or by the side if there is a single pit, the water of the mine, or part of it, is conducted, and the drifts are made available for the ventilation of the distant workings. When there is a pair of pits, the lower of the two horizontal galleries is called the *water-gate*, and the upper the *horse-gate*.

At right-angles to such drift or drifts, and on the rise of the coal, another tunnel is driven from the pit bottom; and as this is immediately connected with the active workings on the coal, it is called the *winning headway*, or, in Yorkshire, the *main board-gate*. If there be a second shaft at a distance, it is convenient that this should communicate with the winning headway, as shown in the diagram No. 13. In the case illustrated here, we may suppose that part of the seam has been removed by crop workings, or by a shallow pit, *p*, meeting the coal at *a*, and that it has been found desirable to put down a fresh pit, *p'*, at a greater depth to cut

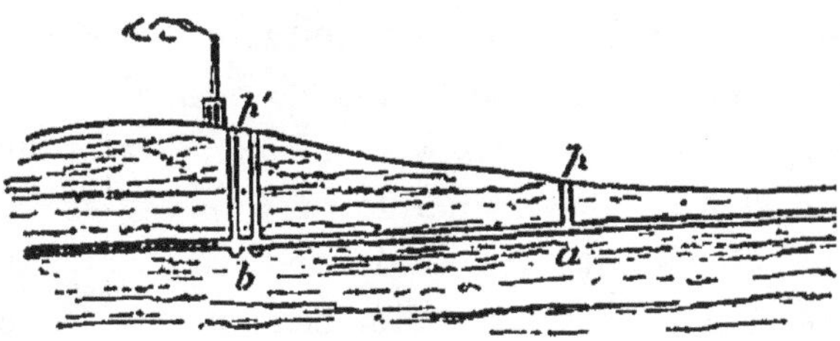

Fig. 13.

the coal at *b*. The level driven from *b* on the rise of the coal towards *a* is the winning headway.

The further working of the mine may be carried on, if the coal is of moderate thickness and not inclined at an angle of more than 20 degrees, by one of two methods, known respectively as the *pillar and stall* and the *long wall* method. The former is adopted in the Newcastle coal-field, and has been introduced with modifications into many other districts; the latter is that followed in the coal-fields of Yorkshire, and others adjacent. There are other methods, intended for very thick seams, for very highly inclined seams, &c., made use of both in England and abroad, but concerning these a few words will suffice. I will endeavour to explain the two principal methods.

In the Newcastle coal-field, where the coal lies deep, where there is much water, and where shafts are very costly, and the coal very dangerous to work, it is found most convenient to divide the whole of a coal property into a number of districts of convenient size, each of which may be opened to some extent independently. These are called *panels*, and they are kept separated by leaving between each two a thickness of forty or fifty yards of coal. Each panel is worked independently, and access having been gained by a drift from the winning headway, it is best to begin with the panel most distant from the shaft. The principle of working is to run levels or galleries at right angles to each other, leaving pillars of coal of very large dimensions. By these the roof is supported till the whole panel is laid open to the full extent to which it is meant to work it. When the galleries have all been completed the pillars may be removed, at first cutting them in half, and then into quarters, and at last carrying away as much as possible, supporting the roof for a time with wooden pillars, and ultimately removing the pillars, and allowing the roof to fall. The farthest panel being removed, the next may be attacked, and so on till the work is completed. The main way is left throughout, and, if properly constructed, remains accessible. It is impossible, however, in a mine where the ground is faulted and the limits of the panels are irregular, to preserve theoretical accuracy, and thus it is rather the general principle than any precision of detail that can be expected.

In Yorkshire, where the mines are not generally on so large a scale as those of Newcastle, where the depth is less and the coal harder, with faults less troublesome, the *long wall* method is adopted. By this, wide levels or drifts, called *gates*, are run through the coal from the main board-gate parallel to the winning-headway; and the coal, instead of being cut up into pillars, is left at first in a number of long walls parallel to each other, and supporting the roof. When the mine is thus laid open, the walls are entered by small cross drifts, and the greater part removed, leaving narrow walls for a time. These also are at length taken, and the roof allowed to fall. In the thick coal of South Staffordshire something of the same general plan is adopted, but the upper part of the seam is first removed. In these works, too, the wall is very irregular. In South Wales, in seams moderately thick, other modifications are adopted. In Belgium, where the bed dips at an angle of 45 degrees or more, it is necessary to follow in some measure the system of mining for mineral veins. The pits are sunk vertically, and the coal is reached by horizontal drifts at successive intervals of depth.

In coal mines generally, although in working some varieties of coal much more than in others, there is a cause of difficulty and danger that I have not yet alluded to. It arises from the quantity of gas, chiefly light carburetted hydrogen, existing in the coal, removable, by distillation, for illuminating purposes after the coal is raised to the earth's surface, but emitted in considerable quantities underground, especially where the coal has recently been broken. Besides this light gas, or *fire-damp*, heavy air, *choke-damp*, or carbonic acid gas, is not unusual. Both have to be provided against by ventilation, and thus the conveyance and distribution of air is one of the most essential matters in laying out a coal mine. Other gases, also dangerous, are occasionally met with, but are less common; olefiant gas is especially dangerous. A certain per-centage of nitrogen and oxygen, varying in different mines, accompanies the light carburetted hydrogen gas.

Mixed with any proportion of atmospheric air, not less than one-fourteenth part and not more than one-eighth, this light gas becomes dangerous, and when exposed to flame or to iron at white heat it explodes, leaving after explosion carbonic acid gas, and a small quantity of water. When a large quantity of gas of this kind issues from coal underground, and mixes with the atmospheric air carried down for ventilation, as soon as the proper mixture is obtained the light from an open candle would explode the whole, burning every thing near the explosion, and leaving behind, instead of air, a poisonous, heavy gas, which must inevitably choke any persons in the mine who have not already suffered by the explosion, and who are unable to escape from its influence.

By the ventilation of mines, dangerous mixtures of gas should be rendered as unlikely to occur as possible, and by a safe method of lighting, the danger of explosion, when fire-damp is present, should be avoided. But a perfectly safe and complete ventilation and equally safe light are not easy to find, and though much has been done towards them in theory, in practice there still occur fearful accidents, arising from the neglect of proper precautions, or from some cause against which it has not been found practicable to provide.

The ventilation of mines is conducted, when artificial means are necessary, by producing a strong draught up one shaft (called for this reason the up-cast shaft) by means of a fire at the bottom, or by exhausting the air by steam or other means at the top. All the air entering the mine by the other shaft or shafts, or other part of the shaft if there be only one, is forced to take a course through the workings, and along all the levels or galleries before reaching the up-cast shaft. Part of the entering air is often split off and sent through one portion of the workings, and part through another, the distribution of the air being regulated by the state of the mine. Extreme care and attention is needed to ensure the ventilation being adapted to the issue of gas, and to avoid a dangerous mixture.

As, however, artificial light is absolutely necessary to carry on the work underground, and open candles or lamps are liable to produce an explosion, a safety-light is needed, even where the ventilation is most perfect and best looked after. Such a light was provided for the miner by the late Sir Humphrey Davy, and it is theoretically perfect, provided the explosive gas in the mine be light carburetted hydrogen, and if also due caution be used. This lamp is a common oil lamp, covered with a metallic gauze so open that little light is intercepted, but so close that flame cannot pass. Many modifications have been introduced, but they all involve the same general principle.

The quantity of gas occasionally poured into a mine from certain kinds of coal, or from empty spaces unexpectedly met with in working coal, is sometimes very large, and it issues with so much force and rapidity, as entirely to overcome all efforts to render it safe by mixture with atmospheric air entering the mine in the course of ventilation. In such mines there is a constant singing noise heard while passing along underground, especially where the coal is newly broken; and there have been cases in which holes drilled into the coal have yielded gas enough to take fire, and continue burning, the whole face of the coal thus resembling a gas-pipe. Some coals are generally free from this excessive quantity, but are subject to occasional blowers or jets, which are often connected with faults. In all these cases the constant use of the safety-lamp is necessary, if indeed it is right to carry on work at all.

Gas is apt to accumulate in old workings, and when by any accident these are reached, either in continuing the works of the same mine, or in any other way, there is great danger. Many of the worst and most fatal accidents have happened in this manner. It is certain that when the coal has been removed the roof or overlying mass, whatever it be, will fall, or if supports are left, the pressure on the floor will drive that up. There must thus in all neglected works be a vast pile of broken rock in which great open spaces are left, and in these the gas becomes stored. Such a pile is called the *goaf*, and the depression that appears at the surface, when the roof of a mine has fallen, is called *creep*.

These are a few of the many points that suggest themselves in reference to the practical geology of coal-mining. I have treated them very briefly, and without more detail than was necessary to indicate their importance; but I have endeavoured not to neglect anything that should belong to an outline of the whole subject.

Lecture the Sixth.

MINERAL VEINS, ORES, AND MINING.

FROM the consideration of bedded minerals, we pass on to the last division of our subject—mineral veins, their contents, and the methods adopted to extract their contents. It is a subject of some difficulty, but of great importance. Except gold, tin, and iron stone, which I have already alluded to, and which are generally found stratified or in surface deposits (though, perhaps, they were all of them originally derived from veins), metals are obtained either native or as crystalline minerals, called ores, from certain fissures and veins in altered rocks. The obtaining of ores from the earth is called metal mining, and is quite distinct from coal mining. I need not say that as a pursuit connected with geology it demands our careful consideration. It will, indeed, be difficult to bring it within any reasonable limits.

I will first explain the nature and phenomena of mineral veins, then the nature and history of the contents of those veins, and conclude with a brief notice of the circumstances and conditions of extraction. Each is a great subject.

All rocks, whether aqueous, metamorphic, or igneous, that are now above the water, have been once below the sea level, and have been raised to their present position by some powerful upheaving force acting within the earth at great depth. They must often have been hardened and dried before being elevated, and this process involves a certain amount of contraction. Now, it is impossible not to see that both contraction and elevation must have produced in any rock a multitude of cracks and fractures. The nature of such cracks must depend partly on the rock itself, and partly on the mode of action of the moving force; but that in all elevated hard rocks fractures exist is as certain as that the rocks have been elevated; for it is not possible to conceive disturbances or upheavals without the occurrence of fissures. Very simple forms of such fissures are shown in the diagram annexed.

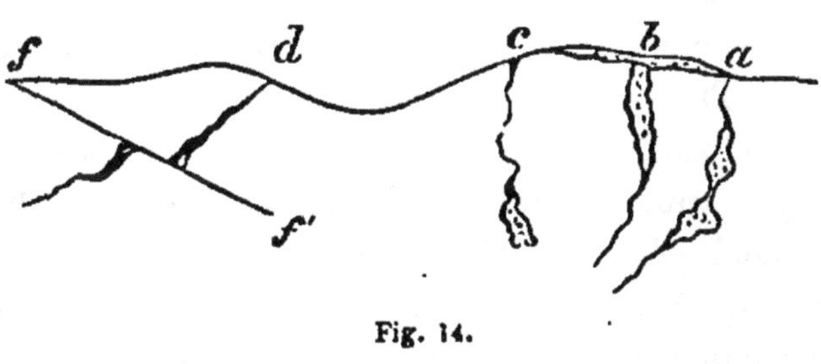

Fig. 14.

Varieties of mineral veins.

a, a bunchy vein not showing at the surface.
b, a wide vein open at the surface.
c, a vein improving in the depth.
d, a faulted vein.
f f′, a throw or fault heaving a vein (*d*).

Fissures in rocks are, however, of two kinds, as being due to two distinct causes. Those caused by contraction will be governed by the chemical laws that determined the hardening, cooling, and metamorphosis of the mass. Those caused by upheaval will be affected and regulated by the amount of force exerted, the weight to be lifted, the direction of the upheaving force, and the mechanical condition of the rock at the time of upheaval. The first kind may have begun almost as soon as the rock existed, and may have been undergoing change ever since. The second kind commenced with the first upheaval. They may, however, be due to any one or all of a multitude of movements that have been going on for a long time, and may still be proceeding. During long geological periods such fissures may have remained unwidened and unaltered. From time to time they may have been crossed by, or interfered with, other fissures, results of upheaval in different directions. The original system of disturbances may have produced systems of fractures in the rocks that have governed all results since; or they may have been small, limited to certain rocks between the disturbing force and the surface at that time, and these rocks may have since been covered up by newer rocks which are not affected by the first movements. Such are some of the complications and modifications that render the study of this subject extremely difficult.

But again, the cracks once formed, and then for a time neglected, have during this interval become filled up. There must have been a constant tendency to fill them, sometimes with fragments of the adjacent rock, and sometimes with crystals which have grown in the cavity. These latter may have commenced from above, from below, or from the walls of the crevice. A crack in a mass of limestone may exist, and though open neither above nor below, it may be occupied with calc spar. A wide fissure in such rock may exist, partially filled with rolled blocks of limestone. An empty space, or a space once empty, may have become filled with lumps of zinc or lead ore. The filling-up may have taken place when, or soon after, the fissure was made, or it may have been gradually progressing during long periods of years. I merely point out these possible conditions of rocks, to show you how full of variety the subject is. I wish you to understand that all rocks present phenomena that have some resemblance to those of mineral veins; that the formation of such veins is an ordinary, not an extraordinary, event in nature; that they form the rule and not the exception in rocks; and that in this, as in other cases, plain common sense, and a knowledge of elementary mechanics, will save a vast amount of wondering and blundering.

The first class of crevices, those formed during the elaboration of a rock, are generally of moderate proportions, and filled up with crystalline material derived from the rock itself. Not, indeed, that the crevice when filled contains such substances as the mass of the rock; this is far from being the case generally, though true enough sometimes. Much more frequently the rock is, as it were, purified and purged of its foreign contents by aid of these cracks, and by the facilities they seem to offer for throwing off substances of which there is only a small and accidental proportion. Thus, in clays we often find the cracks filled with sulphate and carbonate of baryta and calc spar, or with iron pyrites, all crystalline, and evidently brought in by a kind of infiltration from the mass of the clay. In granite, it is very usual to see thin streaks of other granite in the cracks. In marble, coloured veins mark the presence of the oxides of metals; and so on in almost all rocks.

There is, however, a limit to this, and I mention it only as an illustration of a principle. The filling-up of crevices formed in rocks by contraction and metamorphosis need not differ from the filling of wider cracks communicating upwards to the air, or downwards to the unknown interior of the earth. In any case the crevice must be formed before the filling up can begin, and thus every true crack in rocks must have defined walls which were originally separated by an interval. This distinguishes the phenomena we are now considering from instances sometimes met with, where, in an exposed section of rock, differences of condition and of mineral composition are observable, which belong to some process of segregation. A chemical change in rock may be quite independent of any fissure, and cannot therefore be regulated by the mechanical laws that govern fissures. The successive *veins*, as they are called, in slates and granites, including some *elvans*, the *bands* in clays, and the coloured lines and marks in sandstones, are of this nature. They are modifications of the rock, and may afford in many cases admirable and instructive examples of metamorphism, but they are not mineral veins.

Of the two classes of fissures in rocks, that which includes those produced during the formation of the rock is the simpler of the two, and the most frequently met with. In the case of limestones, fissures of this kind are often metalliferous, bearing lead or zinc ore, or iron ore, generally carbonates and sulphides in open natural caverns. A very large proportion of the whole number of fissures are unprofitable, yielding either earthy minerals or ores of metals of little value. In other rocks than limestones the metalliferous contents of such veins are even less important. In some rocks that are highly metamorphised, it would be difficult to decide positively how far a particular crevice was the result of contraction or disturbance, but the existence of a system of such crevices would generally decide the question.

All crevices and fissures in rocks, filled partly or entirely with crystalline minerals, may with equal propriety be called *mineral veins*, but only those which contain valuable ores can be designated *lodes* or *metalliferous veins*. These terms are both useful and distinctive, and are clearly defined. The origin of the vein is of comparatively small importance, but its history as involving the history of the disturbances and upheavals to which it is due, and afterwards the history of the filling with mineral matter, is interesting and will help to guide the intelligent miner in following the traces of the vein when it is lost sight of. It will also help him very greatly in many cases in the attempt to judge of the probable state of a vein when it is only partially seen.

Metalliferous veins in stratified rocks are chiefly confined to accumulations of lead and zinc ore and carbonate of iron in natural open spaces or caverns in limestone. It is found in practice that a particular bed of limestone, or rather the interval between certain beds, distinguished, it may be, by a very insignificant parting of clay or other material, is the recipient of the chief deposits of lead or zinc ore of a district. It is difficult—often quite impossible—to explain or understand this, but it is a law of nature, at least in certain localities, and with certain limitations. Let us see what these veins are like, and what clue we can obtain to their history.

In the diagram before you one of these veins (*a b c d*)

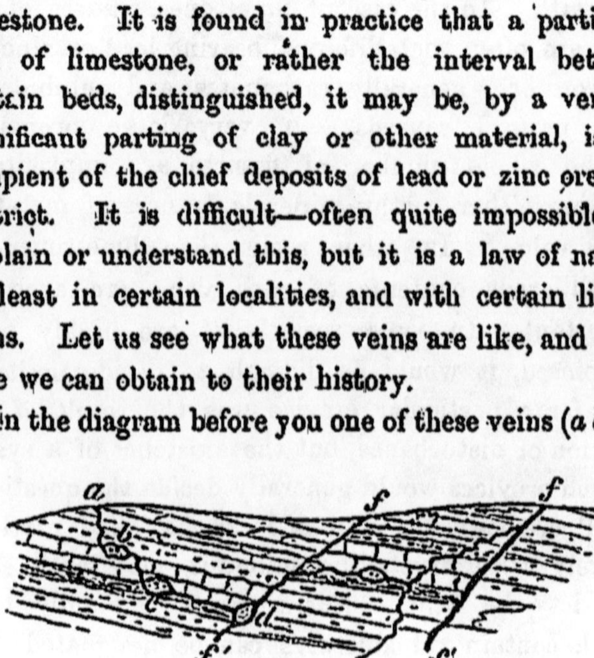

Fig. 15.

is represented. Between and amongst limestones (as at *b*, *c*), where there is no apparent disturbance, where the bedding is regular, and the cavity occurs at the interval between two beds, there may be deposits of sulphide of lead, or galena, carbonate of lead, and carbonate of zinc or calamine. These cavities communicate with others by narrow irregular crevices across and between the strata. How far the natural cracks may have been enlarged and modified by subsequent upheaval and disturbance, bringing up the whole mass of the limestone, it is impossible to say, but in some cases that have come within my experience, in the south of Spain, in Germany, and in England, the main deposits of ore do not seem independent of the stratification. There is, in practice, little guide to the discovery of veins of this kind when lost, beyond a careful and costly following of the slight clue afforded by a thread of ore in a crevice, often extremely narrow, running between very hard walls of rock, and conducting from one to another of the pockets or bunches which alone are profitable.

Useful mineral veins are generally the result of upheavals or disturbances that are in some sense systematic, and they very often show a marked reference to the recognized structure of the country, or part of the country, where they occur. Thus, in the south-west of England (Cornwall and Devon) there is a remarkable chain of granite bosses ranging east and west, or nearly so (see fig. 15). There is also much metamorphic rock (slates, schists, &c.), having a similar range. In the slates, schists, and granite are very numerous and remarkable metalliferous veins or lodes. Of these, some are longer, more regular, and better defined than the rest. Such veins are called *master lodes* or *champion lodes.* They are generally parallel to each other, and though they contain ore irregularly, some portions of the same great lode being rich and others poor, they may be recognized as all belonging to one system. In a general sense, these main lodes range east and west, or in the same direction as the axis of elevation of the district which has brought to the surface the granite and slates, thrusting up, in all probability, large quantities of newer rock at the same time, all of which has since been carried away to form other and newer sandstones, clays, and limestones.

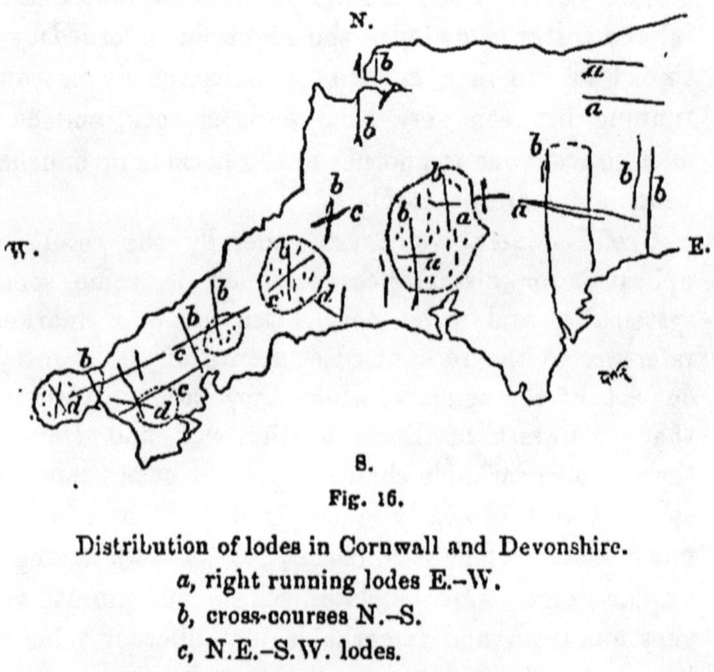

Fig. 16.

Distribution of lodes in Cornwall and Devonshire.
a, right running lodes E.–W.
b, cross-courses N.–S.
c, N.E.–S.W. lodes.
d, contra or caunter lodes.
The dotted lines enclose the districts in which granite comes to the surface.

But besides the main lodes are others crossing them, and for the most part they cross at a right angle. The diagram (fig. 16) illustrates this condition in a rough way; it represents an outline map of the mining district of Devon and Cornwall, in which the general direction of the principal metalliferous veins is marked. The main lodes *a*, *c* at first ranging east and west, are seen to become parallel to the geological axis of the country, bending round till they are north-east and south-west. The cross-courses *b* constantly tend to make right angles with the main lodes, and the comparatively rare exceptions *d* are limited also to particular directions. The relation of the lodes to the granite bosses is also illustrated in this diagram.

What is here observable in reference to the great mining district of England might be discovered with certain modifications in all mining districts. The general range of the local geological axis of the country being made out, the direction of the main lodes will be found to be parallel to it, and the lodes of next importance at right angles. And this law is after all but an expression of the great fact that lodes or mineral veins are fissures in altered rocks, produced systematically by mechanical force elevating the whole district, and, in doing so, breaking up the brittle rocks in a manner that may be, and has been, estimated mathematically. It is certain, that if a rigid solid, tied down on all sides, be exposed to pressure from below, sufficient to overcome the tension of its parts, it must crack on yielding, and that these cracks will follow certain laws. Mr. Hopkins long ago determined that they must be in the main parallel and at right angles to each other and to the elevating force.

It is very important for the right understanding of

the nature of lodes that these laws should be understood, for it is only in this way that the theory of mining can be appreciated. If we must regard the fissures and systems of fissures as due to some mysterious agency, connected in granite, or slate, or limestone, with an immediate in-rush of ores of copper, tin, lead, or other metals, we may well despair of comprehending the phenomena of veins, and may fall in with the hopeless conclusion of the Cornish miner, "Where it is, there it is." But if we find that in the structure and preparation of rocks the inevitable result of the action of known mechanical laws has produced systematic fissures, we have at least some starting point for inquiry, and for this reason I wish to impress on you the importance of observing the general facts as well as the special indications presented in a particular district.

One important conclusion from this mode of considering mineral veins is, that in different countries the systems of veins must exhibit different directions. Thus, while the right-running or ore-bearing veins in Cornwall are east and west, or north-east and south-west, this being the geological axis of the country, in other districts they may be north and south, or with any other bearings. The direction of elevation must govern the formation of each system of veins.

But if veins are due to disturbances that have acted at intervals during a long period of time, and not always in the same direction, the axis of disturbing forces may change, and subsequent elevations may take place in a different direction from that first determined.

In this case there may be a new system of veins crossing the earlier system. Or it may be that successive elevations may produce complication in a different way by fracturing still more the rocks that are already fractured, breaking and heaving the mineral veins after they have been partially or completely filled. Thus are produced *faults* and *throws*. The vein may become broken, and one part removed to a distance. The fracture, once healed, may become re-fractured, and the contents of part of the vein be transferred

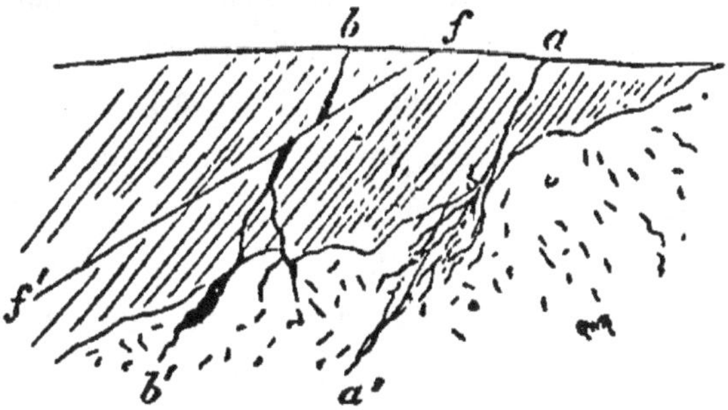

Fig. 17.

a a', a stockwork. (See p. 273)
b b', a branched or forked lode.
f f', a close fault.

The dotted part of the diagram represents granite, and the shaded part slate—the *killas* of Cornish miners.

with the vein to a distance. Thus, in the diagram to which I now direct attention (fig. 17), the vein *b b'* has been heaved from its position by the fault *f f'*, which may have resulted from some elevation subsequent to that which produced the vein. But *f f'* may be an open fault, and become ultimately a vein, and in that case a great complication would be produced if another elevation should affect both crevices.

In the determination of the law that governs the distribution of lodes in a district, it is necessary then that we should know the direction of the various axes of elevation that have affected the lodes, the order of occurrence of the disturbances, and, as far as may be, the rocks they have moved. A knowledge of these points will help us to understand the complications that have been brought about.

The cracks and fissures formed in rocks, whether on cooling or solidifying, or whilst elevation was going on, will necessarily approximate rather to a vertical than horizontal direction. Thus, mineral veins are often almost vertical, or if inclined they are so slightly and irregularly. The peculiarities of form indicated in the veins *a*, *b*, in fig. 17, are by no means unusual. It is natural that such crevices should run down to unknown depth, because we cannot suppose that in any case we reach the actual point of origin. It is natural, also, that they should be to a great extent irregular in width, and also in length. They could not be otherwise if formed by the causes to which I venture to attribute them. All the irregularities of lodes are explained if we consider the probable complications in the history of their upheaval.

But fissures in rocks are not mineral veins or lodes until they have been at least partially filled with mineral matters. These, too, are usually crystalline. The filling-up is the essential part of the whole matter, for it distinguishes the mineral vein from the open fault, or crevice, and the lode from the mineral vein. But in this part of the history there are many obscurities, nor is chemistry as yet able to explain the work that has gone on. There is evidently no reason why a fissure open at the top, or even a crack formed during the construction of an ordinary fault, should not become filled, or partly filled, with fractured stones fallen in from above or from the walls. Such a result may be regarded as inevitable, and thus, when in veins we find angular or rolled stones at the bottom of some open space, we can easily guess whence they came. If large, they are almost always broken away from the rock adjacent, and in limestone districts, where open veins are common, this kind of deposit is also common. Occasionally, however, the vein contains material that has been washed in by water from a distance, including, in some cases, remains of animals or vegetables that may have been living near.

But when mineral veins are filled with spar and ore the case is evidently different. It is true that in some cases the material may have been carried in from above and deposited from water which has held the crystalline mineral in solution. In this way some limestone veins have received cementing medium, which has built together in a solid mass angular and rolled lumps of limestone, cubical galena, blende, carbonate of lead, calamine, and even shells. The cementing medium was carbonate of lime, and the agent water. So, again, it is possible that in some cases crevices open below have received minerals by sublimation, or in the state of vapour. Of these, sulphur and arsenic are familiar examples. These, the former especially, are sometimes found lining the walls of cavities. In volcanic districts examples of this are common. Thus, deposits from above, assisted by the action of cold water, or even without water, and deposits from below, with or without steam, are not only possible, but real methods adopted by nature. But no one familiar with veins will suppose for one moment that all known cases can be thus explained. The vast majority of lodes, and even of such veins as contain little or no metalliferous ore, are lined with crystalline minerals which have clearly commenced to form on each wall of the vein, and not at the top or lower part. When the deposit has begun, the crystals have continued to accumulate with singular order and symmetry, and even when sometimes the filling-up of wide veins has been completed almost without any accumulation of crystals, the history of the deposit is such as I have endeavoured to describe it.

Assuming then that crevices have become filled and converted into veins by some chemical action acting entirely within the rock, it is easy to see that this must either involve the conveyance of foreign material by water circulating through the veins, or by the passage of this foreign material through the mass of the rock itself. Both are possible. Water may, and does, circulate through all free spaces in the interior of the earth. It is often hot, and is often loaded with a variety of minerals, including most of the metals. There is nothing impossible in the assumption that hot water has been largely concerned in bringing the various ores as well as the earthy minerals into the veins. Hot water is a real and powerful agent, and one which is always at hand in the recesses of the earth. Water is not only always present, but always in circulation, and thus an effect, however small in a particular case, may, by repeated multiplication, become very large and significant. Thus silica, in all its forms and all its combinations, may certainly have been the result of water action. Most of the varieties of the salts of lime are clearly obtainable in the same way, and there is no doubt that a great variety of crystals and spars may be accumulated in the manner here pointed out. Nor are the oxides of iron, and combinations of sulphur with metals, free from aqueous influence. Even the compound silicates of alumina, lime, and magnesia, with other bases, are thus formed.

The filling-up of veins is a subject of the deepest interest to the miner. He would willingly discover a natural law of association by which he could convince himself of the existence of ore in large quantities from the nature of the surrounding rocks—the *country*, as he technically calls it—or from the surface appearance of the lode—the *gossan*—or from the intersections of lodes with each other, or with some particular kind of rock; or from the degree of inclination (*underlie*) of a lode. To learn these natural laws he might well be content to study with infinite care all these conditions. Such laws are not yet known, but though no analogies can be implicitly depended on, all are useful guides and afford suggestive facts. It may be long before the observations on these conditions are sufficient to justify any absolute statement in a matter of such importance.

But there is, beyond a doubt, some natural relation between the contents of a lode and the conditions under which it has become filled. By carefully observing facts, and studying their mutual relations, miners have found that a certain development of iron oxide at the top of a lode may—other things being the same—be the indication of the presence of a course of ore of a particular kind. Even the condition of this rusty and unpromising stone is very significant, some iron stones being recognized by the initiated as favourable, and some unfavourable. A "kindly gossan" is to a Cornish miner a tolerably fair indication of a valuable lode. Nor is it in Cornwall only that this weathered outcrop of a lode is thought valuable. It is the *chapeau en fer* in France, and the *Eisenkopf* of Germany, and in both countries is valued and studied as an indication.

So, again, the fact that in lodes crossing each other, or in lodes traversing both granite and slate, there is generally a deposit of ore either at the intersection of two lodes, or at the point where a lode passing out of one rock enters another, must be regarded as tolerably well established as a general rule. But it would not be safe to assert it as invariable. Little is known of the cause of this result of "change of country." It may have been due to an electric or galvanic action analogous to that by which electroplating is carried on. It may have reference to causes altogether distinct. The study both of the examples of, and exceptions to, this rule are well worthy of examination, and cannot fail to be useful; but here again we are met by the great difficulty there is in assigning a satisfactory reason for a phenomenon certainly very common. If one could safely conclude that right-running veins entering slate from granite, or the converse, or crossing from particular bands of limestone to particular bands of shale or grit, would always yield ore, the chances of mining would be converted into certainties. Although this is not likely ever to be the case, there is no doubt that much may be learnt by comparing the various instances that are known—with a view to attain a well-founded opinion in any case that may be submitted.

The condition of the enclosing rock is not without influence on the contents of a lode. An experienced miner will judge, and often very correctly, by reference to this, as to the value of an unworked vein. Certain conditions of slate and granite, in which the rock is not too hard or close in texture, are generally considered favourable. On the other hand, a very compact rock rarely contains large quantities of valuable ore. This applies, however, to quantity rather than quality, as the very small proportion of extremely rich silver ores necessary to make a lode valuable may exist in hard country, while the amount of copper ore that is needed would in such cases not be attained.

Less important, but not without local influence, is the underlie, or inclination of a lode. It is a general fact that the valuable lodes of a mining district have certain mutual relations, but there is not any very clear identification of the cause.

Certain metals and ores are common in rocks of one kind, and in lodes having one general direction, while other ores seem to belong to other rocks and to cross-courses. This is the case in all mining districts, though each has its own peculiar system. Thus, in Cornwall the copper and tin lodes are usually in the direction of the axis of elevation, and are far the richest in ore; the lead veins are in the cross-courses, and are less important. In other districts, where the lead ores are in the main line of upheaval, the copper ores are of small amount, and occur in the transverse fissures. As a general rule, there cannot be a doubt that there is some relation between the external and known physical features of a country and the contents of its fissures.

Mineral veins generally contain either native metals, oxides, sulphides, or carbonates. Other combinations are less common and less abundant. All these are found in veins mixed with quartz, with crystalline salts of lime, and often with clay, in large quantities. In far smaller quantities, but still having manifest influence, and belonging to the history of the lode, are the multitude of double aluminous and other silicates that make up the greater portion of known and described minerals. With these occur combinations of the less common metals. It is clear that the mineral vein is Nature's laboratory. Here, for some reason, are produced the larger proportion of those combinations that seem to have so little importance on the great mass of the earth's crust, but that must certainly have their uses and their influence. Here are deposited the native metals when they can exist without much change; and here it is that all those minerals and metals are bound up together in strange and inextricable bonds, whose mutual relations it has not yet been possible for the chemist to explain.

And, after all, it is but a few metals and ores that we seek for and extract with so much care—iron oxides and carbonates, and iron pyrites; native copper and the oxides, the sulphides, and the carbonates of copper; oxide of tin; sulphides and carbonates of lead and zinc; sulphide and oxide of silver; native gold and silver; native mercury, and the sulphide of that metal. These are all of chief importance, while the ores of cobalt, nickel, manganese, arsenic, antimony, bismuth, and chromium, complete the list.

I do not deal here with metals and minerals of which the supply and nature are such that they are unknown in the general market. For the purpose I have in view it is better to confine attention to the latter, and to consider how and where fissures in rocks have become filled with these very useful substances.

All are not found in abundance in the same district, neither are all found in the same kind of rock, or in the same kind of vein. There are certain laws in obedience to which they may generally be looked for, and these laws must be ascertained by experience and observation in as varied a range of countries as possible. What is true for Cornwall is true in principle, but not in detail, for Wales, for Chili, for Cuba, and Australia; but, if the experience acquired in Cornwall is taken abroad, and there applied without consideration of the change of circumstances of the deposits, it will fail. Copper does not everywhere appear with the same associated minerals; it is not always in lodes having the same direction, traversing the same rocks, or coming to the surface with the same gossan.

Mineral veins containing ore are of very various dimensions. Of their absolute length but little is known. They are certainly traceable in some cases for many miles with little interruption at the surface, and below the surface they probably run on for far greater distances. As, however, they are never uniformly rich along their whole course, the interruptions of the productive parts appear to be interruptions of the lode. It is equally difficult to say what is the inferior limit of length of a metalliferous vein. Those that are apparently without extension in length are known as *pipe veins* and *shoots*, but these are often in sets, and are really connected by narrow crevices. It is, however, certain that veins differ extremely in the extent to which they run, and this is not only natural but inevitable, if they result from elevatory movements from below.

The width of mineral veins is more definite and determinable than the length. Some are regular with distinct walls, and between these walls the distance can be measured. Such veins may vary in width from a few inches up to many yards. One of the widest on record is a silver vein in Mexico, where the width is more than fifty yards, though not for any great distance. Generally it happens that the widest and largest veins are in districts where the mining ground occupies much space. But this is not without exception. Not unfrequently the width of a lode is apparently much increased by numerous parallel fissures filled with ore, and by the existence of threads of ore pervading the rock that encloses the vein. Remarkable instances of this I have observed in the great Cobre copper mine in Cuba, in the remarkable copper lode of Monte Catini in Tuscany, and in some other cases. This condition of veins is called by the Germans a *Stockwerk*, and by it veins are apparently so far widened as to become lost, the passage from vein to enclosing rock being altogether obliterated. Such lateral veins are called also *strings.** They act occasionally as leaders, guiding the miner to some rich deposit. It is possible that they may be due to the general breaking-up of a considerable extent of brittle rock, or of rocks varying in brittleness, and that they have some relation to the depth and distance of the elevating force that has determined the system of fissures forming the stockwork. Of this kind of vein there are cases known in which the lode is several hundred yards in width, as measured by the total range of orey ground. The distance to which a stockwork is continued amounts in some cases to a thousand yards. As may be supposed, it is

* See *a a'*, fig. 17, p. 263.

not generally the more valuable and rarer metals that are thus abundantly distributed. Iron ore is the usual material. The rich iron ores of Sweden afford some of the most remarkable instances; but there are some extremely valuable deposits of copper ore under similar circumstances.

The depth to which mineral veins bear useful deposits of ore is altogether unknown. Certain metals, such as tin and gold, have been sometimes supposed to exist in larger quantities near the tops of lodes than at great depth, but recent experience is unfavourable to this view. It is also quite opposed to any admitted theory of the filling of veins. That the tops of lodes consist chiefly of quartz and iron oxide is true in certain localities, but this is where the lode itself contains throughout a large quantity of sulphide or carbonate of iron, with or without copper or other metals, and where the veinstone is siliceous. The iron oxide is probably due rather to the decomposition of the lode near the surface by weathering than to any difference in the nature of the deposit. In some cases where tin was once found in the upper parts of lodes, and then lost, there has been recent proof that the same mineral recurs below a certain depth, which is great in relation to our mining operations; but if we take into account the probable position of the disturbing force, this depth will seem unimportant.

Veins are usually vertical or nearly so. The inclination (*hade*, or *underlie*) in Cornwall rarely exceeds ten degrees from the vertical. In some great mining districts it is more; but any considerable slope must be regarded as exceptional in all granite and slate districts. The same system of lodes generally shows the same underlie. In limestone the veins are often very different. Occasionally zig-zag, sometimes mere gaps of small depth, and sometimes huge open spaces between certain beds of limestone and shale, they mark everywhere the nature of the disruption, and the nature of the rock disrupted. If metalliferous, they almost always contain lead or zinc, but the lead ore is often argentiferous, especially when it consists of fine-grained galena.

In the filling-up of veins, the deposits seem generally to have been made in a certain order, and with a certain amount of regular system. Thus, in a wide vein, with a well-marked gossan of iron oxide, spotted with copper pyrites or other traces of copper, there may be in one part of the vein sparry iron or iron pyrites near the top, and this may be succeeded by a little copper ore, with spars of various kinds. As we pass down, lead ore may become mixed with the copper ore, till at last we find lead ore only. Such a vein may be assumed to be a lead lode, and the order recognized may be the regular order throughout the vein. In parts of such a vein the lead ore will be absent or poor; in other parts, sparry iron will be replaced by calc spar or silica, or even fluor spar; elsewhere, perhaps, the pyrites will be more rich in copper, but still throughout this whole vein the courses and bunches of ore will be chiefly lead, and all the other produce may be regarded as accidental. If, instead of passing into lead ore, the contents of the upper part of the lode consisted chiefly of tin-stone with copper ore, and the copper or tin increased in quantity with increasing depth, such a mine would be a copper or tin mine, and not a lead mine. So far as this, there seems some system; and we may carry the illustration further, for laws of this kind apply to systems of lodes in a district, and not only to single lodes.

There appear to be certain usual associations of earthy minerals with metals, and some of these have been already noticed. Sulphide of copper and iron, the commonest and most useful ore of copper in England, is generally accompanied by siliceous minerals. Rich ores of silver are often found in gneissic rocks and with quartz, while silver-lead ores and cubical galena, carbonate of lead, and the common ores of zinc, are all more abundant in limestone. These general indications of habitat are useful and suggestive, but they cannot be trusted in all cases.

Such being the usual condition of mineral veins, I must now proceed to point out to you the way in which their existence in a new country, or the presence of new and productive lodes in an old mining district, may best be discovered. The methods must, of course, be such as are within the reach of all who employ ordinary intelligence in the search. But they require some personal experience, for without the latter the most intelligent observer may easily be deceived.

Owing to the nature of mineral veins and lodes, their hardness is, almost without exception, different from that of the enclosing rock. Occasionally harder from the presence of quartzose minerals, veins stand out above the surface as walls. Elsewhere the rock is harder than the vein, and the top of the lode is more rapidly weathered than the walls, leaving a depression. In either case, after a time, the lode is broken away, and carried along the surface to a distance by water. It is, however, left behind at last, and the heavier portions of the whole, which will generally be those containing the ore, will be accumulated in certain places, by degrees in smaller quantities and smaller particles as they are more distant from the lode. By reversing the operation, by following up from point to point these indications, an intelligent and quick-sighted person, accustomed to the work, will soon discover the true position of a lode. Sometimes this may be done by following up fragments of metalliferous gravel, but more frequently the gravels containing the indications are buried. In the latter case pits have to be dug at various points, or trenches cut; but the result is the same. This process is called *shoding.*

When once a lode is reached, it is necessary to prove its direction and underlie, its width, and its condition at various points of outcrop. For this purpose trenches are cut across the direction of the lode, at certain points, where, by calculation, it ought to be found. These trenches will generally bring it to light; and they are called, in mining language, *costeaning pits.* Small pits sunk upon the lode to some little depth reveal the condition and magnitude of the gossan, but will not in most cases show ore of any value. It is rather indications of the lode than profitable results that are looked for by such operations as these.

Nothing seems at first more doubtful and difficult than the attempt to determine the value of a lode by such means, and yet on most occasions these are the only means available without the outlay of much money and labour, and in many cases the lapse of a long period of time. Mining is at the best, and with all possible advantages, a speculative business; and of all kinds of mining that which is most elementary, namely, the discovery of valuable lodes, is the most speculative. At one time a trial and the expenditure of a few hundred pounds will lay bare a deposit of enormous value; at another, the utmost prudence and intelligence, and the employment of a large capital, will only succeed in proving that nature is not tied down by any laws, and that where there seems the greatest probability of success, there are also chances of failure. But we must not omit investigations and inquiries because they are not always commercially successful; and the study of the relation that exists between the country, the outcrop of the lode, and the metallic contents of the lode, can never be out of place.

I have pointed out more than once that lead and zinc deposits in limestone veins are very different from the contents of veins in granite and slate. This is due to many causes; but the search for lead is thus rendered somewhat different from that usually adopted in reference to copper. Lead deposits are perhaps not more irregular in their nature than deposits of copper or tin, but they are irregular after a different law; and the process of shoding adopted on the surface with regard to copper, is applicable in a certain sense, when carried out underground, for lead. In some of the best-known lead districts, where the ore is found between bands of limestone, this method is applicable, and Derbyshire is an example exactly in point; but it is not so in Flintshire and the Isle of Man, which are both very rich lead-mining districts. Still less is it so in Cornwall and Devon, where also lead is found. On the Continent of Europe, the mining ground of eastern Belgium, and that of the Sierra de Gador (in the south of Spain), which are both rich in galena—and the case is the same in the richest galena mines of North America—we find the sulphide of lead in cavities in limestone, but in other places not far off the same mineral may occur in true veins in other kinds of rock. In the limestone cavities angular and rolled blocks of galena are found, either detached or cemented together. These deposits were clearly formed quite independently of the limestone, which has accumulated in a crystalline state on the walls of lodes. Such deposits in different parts of the rock are often connected by narrow threads of ore. On the other hand, many metals are rarely found in limestones at all, and never in rolled fragments. And thus, in seeking for the indications of lodes, although the first methods of shoding are the same, the subsequent discovery and following-up of the lode at its outcrop depend in some measure on the nature of the rock.

The mining districts of the world are to some extent indicated in a good geological map. They occur chiefly where rocks have been metamorphosed; where granites and slates, and certain schistose rocks, called by the Germans *Grauwacke*, are found. They are to be looked for among the mountainous regions, rather than in the great plains or water-worn hills. They belong rather to the barren than the cultivated areas. Where granite or similar rock appears, where the contact of granite with sandy and clayey material has been made evident by changes induced in the sands and clays, and where limestone is hardened, broken, and disturbed—in all these places we may look for, and shall generally find, crevices and fissures more or less systematically grouped, and in these fissures crystalline minerals and ores are distributed here and there. Thus, then, we may know where to expect mineral wealth; and if in such districts ore is found in the streams or gravel, we may trace it up to the rock whence it originally came, and thus learn the nature, direction, and extent of the various lodes.

Some outline statement of the more remarkable of such districts will be useful, if only to illustrate what I have here said. In England, Cornwall, Devonshire, Derbyshire, Northumberland, and Cumberland are the chief mining counties for metalliferous ores in mineral veins. Of these, Cornwall and Devonshire furnish the tin, not only to England but to Europe, and also a large proportion of the copper ore; Derbyshire and the northern counties supply lead and zinc;

North Wales—chiefly Flintshire—supplies lead and copper, and the Isle of Man is rich in silver-lead ore. In Merionethshire, gold has been found, with lead ore in tolerably large quantities. Anglesea was formerly very rich in copper ore. Ireland contains copper mines, in Wicklow, Waterford, and Kerry. The Wicklow mines are remarkable: they contain both iron and gold. Large quantities of iron pyrites are removed from them, and at one time a considerable quantity of native gold was obtained there. Scotland contains lodes in its south-western counties.

France presents five metalliferous districts. The great platform of Central France, in the Puy-de-Dôme, is one, Brittany is another, and the Vosges a third. The French Alps of Dauphiny, and the eastern Pyrenean chain, also afford some metals. Belgium is rich in zinc and lead ores, which are chiefly worked in the eastern and more hilly part of the country, close to Prussia and the Rhine. Spain is exceedingly rich in most of the metals. Poor copper and iron pyrites exist in incredibly large quantities at Huelva, near Cadiz. Cinnabar and native mercury are obtained from the rich mines of Almaden; lead and copper from mines both on the south and north flanks of the Sierra Nevada; and rich silver-lead from the Western Pyrenees. Silver ores and very rich silver-lead ores are also obtained from the mines of the Sierra Almagrera, near Carthagena. Italy is rich in iron ores in the island of Elba, and in copper ores in more than one locality in Tuscany.

Germany has been known as a great mining

country from time immemorial: it is the cradle and school of scientific mining, and the variety of minerals found there is very great. Silver, copper, lead, tin, cobalt, nickle, bismuth, antimony, and iron are all found there, and some under circumstances of extreme interest. Saxony, the Hartz, the Erzgebirge, between Saxony and Bohemia, and Silesia are all rich. Austria also possesses mineral wealth in the Tyrol, while Hungary contains gold, silver, lead, zinc, and iron.

Scandinavia abounds in iron and copper, the mines of each being extremely rich and important, and the localities numerous. Sweden and Norway are the northern countries where the largest quantity of ores are worked. In Russia there are many mining districts; that of the Ural being almost equally valuable for gold and copper. Silver and lead are worked in the Altai mountains. Throughout Asia mining districts exist, and have been rendered available. India and China, and the islands of the Eastern Archipelago are all rich; some in the precious metals, others in copper and tin, and many in iron. Japan also is a mining country; and the larger islands of the Southern Archipelago, as well as Australia, contain important supplies of all the useful metals. The southern part of Australia is especially rich in gold and copper, and appears likely to yield many other metals. The same remark applies to New Zealand.

Both North and South America are metalliferous, and Central America still yields the chief supplies of silver. The gold and mercury on the western side of

North America, and the silver of Peru and other places on the western side of South America, have lately far surpassed the mines of Brazil, which, for a long time, was the richest gold-producing country in the world. The West Indian islands, especially Cuba, Jamaica, and Santo Domingo, are all metalliferous, although the mines of Cuba alone are extensively and profitably worked. The vast hoards of native copper on the shores of Lake Superior are among the richest and most remarkable deposits in the world.

The methods adopted when the existence of a lode is proved and it is desired to extract the mineral wealth, are very different from those that are followed when the minerals are regularly bedded. In the latter case, as in the former, there is an outcrop that may be followed; but the outcrop of a lode affords very different indications from those of the outcrop of a bed. It may be that valuable ore is got from the outcrop; but this is the exception, not the rule; and when it is the case, the lode is generally wide and the quantity of ore large, so that mere digging or quarrying will remove all that is needed. Thus the great iron lodes of Elba and the copper lode of Dalecarlia, in Sweden, are worked from the surface; but this is hardly mining. It involves no search and no special methods either of discovery or working.

In ordinary cases when a lode is known to exist, and there are such indications as to justify the expense of mining operations, it is usual to sink a pit or shaft (*s*, *s'*, *t*) on the outcropping lode, following it downwards to observe its condition, and at intervals driving horizontal galleries, or levels (*l*, *m*, *n*, *o*), to the right and left in the lode to some distance. In the diagram two veins (*p*, *p'*) are represented, one (*p*) between two valleys of different depth, the other (*p'*) only near a shallow valley. These

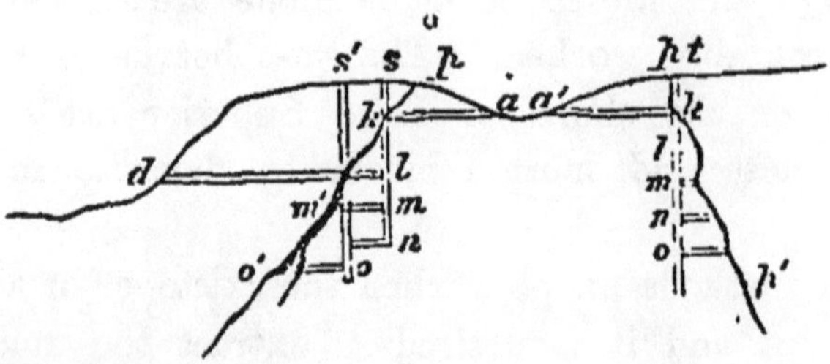

Fig. 18.

valleys may be slight depressions of the surface, and their distance from the lode may be considerable, but they should never be lost sight of. A difference of level of a hundred feet may be so important as to make it profitable to spend enormous sums in order to take advantage of it; for mining involves deep shafts, and the interior of the earth is rarely dry. Water accumulates, and if in large quantity, it is a very serious obstacle to progress. It must be removed, and to be got rid of it, must be lifted and allowed to run off at the lowest attainable level for every foot of lift involves a certain expenditure, going on day and night and year after year. When the quantity of water is large, this expenditure is so serious that it may make the difference between great profit and absolute loss in working a rich mine.

Thus it is that drainage is one of the earliest considerations of the mining engineer, when he has satisfied himself that he may safely spend money in search of ore. But it rarely happens that the early indications of mineral wealth are so certain as to allow him to do much at first, and prospective drainage must be subordinate to the discovery of valuable ore. When, however, it can be done with advantage, a level or tunnel is driven in from some adjacent hill-side to cut the lode at a moderate depth, and at the same time a shaft is sunk to meet this level. Such a level is called an *adit* (fig. 18, *a d'*). If near the surface, it is a "shallow adit" (*a a'*). The adit serves at the same time to prove the lode. If ore is found, it may be convenient to run it out from the adit, and if water comes in, it may be readily drained without cost from all workings above the point at which the adit cuts the lode. Generally, however, there is need of pumps to lift the water, and of a windlass or other contrivance to raise the ore to the surface. Combination is necessary for these purposes, and a number of miners must associate together if the whole is not undertaken by the capitalist.

Assuming that the lode is found to improve on going down, and that profitable works or very favourable indications justify a further outlay, it may be advisable to put down a second shaft (*s'*) to cut the lode at some much deeper point than at first. It is not necessary, however, to wait till the shaft cuts the lode, in order to see the state of the lode at a deeper point than has hitherto been reached. At various depths, generally about ten fathoms (60 feet) apart, cross-cuts may be made towards the lode. These at once prove its position and the state of the ground and of the ore. It must not be assumed that the lode is likely to be regular like a bed of coal, that its underlie is constant, or that it always presents the same appearance, or is equally valuable. All lodes are in their nature irregular. They generally either contain what are called *courses of ore*, or they are *bunchy*, and contain *pockets of ore*. The former condition is that of a tolerably uniform deposit of ore within certain limits of depth and distance, succeeded by barren portions. Such courses may be repeated in the same lode, and though they may not be equally rich throughout, they are always valuable, for they give to mining as much regularity and system as it is susceptible of. Thus courses of ore are always desirable, and the more regular they are the steadier is the work of the miner. They rarely, however, extend very far either in the direction of the lode or in depth, so that because a lode may be worked to advantage in one part, it by no means follows that the mine adjacent on the same lode will be rich. Experience has too often proved that there is no dependence to be placed on the presumed continuance of courses of ore in any direction.

Bunches and pockets of ore consist of expansions of a lode filled with valuable ore, or portions of a large lode becoming within limited distances exceptionally rich. Courses of ore occur not unfrequently in the great copper mines of Cornwall.

Pockets of ore are most common in the lead-mining districts. Under any circumstances the ordinary mining work must include—first, the removing of ore already discovered ; secondly, the laying out, and bringing into a convenient state for extraction, the courses and bunches of ore already discovered; and, thirdly, the organizing of trials and discoveries in those parts of the lode not yet proved to bear ore. Great judgment is needed in laying out a mine so as to secure as far as possible a supply of ore to pay expenses, and yield a profit on the capital invested, at the same time retaining always a sufficient reserve in the event of the supply failing, and expending always a fair proportion of the profits in trial work.

The irregularity of lodes renders a system of working necessary in metal mines that would be quite unjustified in coal mines. In the latter, and in all cases where a regular deposit is being removed, the position of the shafts can be planned beforehand; the depth of each is known, the shafts are all vertical, and almost always open from the surface. In the former, the shafts must be put down to suit the condition of the lode. Sometimes it is even convenient to sink slant shafts on the lode, beginning a shaft at some point in a level far below the surface. After being continued for a time in ore, such a shaft may become useless, and it will not be desirable to proceed with it up or down. Dozens or scores of such shafts may exist in the mine at various depths, and in this way, by perpetually following the ore and removing it wherever there is sufficient to make it profitable, the works become extremely complicated. Where the lode has been large, there will be open spaces left; where it has been small, or *nipped in*, there is nothing but a very narrow and inconvenient passage. But in all these works there is little trouble about ventilation: choke-damp is extremely rare in metal mines, and explosive gases are quite unknown. The risk of metal-mining is not increased by these chances.

Although not to so great an extent as in coal mines, where a vast area of roof has to be supported by vertical props, and where the pressure of the superincumbent load of earth is very serious, it is impossible to carry on mining operations on a large scale in mineral veins without timbering. The principle is in some measure different, since, when the vein is nearly vertical, it requires but little timbering to prevent the walls from coming together, especially when the country is solid, and the walls clearly defined. It rarely happens, also, that the portions even of a rich lode that contain valuable ore are so continuous that their removal causes serious danger, except in the neighbourhood of the main shafts. There are, however, cases where the excavations are so large as to render timbering an expensive operation. Sometimes, also, it will happen that the waters of the mine tend to rot the timbers that are used to shore up walls, and keep the overhanging wall from closing in on the footwall. In the great copper mines of Cobre, in Cuba, the timbering is on the most gigantic scale, and requires the most careful superintendence, since a few months' neglect may produce, and has produced, very serious consequences. Generally in British mines the lode is not so large, or, if it be so, the care taken in this department is sufficient, and the timbering sufficiently strong to render the mine quite safe.

As the ventilation of metal mines is natural and easy, so the lighting is very simple, and there is no objection to the use of gunpowder in blasting the hard rock. In blasting, however, great judgment and experience are needed in deciding on the position and depth of the bore-holes, so as to take advantage of natural joints in the rock, and remove large blocks, instead of dissipating the force of the blast by an ill-placed bore; and in this, as in most matters connected with mining, a good deal of intelligence is needed on the part of the miner. Those who have only visited a mine as strangers, and have been conducted through a labyrinth of narrow passages, up and down innumerable ladders, and through narrow crevices in the rock, to see at the end only a dark dirty wall, imperfectly lighted by a glimmering candle or smoky lamp, have little idea of the clearness and precision with which everything connected with the progress of the work is laid hold of by the guide, who, without any other mark of superior intelligence, can point out here a thread of ore, there a valuable course or bunch, and at another point a favourable indication. You may be sure that such knowledge is not learnt in a day, nor is it ever to be acquired without long familiarity with underground operations.

The plan of a metal mine, except when there are

unusually large and regular courses of ore, as in the Great Devon Consols and a few other great mines, is rarely regular or systematic. But there is always one leading idea, which, as I have already pointed out, is based on the removal of the water, and the best way of connecting this operation with the intersection of the various lodes and cross-courses. In countries where the rainfall on the surface is large, the water that accumulates in a mine, when the workings are deep, may become very considerable. It comes in rapidly from above, it enters from the sides where the lode connects with small branches and strings, and it rises sometimes from below. Now and then springs of hot water well up from the depths of the earth into the workings of the mine. All this water must be removed at the smallest possible cost. Unless, however, great care is taken, the water lifted from one mine may find its way back into the earth into another mine that is adjacent, or it may even be lifted over and over again from the same workings. To avoid this, a systematic drainage of groups of mines on the same lode is desirable, and deep adits are sometimes cut, intersecting many veins and receiving the waters of a number of properties to convey them away to a distance.

In Cornwall there has long existed a work of this kind called the *great adit*, which receives the waters of the numerous mines in Gwennap and Redruth districts, and measures on the whole nearly thirty miles in length. One branch of this adit penetrates ground seventy fathoms, or 420 feet below the surface. The water thus conveyed is discharged into the sea forty feet above high-water mark. In the construction of long lines of deep adit, which exist to a greater or less extent in all mining districts, it is desirable as far as possible to cross at right angles the direction of the principal lodes of the district. These lodes are thus cut across at some depth below the surface, where their condition is determined, and it often happens that other lodes and branches, till then unknown, are discovered during the prosecution of the work.

To complete great tunnels of this kind it is necessary to carry on the work from various points at the same time, and no small engineering skill is needed to bring together in a line all these tunnels. The shallower adits are of the nature of trial-works, but they do not cease to be useful when important works are afterwards carried on in a mine.

Metal mines are generally reached by ladders placed vertically in the shafts; but when the depth is great, the descent and ascent become extremely exhausting, and waste much time as well as strength that might be better employed. Of late years, man-engines and other contrivances have been adopted, by means of which the miners can reach their work and leave it with comparative comfort. One of the most ingenious of these machines was first introduced in the Hartz more than thirty years ago. In its improved state it consists of two vertical beams, working up and down, for a length of twenty-four feet. At equal intervals of six feet steps are placed. A man stands on a step and is let down twenty-four feet, while the other beam ascends as much. He then finds the other beam stationary for a moment before recovering its motion. He transfers himself to a step he finds vacant on it, and when at the next move the beam drops, he is lowered another twenty-four feet. While this is going on, the first beam rises to its original position and presents another step level with that on which he now finds himself. On this he places himself and descends again. This continues till he reaches his destination, when he steps off. Each step may be occupied, and thus a number of men can be lowered or raised at the same time. But this machine can only be used when the shaft is vertical; and the apparatus is somewhat costly, as it will have to be kept in motion almost incessantly, and must therefore be strong. To be of any value it must of course be kept in good order. The original cost of a double man-engine, including the steam-engine to work it, exceeds a thousand pounds sterling for the deeper mines of Cornwall. It is not needed for shallow mines, and would not be advantageous where the depth is less than 100 fathoms. It is believed that where the depth reaches 200 fathoms, the machine more than repays its cost in the increased facility afforded to the miners in reaching their work without previous exhaustion. Below this the gain is still greater. The return to the surface from deep mines, after eight hours' work underground, is exceedingly injurious to the health when ladders are the only means of rising.

Almost all the mining work in Cornwall is executed by contract. The men exercise their own judgment as to the nature of the work to be done, and undertake it on certain terms. There are two classes—the "tutmen," who simply excavate at an arranged price per fathom of ground, and the "tributers," who speculate on the ore-ground when reached. A party of men agree to do a certain work, either sinking or driving. They form into three gangs, each taking eight hours, and the work goes on day and night. If ore is found, it belongs to the adventurers, not to the "tutmen," unless it is arranged in the contract that they shall have a share. Poor mines are sometimes worked in this way. The tutmen bid for the work, judging to the best of their knowledge as to the nature of the ground. If it prove softer and easier to work than had been calculated, they gain; if the contrary, they lose. It seldom happens, however, that when an extraordinary difficulty occurs the men are held to their bargain.

When ore is reached and is good, the tutman engages to raise it at a certain price per fathom; but if doubtful, the tributers come in and speculate. They are men who agree to work a portion of the lode for a given time as well and as completely as they can, receiving as pay a certain agreed portion of the ores raised. The contract is for a certain time, as one or two months. If the ore be rich, they accept a small percentage of the value; if poor, they demand a larger percentage. The captains or superintendents of the mines, having examined the ground on a particular day and decided the value to the best of their judgment, put up a portion or *pitch* to auction, the bidding being downwards, and the parties who bid being each represented by one man. This method, though speculative, is fair, and works well. It has been in force in Cornwall for more than a century, but has not been introduced largely into other mining districts.

In other parts of the country, in England, and in mining districts abroad, the method of setting the work is different; but it is generally advisable, when possible, to interest the miner in the amount of ore produced, as it removes temptation and keeps the men to their work. Where only day-work is adopted, it is difficult to avoid peculation and idleness.

The ores are generally raised by machinery, and broken at the surface. In addition to the quantity of rubbish or *deads* left below, there is thus generally a waste heap, or *attle*, at the pit-mouth. This is produced during the operation of *dressing*, by which the ore is reduced to a convenient size, and is separated from the rubbish by the help of water. Dressing hardly comes under the head of mining operations.

I have now brought to a close this brief account of the practical applications of geology. Commencing with an outline of the structure of the earth's crust, as made known by observation, I have endeavoured to point out to you the way in which every part of that crust becomes available for human wants, and how intimately connected are the details of structure with these practical applications. A certain number, but only a very small number, of elementary substances make up the great mass of the earth's crust. These elements combine, and admit of modifications. They also contain, in limited proportion, many other and rarer minerals. Of the latter, some few, the metals more especially, are eminently useful; but of a large proportion we know no use. They may exercise some influence on us and on nature, or they may belong chiefly to some other planetary system than our own, and be present on our earth as accidental rather than as essential materials. Bound together by certain laws of attraction, kept asunder by the action of heat, apparently permanent in their condition, and changing but little from day to day and from year to year, the various forms of matter are really always subject to change and always undergoing change. The rapid and never-ceasing action of moist air and changing temperature produces at the surface a rapid disintegration and decomposition of all the ordinary combinations, and causes their surface to be covered with a variable thickness of fragments. This is favourable to vegetation, and vegetable matter in a decaying state builds up a soil on which other and higher forms of vegetable life take root and flourish. There could be no life on land if there were no decomposed rock at the surface. But the soil thus formed is not long retained in the same spot. It is frequently removed and as regularly renewed. Whatever it is at any moment is due to the nature of the rock from which it is derived. And thus, if we know the rocks, we may judge of the soil; and knowledge concerning rocks is available and useful to the agriculturist who requires to be informed concerning soils, and in many cases requires to modify them for certain special purposes.

But, in the next place, the soil would not yield the fruits of the earth,—there could be no life on the earth but for the moisture in the air and the rain falling on the ground, when that moisture is for a time parted with. It is this moisture that is one of the chief causes of the destruction of rocks and the formation of soils.

But it is only because of the peculiar arrangement and composition of rocks that the whole of the rainfall does not run over the earth's surface back to the sea when discharged from the clouds: it would be useless for vegetation if such were the case. Rocks and water are intimately connected; each rock exists only because of water; each contains water; and through and amongst all of them water is transmitted. Thus we arrive at the second chapter in this history—the influence of water, the necessity of water supply, and the injury done by excess of water. We then enter upon the consideration of the various relations that exist between rocks and the water that enters them, changes them, traverses them, and emerges from them. It is only when we have mastered those departments of geology that treat of rocks—their nature, origin, and the alterations they have undergone—that we can apply them so far as to understand the bearing of the science on the questions and observations here alluded to.

But again, these rocks are in themselves valuable. They are the materials from amongst which we extract precious stones and gems; from amongst which, also, we take stones to build our houses and palaces, and marble to be cut into the most exquisite forms. Part of them we may distil to obtain illuminating and other oils; part of them we burn in our fires and furnaces; part of them we smelt with the aid of other parts that are combustible, and by them we obtain, and are able to manufacture, the various metals. Besides the rocks themselves, and their actual uses as material, most of them are broken up, disturbed, cracked, and altered; the fissures in the varieties most disturbed and most anciently broken containing these valuable metallic minerals I have been alluding to in this lecture. All that is useful and beautiful, and all that is intrinsically valuable and employed in the arts, and, indeed, all that conduces to life itself, is thus derived from the earth. To seek for it economically you must study the structure of the earth; to obtain it without loss, or at as little cost as possible, you must learn the conditions of its existence—you must, in a word, study geology.

And thus it is that geology, applied to the arts, is a subject of real and vital interest to all of us. In endeavouring to illustrate this, and interest you in the subject, I have confined myself as much as possible to familiar facts and exemplifications. I need not point out to you that to follow these generalizations into detail a very wide range of knowledge and great practical experience are needed. These can rarely be combined in one person; and thus the agriculturist, the engineer, the miner, and the manufacturer must each learn his own department of practical geology, and apply it to his own purposes. The search after this knowledge is as interesting as the knowledge itself is useful, and the interest is increased when the student, before seeking out that which belongs to his own department, will make himself master of so much of the general subject as to recognize its bearings on the details that come before him.

There are other applications of geology that I have not brought under your notice in these lectures. Among them I would especially point out that one which has reference to the fine arts. I mention it now to remind you that the subject of applied geology is far from being exhausted; that, in fact, I have only considered it in one aspect, and that the many-sided science that deals with the earth, its history, its structure, its grand physical features, and the causes that have produced, and are daily modifying these features, is no less calculated to interest the artist and the poet than the farmer and the manufacturer. There is no limit to the study when we engage in the comparison of the works of Nature, with their application to the requirements of man, and the operations of man's intellect.

ADDENDA ET CORRIGENDA.

In addition to the statements made with reference to the water-capacity of chalk and new red sandstone in the second lecture, the following notices are given on the authority of Mr. Homersham :—

CHALK.

Amwell (Herts).—One well yields two and a half millions.

Croydon (Surrey).—Two wells, twenty yards apart. Each yields one and a half millions.

Deptford.—Two wells, not fifty yards asunder, yield together five millions of gallons.

Brighton.—One well, with additions, yields two and a half to three millions.

Hull.—A well with bore-holes, near the town, yields three and a half millions of gallons per day. This supply is affected by the season.

NEW RED SANDSTONE.

Birkenhead.—One well yields two millions.

Liverpool.—Green-Lane well yields more than three and a quarter millions.

PENDLETON (near Manchester).—One well yields more than four millions, but is not in constant use.

In the same lecture, page 53, the reader is requested to make the following corrections:—

Line 11 from bottom, for *ten square miles* read *one square mile.*

Line 8 from bottom, for *ten* read *seventeen.*

CPSIA information can be obtained
at www.ICGtesting.com
Printed in the USA
LVHW022010120422
716028LV00006B/254

9 783752 590647